A LESSON IN GEOGRAPHY

A NOVEL

ROSA JANINE AMONG THE SEA SNAKES

CHARLES JAMISON

Author's Note:

This is a work of fiction.

Any resemblance to actual events or persons, living or dead, is entirely coincidental.

CJ

For Gina,

my own personal Orixá

EAST AFRICA / BRAZIL

They say that the only true regrets in life are for the things you *don't* do—the omissions, the failures of nerve. After forty years of reflection, I can tell you that's an oversimplification.

In 1979, I learned that East Africa and Brazil share a lot of qualities beyond the simple geographical fact that they are both east coast lands on southern continents. I have spent the four decades since then thinking about the other lessons I learned in those two places.

This is my story, without embellishment but certainly with regrets.

Argus Morrison

JAMBA

I am walking slowly across the hard dry ground. The afternoon sun presses on my neck and shoulders with physical force. My shirt seems glued to me, and is stained dark under the arms and down the center of the back. My boots stir the thick layer of dust and my footsteps are silent.

A truck drives past me, filled with laughing Black soldiers clutching FN assault rifles between their knees. They leave a billowing cloud behind them, some of which finds its way into my mouth. I try to spit, but I'm short on saliva and the hot grit stays where I can feel it between my teeth.

It is always the same. I am walking toward a small unpainted wooden building which sits under a large thorn tree. Its corrugated metal roof is shaded, and through the open door and windows the interior looks dark and cool. As I approach I notice that the planks of the outside walls are rough and weathered. This and the way small tufts of grass are growing at the base of the walls makes me think this hut has been here for some time. Perhaps it was one of the first to be built at Jamba.

I step up the one or two wooden steps to the door and peer inside. I can see immediately that the coolness I had anticipated was an illusion. Here there is relief from the searing sun, but the heat is undiminished. The air in the small room embraces the occupants more like a liquid than a gas. There are two men there, leaning over a table covered with maps and papers. They look up and straighten themselves when they hear my boots on the threshold.

Most of what I know about Thomas Morgan came from a Rhodesian pilot named Brooks who beat me in a card game in Loyangalani and then flew me to Juba in his old DC-3. While I had three, perhaps four, encounters with Morgan himself, they weren't the kind of situations where you learn much about the other person.

I know that Morgan was in Jamba two years before our lives crossed. This is one of the things I learned from Brooks, sitting next to him in his cockpit, straining to hear over the roar of the two big radial engines. But at that time I wasn't as curious about Morgan as I am now. So I didn't ask as many questions as I might have.

For those questions I didn't ask Brooks, the ones I would ask now if I had the chance, I have formed my own answers in a kind of self-indulgent arrogance, like a writer who takes liberties with his characters.

Brooks was flying supplies for Jonas Savimbi when he knew Morgan. That was back when UNITA had only recently arrived in Southeastern Angola, that part of the country which the Portuguese called *o fim do mundo* because it literally is the end of the world. Savimbi set Jamba there because that vast region of Cuando Cubango, with its dry sandy floodplains spotted with sparse scrubby forests and occasional grass, was virtually inaccessible to the MPLA forces which had taken control in Luanda. The other advantage to the place was its proximity to the South African Defence Force in Namibia. By that time Savimbi was forced to rely on the SADF for nearly everything. It was a time of survival For UNITA, and of waiting, and Morgan was a part of that.

For some reason I always imagine him at Jamba. It's unclear to me why this should be so, because I have never been there. But I have spent enough time in Africa to have an idea what it looked like. The low buildings and sheds are scattered among trees growing on the banks of one of the major rivers; barracks and workshops and supply sheds and armories built on the hard-packed sandy clay. The trees give some shade from the African sun, but more importantly from the eyes of the MPLA air force. But Savimbi doesn't put all his faith in trees, and there are sandbagged anti-aircraft guns out in the open places.

Because he is at Jamba, Morgan is in uniform. I never saw him dressed that way, but I know how he would look. Unlike most men, who wear army uniforms in a way intended for comfort rather than style, Morgan looks both comfortable and well-tailored. Even in combat dress there is an air of elegance about him which makes him seem out of place here. I think perhaps it is his moustache which does it. It is small and well-trimmed, in contrast to mine, which tended to be a bit unruly and too large for my face. His light brown hair is cut a little longer than I would have expected for the military, not unlike my own. I can see why others might see a physical similarity between us. He is slightly heavier now than he will be two years later, but he is clearly in good physical condition.

Morgan turns and speaks to the other man. "Give us a half hour, will you sergeant? We can pick this up again later."

The sergeant nods mutely and turns to leave the hut. He glances at me as he walks past me toward the door. I feel out of place in my civilian clothes.

After he leaves I walk over to the table and reach across to shake hands. "I'm Argus Morrison."

He grips my hand, and his eyes are steady and clear. "I know. I was told you had come to Jamba to see me."

"Yes."

"Why? I can't think why anyone would travel all this way to meet an ordinary army captain. Is there something in particular that you want from me?"

"Yes. I need to know what kind of a person you are. You see, we won't have time for that later. When events start moving us at their own pace we won't be able to stop and find out about those things."

"Why is that important to you? We all have our roles to play, some forced on us and others taken more or less voluntarily. But we have to play them. There's not much we can do about it, and in any case it's not often that someone else really affects how we behave."

"I suppose that's generally true. But there are times when the other person does make a difference. Haven't you ever met someone to whom you took an immediate dislike, but who eventually became a good friend? That has happened to me more than once."

"You'll have to forgive me," he says, rubbing his chin. "But I'm finding this a bit difficult to follow. If we're going to discuss philosophy I think we should have something to drink."

JAMBA

He disappears into another room, and I hear him opening what I take to be two bottles of beer. He comes back, hands me one, and pulls a straight-backed chair up to the table. I do the same.

"Cheers." We raise our bottles across the maps and I let the warm liquid wash around my mouth before swallowing. In those years Jamba had fewer amenities than it would have later, and a warm beer was much appreciated.

Morgan rests his beer bottle on the Benguela Railroad, which stretches across the map in front of him, and picks up the conversation again. "So what does all this have to do with me? It sounds as if you think we have something in common. Is that it?"

"Not necessarily. But the thought has occurred to me. It bothers me that I have no way of knowing. I want to know for sure."

"In this case I doubt if that's possible. You're probably going to have to reconcile yourself to that. But if it makes you feel better, I don't mind telling you what I think."

"All right. I have only one question: Why are you here?"

"Here?" He motions around the room. "Because it's a job that needs to be done, nothing more than that." He looks at me over his beer bottle as he takes a swig. "Oh, I get it. You want to know if I subscribe to the ideology of the whole thing. Well I can tell you I don't give a damn for the bloody ideology of apartheid. I'm a pragmatist. I'll give you no 'sons of Ham' bullshit from the Old Testament.

"What I will tell you is that I enjoy making life difficult for the Soviets and the Cubans and all the other meddling bastards who're trying to stir things up in this part of the world. But that's not ideology either. I don't delude myself into thinking we're holding the line against

7

Marxism or anything like that. There isn't a Marxist government in Africa that knows or cares a thing about ideology. All it has to do with is power, pure and simple. There are those who have it and those who don't, and I intend to be on the side of those who do."

"So there's no commitment to anything beyond what you want for yourself?"

"I'm not sure I see what you're getting at. I've just told you I can't justify what I'm doing on the basis of philosophy." He hesitates. "But I can see you aren't happy with that explanation either."

"No. I guess I want to believe there's more to it than that."

"Well, if it makes you happier, you can consider self-interest a perfectly valid philosophy. And there are any number of variations to it. Power and money and pleasure are only three of them."

"By that standard, the man who is driven to climb mountains is, in fact, selfish."

"Absolutely. In whose interest is he acting other than his own?"

"Then there *is* hope after all."

Morgan stares at me, uncomprehending, a look of irritation on his face. The warm beer tastes good.

KENYA

LORESHO RIDGE

The garden was a profusion of colors and textures and smells: bougainvillea, papaya, coffee, and a hundred other flowering plants the names of which I have forgotten or never knew. But it was dominated by two enormous flame trees with wide spreading branches and bright crimson blossoms. Those two trees stood over my garden like square-rigged masts over a ship's deck, their variegated green sails luffing softly in the breeze. I carry that picture in my mind's eye even today.

I remember as well that the patio flagstones were warm under my bare feet. There was always warmth in Kenya, of one kind or another. Nairobi is practically on the equator and the sun passes overhead with a regular beat, its cadence unaffected by the season. In the dry months its rays penetrate to the bone. And during the long rains, when the sun labors invisibly beyond a heavy blanket of grey, the fireplaces provide the warmth. Large and stone, their fires push back the creeping dampness and bathe everything in a soothing, wavering light. Of the two, I sometimes think the fireplaces give the greater joy, if only because the alternative is so readily apparent. A short walk through the drizzle of the rains was usually enough to send me back to the hearth, clutching a mug of steaming tea.

But I am thinking now of the dry season, a spectacular Sunday morning about a year after my arrival. There was no possibility of rain that day. The very thought of it under those weightless skies would have seemed strange. Mukami, my steward, was serving breakfast in the garden. He liked to be called Kami, and that is the name which comes to mind now. I watched him set down the coffee as I stood in the warm early sunlight. The small breeze washed around me laden with its fragrances. I listened to a voice in the telephone.

My gaze wandered as I listened and asked a few perfunctory questions. A small monkey chattered briefly in the lower branches of one of the flame trees, and I watched him scamper out of sight in heavier foliage. I closed my eyes to savor the sun's warmth on my face.

The sense of a presence, rather than a sound, made me turn and look back toward the house. Rebecca was stepping through the open double doors onto the patio. Barefoot and slender, she moved gracefully, wrapped in a brightly-colored khanga which reminded me of the flame blossoms behind me.

She greeted Kami as brightly, and a broad smile broke across the older man's face. He nodded and smiled and rearranged some things on the table in a self-conscious way which betrayed his pleasure and his slight embarrassment.

She walked to me, soundless on the flagstones, and she could see from my expression as she approached that the telephone call was business. A call from the Embassy on a Sunday morning was never welcome. She walked to me, put her arms around me and, pressing her body against mine, raised her face for a kiss.

I kissed her with relish, but when I tried to finish quietly she brought her lips away from mine with an audible smack which carried clearly over the telephone. I winced, and there was a momentary silence on the other end of the line. Rebecca giggled and walked out onto the grass, arms spread wide to embrace the whole garden. She was very tanned and her short brown hair was still wet from the shower.

The Embassy duty officer got the hint, and it didn't take long to wind up our conversation. I hung up, and Rebecca turned back toward me.

"Oh, I hope I didn't interrupt anything important." She spoke with her soft Australian accent, and smiled sweetly.

"Not at all, in fact Tony was being even more long-winded than usual. Thanks for breaking up one of his less interesting monologues."

"At first I thought it might be Geoff canceling your tennis match."

"Why would he cancel?"

"Well, you were a bit rough on him last night. I thought his feelings might be hurt."

"Do you think so? I guess we all had a bit too much to drink. Nothing unusual in that, though." I scratched the back of my head. "Maybe I should apologize to him, but I do get annoyed occasionally. Most of the expats here seem genuinely disappointed at how peaceful the whole change of government has been. They seem to feel cheated that Kenya is about the only African country not to have had a coup d'etat."

Rebecca smiled again. "Well, consider that everyone here has spent the last ten years speculating about what would happen when Kenyatta died. Now 'Mzee' drops dead last year, and nothing happens. What a letdown after all those stimulating cocktail party conversations."

"Yes, you're right," I returned her smile. "But last night was about the twentieth time I'd heard Geoff tell the story about the provincial commissioner in Mombasa. It was either stick it to him or pass out from boredom into my Cognac."

The vice president, Daniel arap Moi, had been fortunate enough to have been the first person in Nairobi to be notified when Kenyatta died. That was general knowledge, but should not have been a foregone conclusion. There were others with nearly equivalent claims to the succession, de facto if not de jure, and had that telephone call gone in a slightly different direction the outcome could have been very different.

The conventional wisdom held that a debt of gratitude was owed to the provincial commissioner in Mombasa, where Kenyatta had died. In making his decision while sitting in front of his telephone the Commissioner had come down on the side of the constitution. But a few weeks later he was demoted to a seat on the Kenya Tea Commission, which I suppose is further proof, if any were needed, that there is usually more than meets the eye in such circumstances.

Rebecca looked at me thoughtfully over the rim of her coffee cup. "It seems to me that boredom might not be the only emotion Geoff raises in you."

The monkey chattered again, and I recognized the first tentative twinges of irritation. Rebecca knew very well that I wasn't particularly fond of my British colleague. But there were times when I wasn't receptive to her fondness for psychoanalysis. Sometimes I felt she looked at me as a character in one of the plays her theater company performed.

I sipped my coffee. It was hot, and the aroma soothed me a little. "I wouldn't make a big deal about it." I realized my voice sounded tired, as if I had resigned myself to a vaguely unpleasant task. I wondered if Rebecca would sense my feeling.

She selected a ripe mango from a bowl Kami had arranged and continued, unabashed. "He enjoys playing on the supposed authority of his position," she chose her words as she concentrated on halving the succulent fruit. "It comes across that you resent his assumption that he, as political officer at the High Commission, is the only person in the room who really understands what's going on in Kenya."

"It is a bit 'off-putting' as he would say."

"And you wish you were doing political work?"

"Is that a question?" She knew I wasn't enthusiastic about my work. "You know I didn't come into the Foreign Service to do consular work."

"There's nothing wrong with what you're doing."

"Of course not. It's entirely honorable. I admire those who have the patience to spend their careers doing it."

"Sometimes you seem to enjoy it."

It was true that some aspects of the business allowed me to escape from the office on short notice and brought me into contact with some odd, if not interesting, people: policemen, jailers, physicians, morticians—depending upon how successful I was at solving the problem at hand before it became fatal.

"Too bad I spend most of my time doing visa work." She had heard this before, more than once, but she had raised the subject and I felt it strongly enough to go through it all again. "If I had wanted to be a policeman, I'd have chosen the FBI."

Visa screening, after all, is police work in its purest sense. The process of screening applicants for visitor and immigrant visas amounts to an attempt to apprehend criminals before they have committed their crimes. This is evidently some bureaucrat's idea of efficient law enforcement.

And police investigative work has never appealed to me, perhaps because I have never wanted to involve myself in the lives of strangers. But that business at least enjoys a sense of immediacy and importance stemming from the fact that a crime has been committed. In interviewing a visa applicant I often felt like a detective searching a crowd, looking to arrest anyone who has cleared his throat before he spits on the sidewalk.

I felt the grip of irritation tighten on me.

"But, to return to your original comment," I changed the subject, "you may be right about Geoff, in which case he'll be relieved that *I'm* going to have to cancel our tennis match. To be honest, now that I think about it I'm not in much of a mood for it. I don't think I would have much patience today for the old tennis crowd. The conversation would be a continuation of last night, or, worse yet, a replay."

"Why do you have to cancel?" She was curious now about the phone call.

"Tony is Embassy duty officer this weekend. He was telling me about a call from the police. An American was arrested in Mombasa last Wednesday, four days ago." The warm breeze ruffled the edge of the tablecloth in front of me. "I guessed it was drug-related, as most of them seem to be, but I was wrong.

"There aren't many details from the police, but it seems it's a mental case. He had locked himself in a public toilet. The police had to break the door down.

"Tony ignored me when I said I didn't know Mombasa had any public toilets. The name is David Huntington Haverton III. I said with a name like that he shouldn't have been in a public toilet in the first place. Tony thought I was being serious."

"So what do you have to do about him?" Rebecca had finished the mango.

"I guess I should fly down to the coast. He's been four days in Shimolatewa Prison already."

"Well that, at least, is pleasant. We'll have a few days down there together." Rebecca was in Kenya on contract with a repertory theater company and was scheduled to do a play in Mombasa the next week.

As Kami set a basket of warm muffins down on the table in front of us, I reflected that my irritation had, in fact, left me at that thought.

SHIMOLATEWA 2

Travel to Mombasa was routine for me. I liked the relaxed Swahili culture of the coast, that mixture of Arab and Bantu which developed during the centuries the Sultans of Oman controlled trade and governance in that part of the world. I have always liked the tropics, and Mombasa's beaches are among the most beautiful I have seen anywhere. I told myself that I liked Nairobi too, but I escaped to the sweaty heat of the coast whenever I could.

I managed to reserve a seat on a Kenya Airways Fokker going down in early afternoon. Rebecca was scheduled to fly down with some of the other actors that evening, and we agreed to meet for dinner.

My flight had a good view of Kilimanjaro, ringed with clouds, off to our right. That sight had always before sent a small thrill through me. But I remember clearly that time it seemed somehow a mild reproach. I saw it as the point on the globe farthest removed from my office in the Embassy with its small windows and the undiminishing stacks of visa applications on my desk. The mountain seemed as inaccessible as it was near, and I felt more than a little depressed.

The flight by propjet takes about an hour and a half, and during that time I was able to bring my thoughts around to the task at hand. In my year or so in Kenya I had handled only one other "protection" case involving psychiatric problems. An American tourist had been found wandering around Nairobi, incoherent. It turned out that she was a nurse, and when I walked into her holding cell at the police station she was naked. She had arranged all of her clothes on the damp concrete floor as if someone were wearing them, and was administering artificial respiration to them.

I had learned in handling that case that there was only one mental hospital in Kenya, at Mathari just outside the capital. It had taken me two days to get the legal approvals and to make all the other arrangements to transfer her from police custody to medical care. On top of all that, she had managed to stick her thumb in my eye during her transfer.

In Mombasa it would be all the more difficult, three hundred miles from Nairobi. Everything always took longer in the provinces. My eye began to ache.

My arrival in Mombasa was well-practiced. I never took more than a carry-on bag, and always had a rental car waiting at the terminal. Normally no more than 45 minutes elapsed from the time the plane's wheels touched the runway until I was stretched out on the hot sand of Nyali Beach.

This time, however, after leaving Mombasa Island I drove straight up the coast road, several miles past Nyali, to Shimolatewa Prison. Tall palm trees fringed the road and every few minutes I caught glimpses of the Indian Ocean off to my right. The blue of the water was electric.

I had never been inside the prison before, but I knew the high green walls topped with barbed wire, which lined the main road. My diplomatic identity card got me through the main gate without any difficulty, and I parked my car in the shade of a thorn tree in the dusty outer yard. The policeman at the gate had motioned toward an open door in the wall of the main building. I walked toward it, feeling the heat of the late afternoon sun on my forehead.

It's my experience that government buildings in general, to say nothing of penal institutions, are dreary and ill-kept places. Those in the developing world have their own special charm in that respect. The climate has something to do with it. The concrete walls of Shimolatewa had at one time been painted a neat, bureaucratic green. But seasons of baking heat alternating with torrential downpours had left them faded, cracked, and stained from the bottom with a residue of reddish brown mud. In the dry seasons, as on that day, the buildings of Shimolatewa Prison were landscaped in heat, light, and dust.

I stepped through the doorway into the relative cool of the building. My eyes took a few moments to adjust to the absence of the outside glare. The room I entered was fairly large, also of concrete, but with the green paint somewhat better preserved than on the outside. The only furniture was a number of unfinished, backless benches scattered about, and a small wooden desk next to a doorless opening on the far side of the room. Behind the desk sat a young constable in neatly pressed grey uniform, his face shining with perspiration. Above him hung the only decoration in the room, the new president's official photograph, distinctive in its newness and lack of dust, and hanging a little askew.

It was a slow Sunday afternoon. There were only the two of us in the room, with the President peering mutely over our heads.

"I'm from the American Embassy in Nairobi," I said, extending my red identity card to the constable. "Police Headquarters in Nairobi informed us this morning that there is an American citizen here at Shimolatewa, and I have come to see him. His name is Haverton."

The constable digested the contents of my identity card and handed it back. "Just a moment." He picked up the handset of the old-style bakelite telephone which was the only object on the desk, and sat listening silently for fully a minute without dialing. After a while he replaced the handset, and motioning for me to remain where I was, disappeared around the wall behind him and down a windowless corridor.

I entertained myself by scrutinizing the myriad scratches and grease marks on the top of the desk, where generations of constables had carried out their duties through the long hours. I noticed that the room was lighted by a single shaded bulb suspended from the middle of the ceiling, although much more light came in through the outside doorway.

Meanwhile, rumblings of conversation approached down the corridor. It was Kiswahili, which meant that even had I heard it clearly I wouldn't have been able to understand most of it.

Around the corner a police officer swung into view. I guessed he was in his mid-twenties, and I noticed the pips on the shoulders of his khaki uniform coat. The constable struggled into view behind him.

"I am the duty officer," he said in his best formal-official voice. "May I see your identification?"

I gave him the card, which I still had in my hand. "Police Headquarters in Nairobi was to have informed you of my arrival," I said.

"Thank you," he smiled thinly as he handed the card back. "Please come into my office."

I followed him into the badly lit concrete corridor, and smiled my thanks to the constable. He stared back at me without expression.

After turning the corner, we walked past several office cubicles, the kind with glass in the upper halves of the partitions. All of them seemed to be used for storage, except for the last one, which had "D.O." stenciled on the door. Here was another shaded bulb hanging over another small wooden desk, this time with a second straight-backed chair in front. The door and frame to the cubicle were heavily soiled from a thousand shoulders leaning against them in conversation, and I noticed a number of greasy noseprints in the corner of the dusty glass partition. No doubt it would be normal for a subordinate to check on the status of the duty officer before knocking.

"Please sit down," he motioned to the extra chair as he moved behind the desk. "We have received no word from Nairobi as to your arrival," he added pleasantly after having seated himself.

"I'm surprised to hear that," I lied, "but I hope there's no problem in my seeing Mr. Haverton in any case." I added a smile to my lie. "I'm sure you are aware how seriously we take our responsibilities in prisoner cases." The Embassy would protest later the fact that Haverton had been in jail four days before the police had notified us. But I was prepared to play that card now if necessary to see Haverton immediately.

"No, there is no problem with your seeing Mr. Haverton, but of course we take our responsibilities in these cases very seriously as well."

"Of course." Ease up, I said to myself. I smiled again, unconvincingly. "Can you tell me about Mr. Haverton's arrest? Is he charged with anything?"

"No, he is not charged with anything. We have taken him into protective custody. You see, when we found him he was behaving strangely. He had barricaded himself in the toilet of a bar in the old part of the city. He would not come out, and no one else could go in. Eventually the bar owner sent for the police. Our men had to break down the door to the toilet. The bar owner, however, not wanting to become involved in legalities, has not filed a complaint."

"I see." The DTs, I thought. Maybe if we could get him someplace to dry out he'd be okay. "Had he been drinking heavily, then?"

"Apparently not. We thought at first that he was merely drunk. That wouldn't be altogether unusual for a sailor, particularly one who had missed the departure of his ship. But we could detect no sign of alcohol, and his behavior hasn't changed since then."

"You say he came in with a ship?"

"Yes, the *Molucca Victory*. That was in our report to Nairobi. The captain reported his absence before leaving port."

Great. "When did the ship leave?"

"Tuesday night."

"You seem to be very well briefed on this case. Is there anything else I should know before seeing him? How about his papers?"

"He has his papers with him. As it happened, I was on duty last week when he was brought in. I should tell you that he hasn't been cooperative since he has been here. In fact he sometimes gets quite agitated and shouts a lot of nonsense. I will have a man right outside the cell in case you need him."

"Thank you very much. I expect that we will want to transfer Mr. Haverton to medical treatment in Nairobi as soon as possible, but I understand I will have to speak with a magistrate about that."

He nodded and got up. I followed him out of the cubicle and on down the corridor toward a pool of light which indicated a doorway to the outdoors. There we found a set of bars between us and the inner courtyard of the prison. On the other side of the bars, several paces away, stood a sergeant and three constables.

"Sajini, kuja hapa."

The sergeant jumped, unlocked the gate, and held it open for us. I had the impression of stepping from a barn into a barnyard. The entire courtyard was in shadow, and the air had cooled noticeably in the short time I had been inside. The duty officer and the sergeant exchanged some words, whereupon the officer turned back to me, his part of the process evidently complete. I thanked him again and waited for the sergeant to lock him out of the courtyard.

In turning to follow the sergeant across the yard, I noticed that all three constables were following along. Is this really necessary, I wondered, or are they just tagging along for the show? After all, with a name like David Huntington Haverton III how dangerous could he be?

From the moment I had first heard his name, I had pigeonholed Haverton as an upper-crust drug case. I fully expected to find a worn out individual, but still someone at least vaguely recognizable as out of a designer sportswear catalogue. The merchant seaman part didn't quite fit, but I hadn't had much time to think about it.

The sergeant unlocked the cell door and pulled it open. Inside were more concrete walls, their original color indeterminable under stains and dirt. Yet another shaded bulb hung from the ceiling, too high to reach. There was no furniture. As I stepped into the cell, I thought of some subway stations I had seen in New York. Only the sparsity of graffiti marred the comparison. The sergeant left the door open a few inches behind me.

Haverton was sitting on the floor with his back in a corner, his knees pulled up to his chest and his head thrown back, mouth agape. He snored softly. My first impression was that I had entered the wrong cell. He had a mop of matted grey hair, and about a week or ten day's growth of grey beard. He wore an old pair of canvas trousers which showed no history of a crease and had probably been white at some time, an old white t-shirt, and red plastic thong sandals.

He was stringy. I couldn't tell in that posture how tall he was, but he looked thin and wiry, and where his skin was exposed—arms, ankles, and neck—the sun had given it the complexion of jerked beef. The backs of his hands rested on the concrete floor of the cell. Though he was thin he looked strong. The bottom half of a tattoo, faded and blurred by time, showed from under one sleeve of his t-shirt.

As I stood just inside the doorway taking all this in, he broke wind, long and luxuriously. Then he closed his mouth and swallowed, and without opening his eyes or raising his head to look at me, he said, "You here to sling some more of that goddawful shit you call food in this fuckin' place?" He spoke with a hoarse baritone in a neutral American accent. I couldn't place it, and somehow the voice didn't seem to fit the body in front of me.

"No, I'm here from the American Embassy to see how you're doing."

His head shot up and his eyes opened wide, then narrowed on me. "If you expect me to believe that you're a bigger fool than any of the other assholes on this ship." He hesitated a moment and cocked his head as if listening to a distant sound. "Whatever it is you're after, fuck off."

This, I said to myself, is going to be more difficult than I had expected. "Actually, I just want to see that you're all right. In fact, I hope we'll have you out of here in a day or so, to someplace where you can rest up."

"When I get outta here I'm *gone*."

"Certainly, as soon as you're in good shape."

"What're you talkin' about, you stupid shit? When I get outta here I'm *DEAD*. He'll see to that."

"Who will?"

Haverton snorted disgustedly, hawked and spat. My eyes followed involuntarily, and I watched for a moment as his gob hung on the filthy wall across from him, sagging a little. When I turned my gaze back on him he had laid his head back against the wall. I took the opportunity to pick up his passport, which was lying on the floor a few feet from him. It had about six months to go before expiration, and was full of entry and exit stamps, mostly from Africa and Latin America. A seaman's card was stuck in among the pages. The names in the passport and on the card matched what the police had given our embassy duty officer. His date of birth made him fifty-four. He seemed twenty years older.

As I looked at him, his mouth slowly fell open and he snored a little. I noticed that he was missing a couple of teeth. Just as I was about to speak he broke wind again, and I made a mental note to get him some vitamin supplements. His diet couldn't have been very healthy for some time.

"Mr. Haverton, do you have any relatives you'd like me to notify? Anyone in the States or anyplace else?"

He slowly raised his head and stared at me with those same narrowed eyes, lips compressed. "Who the fuck're you and whaddaya want?"

"Like I said, I'm from the Embassy. I asked if there was anyone you wanted me to notify about your situation here."

He stared at me and scratched his beard with dirty fingernails.

"All right, how about money? Did you have any money when you were arrested?"

Suddenly his eyes widened and he leaned forward. "*MORGAN!*" It was a hoarse whisper.

I actually turned and looked behind me, but no one was there. "What?"

"Morgan. I didn't think you'd come here. I mean, it wasn't my fault. I was makin' good way, well along the Brazil coast when up come this godawful weather an' just kept gettin' worse. Before I knew it, all I could do was ride it to a storms'l with a sea anchor out an then came this fuckin' huge wave an we took a goddam roll like I never want to see again. Snapped the goddam stick, and we started to take on water. Wallowed in the goddam trough 'til she hit some rocks, slipped under an' settled."

He had planted his palms on the grimy concrete floor, and seemed to be trying to press himself farther into the corner. His face had a look of wide-eyed terror to it as he looked up at me, and his speech was one long hysterical whisper.

"Look," I said, "you seem to be pretty upset. Why don't you just get some rest, and I'll..."

"But don't worry. Everything's okay. It's still there. The gold. No problem with the ballast." He licked his lips. "I know I wasn't supposed to know about that, but I found out when we were fittin' out in Cape Town. Not that I give a shit for them UNITA bastards. I didn't care what was in that boat. It's there, I'm sure. No more'n thirty feet a water, max, right off a set a rocks easy to spot. Here, I swear, I been keepin' this to give you. We were in sight a land when she settled. I stuck around after I made it ashore. A month at least. Figured it exact. Here."

He scrabbled in the waistband of his trousers for a few moments and came up with what looked like a fat toothpick. He held it out to me nervously. I had concluded it was high time to bring this conversation to an end, but it seemed very important to him, so I took it.

It turned out to be a small piece of paper, greasy and rolled up tightly, as if it had been fingered constantly for a long time. I unrolled it and recognized a scrawled notation for a navigational position—latitude and longitude down to the second. Suddenly I had the absurd feeling that I had been transported to some old pirate movie. Here in front of me was a very lean Wallace Beery, who was bound to say "Arrr, matey" any moment and leer at me out of one eye.

I let the scrap roll itself back up and started to hand it back to him. "That's fine, but I think you're confused. My name's Morrison, not Mor..."

"Keep it. I don't want it." He literally cringed from my hand.

"All right. We can talk more tomorrow. I'm going to see a magistrate in the morning about getting you to a better place. I should be back by early afternoon with some news."

He stared at me, still with the look of terror. I turned and stepped to the door, hoping he wouldn't launch into another soliloquy until after I had left. The heavy door yielded to my push and I stepped out into the corridor.

I slipped Haverton's piece of paper into my pocket as the sergeant locked up behind me. On the way out, I noticed that my heart was beating a little too fast, and I was sweating a little more than the heat would justify. That man definitely had problems; hallucinations and paranoia just for starters.

I saw the duty officer again briefly, and wrote for him on one of my business cards the telephone number of the friend's house where I stayed when I was in Mombasa. He promised to keep an eye on Haverton, but I knew there wouldn't be any real help for him until I could get him to a hospital. It was dusk when I climbed into my car and drove back toward Nyali.

I tried to put business behind me for the day. I noticed the moon had already risen over the ocean, and I thought forward to the evening. I leaned over and rolled down the passenger window to let the warm evening air sluice through the car.

My thoughts turned to Rebecca, and my earlier irritation was completely gone. I felt a little guilty about the way I had reacted at breakfast. I looked forward to seeing her for dinner.

First, however, I had to get myself situated. I knew that the friend I normally stayed with in Mombasa was out of town. But I had stayed there many times before, and his cook let me in when I rang the bell at the gate. It was dark, but I could hear the surf down on the beach as I carried my bag into the large Arab-style house and down the tiled gallery to my room.

After showering off the day's dust and sweat, I lay naked on the bed and felt clean and relaxed. The breeze passed between louvered screens at opposite ends of the room and played lightly over my body. It carried with it the sound of the surf and the smell of sea salt mixed with the fragrance of honeysuckle. My freshly scrubbed skin throbbed slightly to my heartbeat. I drifted off to sleep.

NYALI BEACH 3

The Coriander Restaurant was a favorite of mine in Kenya; another Arabic-style building with lanterns hanging in the dark breeze, arbors filled with flowering vines, and a large patio overlooking the lights of the old port of Mombasa. On warm, clear nights it was a wonderful place, especially when there was a moon.

Rebecca sat opposite me at a small table near the edge of the patio. The candlelight played on her suntanned face and arms, and her skin glowed. When she laughed, which was often, her short brown hair danced and shone and her eyes sparkled. She wore a sheer silk dress with thin straps over her slender shoulders, and when she leaned forward to speak I could see the curves of her breasts through the material.

She was pleased with the way the audience in Nairobi had reacted to the current play. "Argus, do you remember that one set of lines I rehearsed in your garden? The ones when you took the role of the physician? Remember how many times we had to go through those lines until I had it just the way I wanted it, with just the right twist?"

We were sharing my favorite Coriander meal: crab claws washed down with Soave. I picked up the last claw on the plate and held it out to her, but she declined with a shake of her head as she finished her question.

"How could I ever forget?" I said, inspecting the claw and savoring the thought of it before taking a bite. "I think I could do the part of that doctor in my sleep. We must have gone through those lines a hundred times."

"Well, it all paid off. The audience loved it. I think I told you, at first in rehearsal Tim didn't want me to do those lines that way. But I talked him into it, and tonight he admitted I was right."

"Bravo. I think that's the second or third time now you've brought the director around to your way of thinking about a part. I guess I'll have to see this play, maybe later this week."

"You'd better. If you stay down here all week and miss the show I'll be forced to let you go as my rehearsal partner."

"And here I was thinking I had become crucial to your success."

"On the contrary. I'm finding it increasingly difficult to concentrate on my lines. I keep seeing you in my mind's eye in candlelit poses, at very close quarters, and wearing nothing at all. Perhaps I should say I keep feeling you like that."

I looked at her over the top of my wineglass. "It's a good thing I'm sunburned, or I'd have to admit I'm blushing."

Our eyes locked across the table, and I think it's safe to say our thoughts were moving to after-dinner activities.

Suddenly a strange voice forced its way between us. "May I?"

I hadn't noticed the man approaching the table from behind me. He pulled up a chair and sat down before I could respond.

I was certain I had never seen him before. Compact and elegant, he wore a white dinner jacket, with a bright red carnation on the lapel. I had never seen anyone dress that formally in Mombasa. I thought perhaps he was somehow connected with the restaurant: an East African Rick, à la Humphrey Bogart.

"Please excuse the intrusion," he nodded to Rebecca and then turned back to me, "but I have a matter of some urgency to bring to your attention."

"Yes?"

"I spoke a short while ago with an employee, a former employee, of mine whom I believe you have met: Mr. Haverton?"

I was too surprised to say anything.

"The poor fellow was quite confused. He swore that he had already spoken with me today. It was quite some time before I was able to put the pieces together. You see, it seems he mistook you for me when you stopped in to see him earlier this afternoon."

He spoke with a South African accent.

"He did seem rather confused when I saw him." I noted that we were of generally similar height and build, and we both had moustaches. It was plausible, particularly in Haverton's state of mind, that he could confuse us. I wondered if this man's name was Morgan.

"Well, to make a very long and tedious story as short as possible," he continued, "Mr. Haverton had been on an extended holiday until I terminated his employment today; two years, to be exact. During that period of time he has had some property of mine, a fairly substantial amount of property. For that reason I have spent a considerable amount of time and trouble in locating him."

I thought back to my conversation with Haverton and tried to see how all of this fit together.

"Now that you've found him, perhaps you could tell me if he has any relatives I should notify concerning his situation?"

"I think not. The point is, Mr. Morrison, I believe Haverton gave you a piece of paper with some numbers on it. He said he gave it to you. I don't know what kind of nonsense he may have told you about it, but that piece of paper is my property and I would like you to give it to me. I assure you it is of no use to anyone but me."

This was getting interesting. "If Mr. Haverton gave me anything when I spoke with him," I said, "I would have to have his permission before passing it to a third party."

"Don't play bloody games with me Morrison. I want that paper, and I'm deadly serious about it. Give it to me."

I felt the blood rise in my face. "If you have business to conduct, Mr.—"

"Morgan," he said after a moment's hesitation. "Thomas Morgan."

"If you have business to conduct, Mr. Morgan, I'll be happy to see you tomorrow. In the meantime, get lost."

His face started to approach the color of the carnation on his lapel. "Tomorrow will be too late. I need it now."

Cool down, I said to myself. Just get rid of him. "Even if I wanted to oblige you, Mr. Morgan, I don't have my briefcase with me here at the restaurant. You'll have to wait until tomorrow. I'll be seeing Haverton again early in the afternoon, and after that I'll see what I can do. Where can I reach you?"

Morgan slowly stood up, his eyes boring into me. "I had hoped this wouldn't be difficult, but you've disappointed me. Don't worry about reaching me. I'll reach you." He turned on his heel and stalked off through the other tables.

That was a bit disruptive to the mood of the evening; not so much what Morgan had said as the peculiar vehemence with which he had said it. I think I downed the rest of my wine in one slug. We decided to order coffee and Cognac to give ourselves a chance to settle down, and it was certainly after one thirty when we left the restaurant.

I drove back to Nyali Beach circuitously, keeping an eye in the rear view mirror to make sure our friend wasn't following us. After ten minutes or so I decided I was overreacting, and by the time we got to the house my thoughts were again running as they had been before we were interrupted.

I helped Rebecca out of the car, and led her by the hand through the house to the main balcony overlooking the beach. Below us lay the Indian Ocean, bathed in moonlight out to the horizon. A ship's lights shone faintly several miles out. We kissed, and slowly my hands molded the sheer fabric of her dress to the firm curves underneath. The night breeze moved softly around us. The surf pounded.

Before long, she detached herself and led me by the hand to the bedroom. I lit a candle on the table while she kicked off her shoes. We faced each other about ten feet apart in the candlelight. Slowly she reached up and slid the straps of her dress off her shoulders. It fell to the floor with a barely perceptible rustle of silk. She wore only the smallest of bikini pants, a tiny white triangle against her golden skin. The candle flickered shadows across her body and highlighted the curves of her breasts and thighs, the flatness of her stomach. Her skin looked smooth and moist.

We looked at each other and smiled. She walked to me and began to unbutton my shirt. I heard the telephone ring like someone shouting to wake me from a wonderful dream. We both ignored it. She pushed my shirt off my shoulders and it fell to the floor. Her hands moved caressingly across my chest and stomach and started to unfasten my belt buckle.

Suddenly, there was a light knock on the door. It was the cook. "Mistah Morrison, sah, the police, they want to talk with you."

Damn! "All right," I croaked, "I'll be right there." I kissed Rebecca. "Why don't you get into bed, darling. I'll be right back."

I walked down the corridor shirtless, thinking my job didn't pay enough.

"Morrison speaking."

"Hello, this is police Assistant Inspector Kimathi. I am most sorry to disturb you at this hour, but we have been trying to contact you all evening. It is about the American at Shimolatewa, Mr., ah, Havington."

"Haverton," I said, not liking the sound of this.

"Yes, quite, Haverton. I am afraid that I must inform you that he died in his cell early this evening."

I started to get a queasy feeling in my gut. "What? How?"

"We are not certain. There are no outward signs of the cause of death. We thought perhaps an autopsy would be in order, but I wanted to speak with you first."

"Yes, by all means, please order an autopsy. Where is the body now?"

"It has been taken downtown to the morgue."

"I see. Will you be the investigating officer, Inspector? Is there anything to be done tonight?"

"Yes, I will be the investigating officer, and I think there is nothing more to be done now. We could meet at my office in police headquarters tomorrow morning at, say, ten o'clock. Would that be convenient?"

"Yes. Fine. Thank you very much, Inspector, I'll see you then." I rang off and stood looking at the telephone for a moment, wondering if I should have mentioned Morgan to him.

With the benefit of hindsight I can see that I was foolish. But at the time I reasoned that Haverton's death just might have been from natural causes. He clearly hadn't been all that healthy when I had seen him, although I hadn't thought him on the brink of death.

Given the possibility that Morgan hadn't been responsible, I didn't want to make what would have amounted to an accusation of him to the police. I can't deny that he hadn't endeared himself to me at the restaurant, but I nevertheless felt it would be going a bit far to accuse him of murder. Presumably the police knew he had visited Haverton anyway. If the autopsy turned up anything suspicious he would be on their list of people to talk to. I decided to mention Morgan to Inspector Kimathi the next morning.

All the same, I was more than just a bit unsettled as I walked back to the bedroom. I kept thinking back to my conversation, such as it was, with Haverton. It made a lot more sense to me after that phone call than it had when I was in the cell with him. If what he had said hadn't been complete nonsense, he must have been smuggling some-thing for Morgan when his boat was wrecked in Brazilian waters. I thought I remembered him mentioning gold.

By the time I reached the bed I knew I wouldn't sleep much that night, but not for the original reasons I had in mind. Rebecca was asleep, looking very tempting with one tanned arm lying on top of the sheets. Her bikini underwear lay on top of her dress, still in the middle of the floor.

I walked over to the closet and felt in the pockets of the clothes I had worn that afternoon. Haverton's rolled up scrap of paper was in the third pocket I tried. Moving as quietly as I could, I left the bed-room and walked down the corridor to the library. I switched on the desk lamp and began searching the shelves for an atlas. If Haverton's coordinates turned out to be in the middle of the Amazon rain forests I could forget the whole thing.

Down low on the shelves, among the other big books, I found what I was looking for. I opened the atlas under the light of the lamp, and found the right plate, in the section covering South America. The map was very small scale; too small to use for anything but a general idea. But it looked like Haverton's latitude and longitude would plot on the coast south of the city of Salvador, in Bahia.

The queasy feeling returned to my stomach. I sat there for a long time, with the atlas open in front of me but not really looking at it. The more I thought about it, the more unsettled I became. I even considered calling the police, but I kept telling myself not to overreact.

Eventually I got up, put the book back, and switched off the lamp. I went back to the bedroom and woke Rebecca with a kiss.

"Mmh, that's a nice way to wake up." She smiled sleepily and ran her hand down my back until she felt my trousers. "But you are definitely overdressed for this occasion. I think you should rid yourself of those nasty garments, sir, and climb into bed with me. I'll keep you warm."

"I'd love to, darling, but I think we'd better not tonight. I'm sorry, but something's come up, and I'm a bit worried about it. I'd better take you back to the hotel."

"I don't like that idea at all." She looked at me and frowned. "I bet it has something to do with that naff South African at the Coriander, doesn't it?"

"It may, I don't know. I don't like it either. But the fellow I visited at Shimolatewa today, the one Morgan was talking about, has died, and I've got a bad feeling about it." I hesitated a moment. "Haverton, the dead man, mentioned some very strange things to me about Brazil and a sunken boat, and I think perhaps his death wasn't altogether natural. I've got to look into it first thing tomorrow. I'm sorry, darling. Let me take you back. Hopefully everything will be cleared up by tomorrow night."

I kissed her again. She pulled me down onto her, and my resolve wavered with the feel of her breasts against my chest. But persistence, or perhaps obstinacy, on my part prevailed. I watched her get dressed as I buttoned my shirt.

The drive into town and back took me roughly forty-five minutes. By the time I returned to the house, I was starting to get pretty tired. I parked the car, let myself in the front door, and walked to the bedroom.

I switched on the light, and there, sitting in a chair across the room, was Morgan. He had traded his evening attire for a khaki safari suit, and was holding what looked like a 9mm Browning pistol. I hope I never get another surprise like that as long as I live.

"It's not here, so I assume you have it with you," he said.

My briefcase was open, as was the closet door. "What the hell are you doing here? How did you get in?"

"Save your indignation. I told you, I want that piece of paper Haverton gave you." The Browning was pointed at me. "I'll take it now, thank you."

It suddenly occurred to me that this whole thing had gotten out of control. "Right. I can be reasonable. Don't shoot."

I tried to remember what I had done with the paper after I had looked at the atlas. Just as I remembered that I had put it in my shirt pocket, the thought hit me that even if I gave it to him, Morgan would probably kill me anyway. Haverton had known too much. Morgan didn't know exactly what I knew, but he had also heard Haverton's speech, and he probably guessed that I knew more than he would like.

"Well, where is it?"

"I'm trying to remember where I put it," I stalled. Morgan was being a little casual with his pistol, and at that time I didn't know that he was a trained army officer. I knew from my navy experience that very few people could hit anything with a pistol at twenty feet, even if they tried to sight carefully. Morgan was holding his pistol at waist level, and he had his legs crossed, trying to be nonchalant. The distance was probably a little less than twenty feet, but I was convinced I had to do something.

I lunged for the door. Morgan fired, and the doorframe splintered next to my head. I felt a sharp slap in the face, but I could still see and move my legs, and I kept going. Right outside the bedroom was a stairwell which led down to the patio and swimming pool. But I remembered that the door there had two locks, each of which took some time to open. The same thing was true for the front door. I wasn't sure about the servants' quarters on the other side of the kitchen. The only other way out was a way I had tried only once before, during a party.

I pounded down the tiled corridor, through the sitting room, and toward the balcony. I knew if I pushed out enough, and slightly to the right, that I would hit the swimming pool one storey below. As I reached the spot where Rebecca and I had been earlier, I launched myself over the railing into the void. I heard another shot, but didn't feel anything.

By that time I was having trouble seeing, and it would be difficult to describe how it felt to fall toward that pool, not knowing whether I would hit water or concrete. The horrible thought occurred to me that my friend might have drained the pool before leaving on his trip.

But before I could continue that line of thought, I landed in the water with an impact that knocked the wind out of me. I struggled to the side of the pool, pulled myself out with what seemed like the last of my energy, and started off again. The water had cleared my vision a little. I sprinted toward the beach and took the fence there like a hurdle. Onto the soft sand, I found it harder going. But I guess I got to the water before Morgan arrived at the beach because I didn't hear any more shots. I threw myself into the waves, swam a few strokes out and then lay as quietly as I could on my back. I knew there was a strong current parallel to the beach that time of year, and that it would soon have me quite a distance away. I hoped the moonlight wasn't bright enough for Morgan to spot me if I lay very still in the water.

I stayed that way for what seemed like a very long time, trying to get my pulse rate back near normal. The left side of my forehead stung ferociously, and I guessed I was bleeding from a splinter wound there. I thanked God for the Nyali reef, which keeps sharks away from the beach.

After a while I calculated by the lights I could see that I had drifted past the big hotels, which put me farther south than I figured Morgan would be looking. So, with the first faint signs of dawn over the eastern horizon, I chose a place where the waves were washing over some rocks, clambered out of the water, and ducked into the undergrowth. There I found a spot where I was well hidden but could watch the beach in both directions.

An objective observer might well say that anyone in his right mind would have made it for the police right away. I still don't think that would have done any good. I was convinced Morgan was a psychopath. Whether that was true or whether he was simply a very tough and determined criminal, lousy marksmanship notwithstanding, he had managed to murder Haverton in the middle of Shimolatewa Prison and get away without raising any alarm. I didn't doubt that he could get to me eventually, regardless of what the police did to protect me. I just didn't have that much confidence in the police.

Even if I contrived to get Haverton's grubby little piece of paper to him, I thought he would still want to shut me up permanently. I was convinced that I had been drawn into this thing past the point of no return.

But other thoughts also passed through my mind as I sat there in the underbrush. I was sitting cross-legged on the hard sand, my back against the trunk of a palm, and I could feel its roughness through the damp fabric of my shirt. A dawn breeze gently ruffled some of the foliage around me. I leaned my head back and listened to the sound of the surf on the beach. The eastern sky was turning a cool rose-blue, but stars were still visible between the colorless palm fronds high above me.

It would be untrue to say that my life in Kenya had been boring. But I thought back to my reaction when I had seen Kilimanjaro earlier that day, and I realized with a little surprise that it had been some time since I had really been happy. It wasn't so much anything bad as it was the absence of something good which I sensed: a lack, or more aptly, a rarification where there should have been a compression, an intensity.

I tried to identify the source of my emotion, and it was a little like waking from a dream not fully remembered, but one which has left a residue of unease. I searched my mind, not knowing where to begin, hoping vaguely that I would stumble on the answer, and hoping again that the answer would be trivial—one which made the question not worth asking.

But I knew without really thinking about it that the question *was* worth asking. What surprised me was that I hadn't asked it before. It seemed so insistent there in the underbrush that at first I wondered if I was overreacting from loss of blood or exertion, or shock. But that wasn't the problem. I realized dimly that I had been asking it for months—of the stacks of visa applications on my desk and of the empty faces explaining things to me across my desk and of the desk itself, with the cup of coffee steaming gently off to one side.

I remembered a film I had seen a few years earlier. The images were as sharp as the pain in the side of my head. A journalist on assignment in North Africa. A dusty Land Rover and a seedy hotel in a flyblown village. Heat and dust and sweat, unremitting. In loneliness and frustration I take a bottle of whiskey to the next room to have a drink with the other European there. But he isn't drinking. He's dead. I sit in his chair and have a drink, calmly regarding his corpse on the floor at my feet. No signs of a struggle. Natural causes.

I am intrigued. I remember stories I have heard of people given the opportunity to lose themselves, to disappear from their lives; to change identities with a corpse, perhaps. I have the strong sense that I am facing a once-in-a-lifetime decision, and I am morbidly fascinated.

But that fascination isn't driven by boredom or despair or even by mere frustration. It is driven by the realization that there is more than there has been. It is driven by the knowledge that you have forgotten things without knowing it—things which are valuable and which make a difference—but things which are gone now because you don't even remember you've forgotten them.

The answer began to form itself in my mind like half-spoken words on the lips of a sleeping man. I tried to concentrate on the words. The faintest breath of a breeze washed over my throbbing forehead and pulled with it the first pale rays of the sun, bursting over the rim of the horizon and cascading over the waves toward me. I closed my eyes and savored the faint warmth on my skin.

I tried to concentrate on the words. There had been a time when my world had been the surface of the sea, with all its moods and states—sometimes boiling furiously, sometimes glasslike and solid in its calm. And my life cut through that world like the stem of a ship, not large or even particularly noteworthy, but undeniably there. My passage cut through the surface and peeled it back in white foaming curls and sent it out behind me in wake and wavelets, nothing permanent, but testament nonetheless to my passage. At least it had seemed that way to me.

The early rays of the sun had seemed the same to me then, like cold fire, reflecting off the waves with an intensity which made me squint and shade my eyes, but warming at first only faintly. But later, that sultry beginning would blossom into a heat and a glare which made the railings impossible to grasp. The steel surfaces of the ship, faded grey from salt and sun, became one huge, convoluted heat magnet, and inside the air pounded in your ears from the transmitted energy and from the faint sounds and vibrations of the machinery far below.

I tried to concentrate on the words. A trickle of sweat ran down my chest and into the waistband of my trousers. I lifted my arm from the nautical chart spread out in front of me and the place where it had rested was dark from moisture. I moved the sharpened point of my pencil to another place on the chart and made my mark and a small notation from the reconnaissance report. With each mark and each notation we moved closer to our nightly climax. A drop left my chin and obliterated a small island, the moisture expanding quickly outward through the fibers of the chart paper. I tried to wipe my face on the short sleeve of my shirt, but the khaki material was already soaked.

The charthouse eventually became unbearable. It always did. I moved out onto the bridge wing. The only breeze was from our slow movement through the water, but the air was cooler, even out in the sun. The officer of the deck was standing with his hands on his hips and his feet apart, looking out over the oily calm and trying to let the air move around his limbs. When he saw me emerge he pointed to the surface, thirty feet below. The sea snakes coiled and stretched in groups just below the surface, like animated seaweed. I unholstered my Browning and sighted downward. The shot shattered the peace of the morning and sent a tiny waterspout back toward us. But the snakes were difficult targets and I always missed. The only real question was how long we could keep it up before the captain demanded a return to peace and quiet.

I tried to concentrate on the words. But the nights would always come. That was the time of exhilaration and dread. We were at our stations before the general quarters alarm sounded, checking our equipment one last time. In the late afternoon and early dusk the heat receded and the sultriness returned. We ran darkened up the coast to a point I had marked on the chart where our approach course angled through islands or past shoals toward the other marks and my small penciled notations. We increased speed as we turned in toward the target zone. At thirty-four knots the ship strained with a well-oiled tension and cut cleanly through the small seas.

Sooner or later the coast began to flicker like a summer garden heavy with fireflies in the muggy heat. But some of the flashes were larger than others, and those were the ones we had to deal with first. The largest were two hundred millimeter batteries, with a range exceeding that of our own five inch guns. We had to endure their attention until we had closed the coast and unloaded the allotted number of rounds on our assigned targets.

The flashes were silent, which added to the summer garden image, until the incoming rounds arrived at our end. Then the detonations ranged from alarming to heart-stopping, depending upon the quality of the North Vietnamese gunnery. Tall geysers grew into the air, shining faintly phosphorescent in the moonlight. The conning officer gave orders to the helmsman which took the ship toward the last point of impact, sometimes through the spray still suspended in the air, in order to confound their sight corrections. All the while the boilers and turbines in the machinery spaces sent out vibrations with an urgency which made itself felt through the soles of my shoes way up on the bridge.

On the way out we were free to engage in counterbattery fire. Most of the notations on my chart were the latest observed positions of coastal batteries. I read the coordinates to our main battery controllers as my men recorded our position every thirty seconds. Rapid-fire salvos from all three mounts shook the steel plates under us and sometimes broke light bulbs. And occasionally there was a secondary explosion ashore where our rounds found a small ammunition dump. Those fires flickered more brightly than the muzzle flashes, and reflected off the clouds and the surrounding hills.

I tried to concentrate on the words. Then there would be the next night.

I felt the cool hard sand under the palms of my hands and stretched to ease the ache in my back. The sun was a bit higher and the color of the sky had shifted away from the rose and toward the blue. The foliage around me had come alive in various shades of green. I thought of Haverton, and realized that he was the corpse in my cinematic North African hotel room. I sat there on the hard sand and sipped on my imaginary whiskey and watched him lying dead on the threadbare rug under my feet.

And then I thought about Rebecca. And when I thought of her I thought of the rarification of my life. It wasn't clear to me why I felt that way. I thought I should think of her as a compression of everything rich and full and profound. I stared unblinking at the contradiction.

I tried to concentrate only on the words forming on the sleeping man's lips. That was it. Everything pointed in the same direction. It was the thing I had forgotten without realizing it. It was the thing which wasn't pain, and wasn't really frustration, and wasn't even boredom. It was the lack of an identifiable edge. It was the absence of the cutwater moving through the seas, even if without real purpose. It was the absence of motion.

As the lips formed around the final syllables I felt myself starting to move.

RAS MKUUNGOMBE 4

Mombasa has the most virulent sand flies on earth. Their bites, which pass unnoticed at first, fill with inflamed liquid, drain for several days, and usually leave a small scar when they finally heal.

As I sat in the underbrush the sun slowly rose in the sky and the tiny gnat-like insects began to explore my eyes, ears, nose—and the cut on my forehead. It still stung, but had long since stopped bleeding. In the predawn darkness it had throbbed lightly. That gave way in the increasing heat to a deep, crashing headache which stabbed to the center of my skull. I began to sweat freely.

But having come to a decision of sorts, I felt a strange sense of relief. What I was going to do seemed completely natural to me. Everyone I knew would think me insane, but I was comfortable with the idea.

I ran through the contents of my pockets: money, keys, identification, and Haverton's coordinates. The unpleasant thought surfaced slowly in my pounding brain that the scrawled numbers might be illegible after my nighttime swim. I unbuttoned my shirt pocket and carefully fished out the scrap of paper. It was still damp, and I unrolled it slowly. But it had gotten so greasy during the two years he had carried it with him that the inked numbers hadn't blurred at all. I realized I had been holding my breath, and exhaled slowly through pursed lips.

I shifted my position on the hard-packed sand, leaned back against the bole of a palm tree and swatted at the sand flies swarming in front of my face. I would somehow have to get out of Kenya without being caught by Morgan. It occurred to me then that I would also have to avoid the police, since they would have all kinds of questions I didn't want to take the time to answer. A powerful urge for evasion welled up inside me. I knew my decision would seem strange, and that virtually everyone would conspire to keep me from fulfilling it.

My white short-sleeved shirt, khaki trousers, and brown leather boat shoes all looked like they had spent the night in the Indian Ocean. Fortunately half the tourists in Kenya normally looked that way. But if looking like I had slept in my clothes wouldn't raise any eyebrows, my head was another matter. I had no idea what the cut looked like, but it felt nasty and probably bad enough to raise a comment from anyone who saw me.

I decided I should find some place to clean up and perhaps get a hat to wear. I couldn't go back to my friend's house, but there were other beach houses all along that part of the coast. Many of them were owned by people living in Nairobi and often went unoccupied between weekends.

No one had come by on the beach during the hours I had kept watch, and it looked clear. At a crouch, I began to pick my way through the undergrowth, moving south. The first few houses I passed were occupied. At one a man and a woman were eating breakfast on the patio. I thought back to my breakfast the previous morning and realized that I was ravenous. The Coriander's crab claws were not made for a long-lasting meal.

The fifth or sixth house I passed looked promising. I considered crawling around it in the bushes to take a look, but my head pounded, my back and legs ached from crouching, and I was tired and hungry.

I walked quietly toward the house. The hard sand and sparse grass on the inland side was well shaded with tall palms, and fallen fronds littered the area. I stepped tensely among them, straining to catch the least sign of life. Shutters closed, the house looked thoroughly abandoned. The air was absolutely still and the faint sound of the surf was barely audible from the other side of the house. The sand flies still swarmed around my head. I inhaled one and coughed it back up into my mouth. The tiny insect squirmed for a moment on my tongue before I quietly spat it out. A trickle of sweat ran down my spine.

The patio on the ocean side was empty except for some cushionless chairs and a small table. All the shutters were closed. I completed my circuit of the house and came to the entrance to the service yard.

My original thought had been to break into the kitchen door, perhaps through a pane of glass, but on the wall facing me was a light fixture mounted above and to the right of the door. The paint next to it was soiled from dirty hands. I walked over to the light, reached up and behind the glass lens, and pulled out a key which opened the kitchen door. I went in quietly and relocked the door behind me.

* * *

I awoke in darkness, totally disoriented. Running both hands over my shirt, trousers, bare mattress, I struggled to remember where I was. My eyes began to pick out faint shapes in the void; almost unnoticeable light coming in through the slats of shutters. I remembered.

I swung my feet onto the floor and rubbed my face with both hands without thinking of the cut there. Pain stabbed me awake. Still, I was refreshed after what must have been hours of sleep. I sat on the edge of the bed trying to think what I should do next. I had half thought that with a fresh mind I would see my decision to find the boat as stupidly irrational. I forced myself to contemplate going to the police. But I didn't want to, and turned back to my plans with the same sense of exhilaration I had felt earlier.

Having decided to leave, the longer I remained the greater the chances that Morgan would find me. I had no way of knowing whether he was operating alone or within a larger organization. I was on my way to Brazil, but I didn't want him to know that for certain, and the best way to keep him in the dark was for me to disappear completely. I would have to give up any thought of traveling by normal means.

The main road out of Mombasa to Voi and Nairobi is the shortest and fastest way to the capital. But it is also the easiest to watch. I decided to go north to Malindi and from there across on the much less used road through Tsavo East, picking up the main road at Manyani. It would take longer, but the chances of being spotted by Morgan or anyone he had working with him were much more remote.

In a bathroom I washed my face and found some small bandages for the cut. I also found a khaki bush hat, the canvas kind with a floppy brim, which fit well enough. By flashlight in the bathroom mirror

I checked the results and thought I would pass muster in daylight: disheveled certainly, but unremarkable.

Downstairs I stopped by the telephone. There were two calls I had to make, and I chose the easy one first.

The chargé d'affaires told me I was crazy. The police had been in touch with him most of the day, and he was relieved to hear from me. But when I told him I wasn't coming back he decided I had gotten into something illegal. He tried to talk me into turning myself in. I told him it was something more important than a criminal act. It turned into a longer conversation than I had intended, and I finally told him to consider me on leave without pay, if it made him feel any better.

The second call was much more difficult.

JAMBA   5

And there are times as well, or were, when Rebecca is at Jamba. She is in there with me in the heat and the light and the dust, but never in the company of Morgan. That seems natural.

When I go there it is for a purpose; always a purpose, but not always the same one. There are the matters to be worked out with Morgan: Those empty spaces to be filled the way a painter addresses himself in turn to each portion of a portrait, or more aptly, as a sculptor gradually removes the chips of stone which cannot be a part of the form he is bringing to life. As I have said before, Morgan is more the block of granite to me than the sculpted being. His personal mystery lies behind the rough opaque facets of stone. It is left to my imagination's chisel to release what will pass for the truth for me.

And how many possibilities are there? The fact that I always set my chisel aside to the same result is not convincing to me. When the sculptor begins his work does he know the result? I don't think so, but I will never know. I want to think the final form is somehow preordained by the collision of the artist's will against the raw stone.

I want to believe that because it would allow me to set aside my doubts in favor of certainty. That would be a relief. My uncertainties toward Morgan are a burden I would happily surrender.

But my encounters with Rebecca at Jamba are of a different sort, less a need to fashion a being from incomplete materials than an urge to explore my own character and motivations. Or perhaps it is a wish to explain myself. It is all the same in the end, in spite of the fact that Rebecca would never demand explanations. I know that. But it is that quality of not asking which makes all the more imperative my answers—to her and to me.

What I see of Rebecca at Jamba was drawn from that final telephone conversation, perhaps embellished later with details here and there. But the arguments are always the same.

She sits next to me on the bank of the Cunene. It is a time of the year when the river fills perhaps half its bed, moving with purpose but not with haste, furrowing channels in the sand among the large scattered stones. The sand is hard under us and the grass grows sparsely in tufts at haphazard intervals. It is the late afternoon and we sit in the accumulated shade of the thorn trees behind us. The sounds that come to us from the workshops and armories are the sounds of the late afternoon, the sounds of an end to the day's work. Slowly, as we talk, the shadows creep out into the riverbed until they touch the flowing water and gradually mask the reflected light there.

The heat, as always in the African evenings of my memory, is subdued but not quenched. When I turn to look at her there are small beads of perspiration on her brow. But when she turns her head toward me her brown eyes have the same depth and clarity they have always had. Whether reflecting the flame of a candle or the flow of the river, the illumination is the same, and it comes from within. Next to her I cannot help but feel that my eyes are opaque by comparison.

Wanting to take her hand, instead I explore in my mind the explanations I have always found lacking in trying to communicate why I left her. But I always come back to the unvarnished fact. She smiles, and I feel a twinge inside me.

To explain the impulse that drove me, I search for a word more suitable than "purpose" because surely that word carries with it a concept which was not present in me when I left Kenya. That concept has to do with the end rather than the means. I was concerned—obsessed—with the means, with the doing rather than the result. After all, I was never certain there would be a result, but I was drawn to the act nonetheless.

Some would call it a challenge, and that captures a portion of the meaning for me. But a challenge to what? Simply to the doing? To see if it could be done?

Like the tribal *moran* who chooses, armed only with a spear, to face a lion in defense of his cattle, it is a personal choice which has much more to do with the individual than with the intended result. The moran doesn't have to put his life at risk, in fact it is against the law for him to challenge the lion. The government has told him he must ask for help from the proper authorities. But he gladly accepts the opportunity to break the law. The lion gives him a chance to define himself as a moran. A primordial pact exists between the two of them. In their clash lies the means for them both to define themselves, in a way which the modern world rejects as anachronistic, but in a way which carries meaning, at least for the moran.

In that sense Morgan was a challenge to me to define myself: a challenge not for definition by result, for the completed thing which rises from the labor, but for the act itself, for picking up the tools and plunging into the labor. And in the doing, the individual recovers control of his life. So, then, I stood up and, turning my life away from its apparently well-laid path, prying it out of the comfortable mold to which it had adapted, said, "This is who I am."

So that is the why of it, as nearly as I can tell and as well as I can express it. And she smiles again, timidly, understanding some but not all. Most of what she doesn't understand is the how of it. I anticipate her next statement: "But you could have taken me with you."

That is exactly the point. The meaning to me lay as much in the how as in the why. The extremism of it was central. It was as if I needed pain to complete the catharsis.

And she responds that it was her pain as well as mine—overwhelmingly selfish and self-destructive at the same time.

But in the end the arguments run dry, like the river in front of us when the season comes. And to me that is a relief. The thing gets done from the gut, not from the brain.

But there is one final argument. It is the last of the arguments. I have struggled with them all, but this is always the last. Isn't loving someone enough? It is the final argument of romantics, and since I am a true romantic—why else would I have done what I did?—it carries the most weight with me.

Yet for the same reason the answer comes most readily. My decision was one of those which forever changes the person faced with it. Like some situations in war, neither common nor rare, when the soldier must choose between bravery and cowardice. There is no middle ground. There was no middle ground for me as I sat in the light of that Nyali dawn, although I will admit I didn't see all of it clearly then. Morgan triggered an impulse in me as surely as he triggered the bullet which hit the wall next to my head.

I look into her eyes in the fading light and feel drained. I wait for a sign from her. The river, in darkness now under the lowering skies of the tropical dusk, moves purposefully next to us. She smiles again in the gathering gloom, and with one deft stroke, like sweeping away an intricately wrought spiderweb with a casual gesture of her hand, strikes away my feeble pompous arguments.

"In the end it all means the same thing," she says, among the only words she utters in my encounters with her at Jamba, without rancor, incredibly.

"You didn't love me, and you left."

KILIFI 6

In the late dusk my watch showed seven o'clock. I had been in the house about nine hours.

Before that day I had never thought about walking from Mombasa to Malindi. The drive normally takes about an hour and a half or so, if you make time, so I thought I could do it on foot in about eighteen, given luck and stamina.

But the trip was more complicated than I had thought it would be. I had to keep an eye out for headlights and duck off the road whenever a car drove by. Early in the evening I didn't make as much progress as I would have liked, because the traffic was regular if not particularly heavy. When I reached Shimolatewa, I didn't want to use the bridge over the creek next to the prison, and it took me a long time to work my way cross-country, about a half mile from the road. As I waded across the stream I thought about the cell nearby where Haverton had so recently pulled me into all this.

By the time I got back to the road beyond Shimolatewa it was almost midnight, and I made much better progress with the lighter traffic. The moon was up again, and I walked in the middle of the road, casting a distinct shadow across the sun-bleached asphalt. The beach was too far away to hear the surf, and as I walked the only sounds were the night breeze rustling in the palms and my shoes occasionally scuffing the road.

I reached Kilifi Creek just past dawn, and I thought briefly about stopping there. I knew a small hotel run by a Frenchman on the south side of the river, out by the ocean, and my mouth watered thinking about the meals I had enjoyed there. But they knew me, and the risks were too great.

Rather than take the ferry, I found an early morning fisherman on the riverbank some distance away, and paid him a few shillings to take me across in his boat. I had to wait while he finished patching some holes in his net, and by the time we reached the north side of the river the sun was getting strong. He dropped me at the upriver edge of the town of Kilifi.

I had never been there before. There wasn't much to it at that time, and I suppose it looked the same as thousands of other coastal towns in the tropics. I walked up from the creek and found myself in the middle of a street, a rutted expanse between two rows of one-story, tin-roofed buildings. I walked slowly over the pebbles and the scattered tufts of grass, looking left and right trying to spot a likely place for something to eat. I wanted to avoid the center of town.

Nothing else moved in that street. Most of the buildings were shops of one kind or another, but in one I saw some trestle tables and benches. I stepped in out of the still heat and the dust. An elderly man sat propped in a corner, dozing. Flies buzzed. A Tusker beer poster hung from a nail on one wall. A dark head bent behind a counter with an empty glass case on top.

"Jambo."

She looked up, surprised. "Jambo sana." I thought she looked young.

"Do you have anything to eat?"

She hesitated and glanced toward the rear of the small building. "Oh, yes."

"Any eggs?"

She frowned.

"Um, how about fish? Can you get some fresh fish and fry it for me, and some bread?" This was, after all, a fishing village.

I followed her to the rear door. A teenage boy was cleaning fish out back.

"You like?" she said, pointing.

"Yes, great." I picked out two medium-sized fish. I had no idea what they were, but I was starting to get very hungry. I pointed to a charcoal fire with a kettle on it. "Can you fry these for me for breakfast? And some bread?"

She nodded and set to work. In twenty minutes I had a meal in front of me at one of the trestle tables. The fish was delicious, whatever it was, and with the bread I ate my fill. To wash it all down I had a choice of Fanta or Tusker, both warm. I chose Tusker.

I will never forget that breakfast. Halfway through, the old man in the corner woke up, peered at me incredulously, and shuffled out. I was really enjoying myself.

When I finished picking the bones, I leaned back against the wall and downed the last of the beer. My hat pushed onto the back of my head made a thin cushion against the rough wall. "That was very good," I said when the girl came over to get the plate and the bottle.

"You want more?"

"No, thanks. But maybe you can tell me if there is anyone around here driving up to Malindi today. I need a ride."

"There is bus," she said.

"I know, but I don't want to take a bus. I will pay, but I want to go in a car or truck."

She thought for a moment. "Nguji, he drive to Malindi sometime."

"Where can I find Nguji?"

She walked to the open door. I got up and followed. From the doorway she pointed down the street, back toward the river. In front of one of the shops stood an old green Land Rover, the long wheelbase model, with an enclosed rear section. I remembered I had walked past it on my way in. The bonnet was up and a heavyset man was leaning over the engine, a toolbox next to his feet.

"Is that Nguji?"

She nodded. I paid her for my breakfast, thanked her, and left.

The fish and bread filled my stomach nicely as I walked toward the Land Rover, and I belched a little from the Tusker. I would have to remember to have that breakfast again sometime.

"Good morning," I said from alongside the open engine compartment.

"Unnh." Nguji had the air cleaner off the carburetor and had pulled a couple of spark plugs. He was removing a third. The Land Rover had seen better days. Its dark green paint had faded and worn away in places, and little of the bodywork was unmarked by scratches or dents.

I waited for him to finish and heave himself upright from the radiator. "I understand you might be driving to Malindi today," I said. "I'm looking for a ride, and if you have room it would be a great help to me if I could go with you."

He glanced at me with big eyes set wide in a massive face, and then held the spark plug up to examine it closely in the sunlight. His red checked short-sleeved shirt was soaked in sweat under the arms. He set the plug on the fender next to the other two, apparently satisfied with its condition.

"Why don't you take the bus?"

"I don't like buses."

He looked at me for a moment. "I drive to Malindi almost every day," he said. "Sometimes on to Voi as well. Like today. But I can't say I have room for passengers. I carry fish, and I don't have much space."

This was good news. Voi is on the main road to Nairobi, and I had been wondering how long it would take me to get a ride there from Malindi.

"I know there are expenses involved, and I am willing to help cover them. In fact, I would be interested in going all the way to Voi with you. Do you sell fish there?" I couldn't imagine there was much of a market for fish in a small rail junction and crossroads like Voi.

Nguji nodded slowly without taking his eyes off me; "To a man who sells to the game lodges." He leaned against a headlamp and regarded me thoughtfully, pinching a nostril between thumb and forefinger, other hand jammed in his wet armpit.

"In fact," an idea struck me, "do you ever drive all the way to Nairobi?"

He cocked his head to the side a bit and frowned. "You want to go to Nairobi, it's a lot faster from here to go down through Mombasa."

"I know, but I've already been to Mombasa and I want to go through Tsavo Park."

"It's an expensive trip to Nairobi."

"I can pay a fair price to make it worth your while."

Nguji stared at me again, calculating the price of his doubts about me. He quoted me a figure which was more than I had with me, and twice what I thought I should have to pay. We went back and forth two or three times before settling on a price which was still high.

Nguji said he wanted to leave as soon as possible, by ten o'clock at the latest. It would be a long drive to Malindi and Voi to make his deliveries, then on to Nairobi. He called a boy out of the shop. He must have been about thirteen, and I took him to be Nguji's son. I gathered that his father gave him instructions to start loading the Land Rover. Nguji turned back to his engine without looking at me.

"Is there somewhere I could rest until you're ready to go?"

Nguji nodded and called to some children who were playing nearby. A little trouserless boy ran over and looked at me nervously while Nguji spoke to him and pointed into the shop. The big man turned back to me. "He will show you."

I followed the boy through the nearly empty shop to a walled area in the rear. Old baskets and fish bones littered the place. There was a rough work table against one wall with two or three knives on it. The boy showed me a hammock stretched in the shade between two palms.

I smiled when he pointed to it, and he ran away. There was an open gate nearby through which the older boy entered carrying a basket of fresh fish. I settled myself comfortably and set my hat over my eyes. I hoped the bustle of Nguji's family assembling his cargo wouldn't rob me of what could be two or three hours of sleep.

VOI

7

We got started somewhat later than Nguji had hoped, but still before eleven. It would be late evening before we would arrive in Nairobi, but that fit well with my plans.

I walked out of the shop wiping my face with my handkerchief, which I had wetted from a basin of water. It smelled like fish.

Nguji was standing next to the right-hand, driver's door, and next to him was a girl in her teens, wearing a faded blue smock and clutching a baby. Beside her on the ground was a basket filled with clothing, and she looked vaguely as if she were ready for a trip.

I wasn't at all certain I liked the looks of this. My nap had left me a little better rested, but my head ached, and I didn't savor the prospect of three and a half of us in the front seat of the Land Rover for the long drive ahead.

"This is Wambui," Nguji announced expansively, with a theatrical sweep of his arm and a broad grin on his wide face. "She is going to Nairobi with us. To visit relatives." Wambui smiled shyly and squeezed the baby. It cried.

I walked to the rear of the vehicle and looked in. Baskets of fish filled the cargo area, with a few small blocks of fast-melting ice set on top of them.

Nguji preempted the complaint which was welling up within me. "Plenty of room up front. No problem. Wambui has not seen her Nairobi relatives since she was a girl. Now she has a baby of her own, we call her Mama Wambui." He threw his head back and barked several short laughs.

I put a hand against the hot metal of the Land Rover and closed my eyes for a moment. My head pounded from a point beneath the cut. I opened my eyes and focused them on a long scratch through the paintwork next to my hand. I felt the scratch with my thumb while the others watched me expectantly. "Okay, let's go," my words sounded heavy to me.

Wambui, obviously relieved, climbed in the driver's door with her baby and slid over to the center. While I walked around and opened the left door, Nguji got behind the wheel with Wambui's basket, and after some experimentation managed to wedge it under her legs, next to the gearshift. He slammed his door, started the engine, and we bounced forward over the ruts.

The ride to Malindi was uneventful. The road up the coast from Mombasa is well paved and I dozed a little, left arm cocked out the window, and enjoyed the wind and the engine noise. We talked very little, but Nguji did explain that he had decided to forego his usual business in Malindi in order to arrive in Nairobi at a reasonable hour.

So we passed through the town without stopping. I was jolted awake at intervals and snatched images through the dirty and insect-studded windscreen of dusty streets filled with humanity, market wares under sagging canvas, and an occasional bus. Soon we were heading west on the unpaved road to Ganda. Nguji was making time, and I gave up any idea of sleep. We bounced and skidded along the road through the coastal forest.

Ten or fifteen miles west of Malindi, small clusters of buildings appeared and disappeared rapidly. Jilore and Kakoheni, Nguji named them. The road slowly climbed, following the Galana River, and the vegetation thinned out into the more arid strip between the coast and the high plateau farther inland. The world became browner, less richly alive in its flora.

After Kakoheni we didn't see any further sign of habitation until Sala, where we passed through the gate into Tsavo Park. But women walked the road, wrapped in brightly colored khangas and carrying baskets and jugs on their heads and bundles of sticks on their backs. There were men as well, in jeans and t-shirts. The foot traffic attested to a local population, but their homes were hidden down rutted tracks to right and left; how far, I had no idea.

Once inside the park, the road ran closer to the river, and I entertained myself watching the game. We passed two herds of giraffe grazing in the high branches of thorn trees. I could see their long black tongues picking the succulent leaves from among the thorns.

About halfway through the park we came to a standstill among some elephants, face to face with a young bull standing in the road. He swung his trunk at us and rolled a small boulder a few feet in our direction with his forefoot. Nguji revved the engine and sounded the horn. The elephant swayed slightly but remained planted in the road, eyeing us truculently. Nguji swore under his breath, put the Land Rover in gear, revved the engine again, and pumped the clutch a few times. The vehicle lurched forward, and like a schoolyard bully who suddenly realizes his victim is holding a baseball bat, the young bull trumpeted defiantly and trotted after his mother.

That trip had, I thought, more than its share of mother-child relationships. Wambui's baby cried at regular intervals, at which she would open one side or the other of her dress. The infant would suck away contentedly until Nguji hit a rut or skidded on a section of washboard road. Then Wambui would bounce, the baby would cry, and either Nguji or I would be spattered with milk.

About two in the afternoon we turned south, away from the river, and headed down a smaller road toward Voi. Nguji was still pushing it about as fast as he could, and a layer of dust covered everything in the vehicle. I was getting cramped from bouncing around when we finally entered the town from the northeast at about three-thirty. It was a relief to get out and stretch while Nguji unloaded the fish.

From Voi it's paved road all the way to Nairobi. It would be a lot more comfortable than the drive from Malindi, but the risks were also greater, and I was a little worried that someone might recognize me. So I resolved to pull my hat down over my eyes and try to sleep some more.

The idea was a good one, but I was a bit slow in the execution. As Nguji approached the main road at the Voi junction, I took my hat off to scratch my scalp. We bounced through the last few potholes in the dirt road, me yawning and scratching contentedly. We climbed up onto the asphalt camber, each wheel in its turn. At almost the same time a car parked alongside the main road came into view from behind a shed. Something about that car immediately caught my eye and my curiosity.

It was a green Peugeot sedan, parked at right angles to the road about fifty yards ahead of us. As nearly as I could tell no one was in the car. But what had caught my attention was what appeared to be a small animal on top of the car.

I stopped yawning and leaned forward a little in my seat to get a better look. Nguji was shifting through the gears and the distance to the Peugeot narrowed rapidly. I strained to see what it was on top of the car, and my gaze was answered by a sudden flash of light. The small animal leapt into the air and became a man's head, standing up from behind binoculars braced on the car's roof.

Shit! A wave of anger rolled over me. I couldn't have given him a better view if I had tried. Clearly Morgan had staked out the road to scan the passengers in every vehicle driving toward Nairobi. It wasn't a foolproof tactic, but it had worked, thanks to my stupidity.

I immediately slouched in my seat, hoping it wasn't Morgan, or that he hadn't seen me. But as we accelerated past him I could see in the big side mirror that he was getting into his car. It was Morgan, and he had certainly recognized me.

My first reaction was rage that all the trouble I had taken to avoid him had gone for nothing. But that passed in a moment, replaced by a seed of fear which I could feel starting to grow in my stomach. I glanced at the three people sitting next to me before speaking.

"Nguji, we've got a problem. There will be a green Peugeot coming up behind us in a minute or two. The driver may try to force you off the road. Don't let him. If he gets us, we're all dead." I had no idea how Nguji would react to that news, but I figured I had best lay it all out, and I didn't mind being a bit dramatic about it.

He looked at me and frowned. "Who is he? What does he want?"

"He wants me, and anyone I've been with." I thought I'd better give him some incentive to try to lose Morgan.

Nguji looked at me and I knew he was trying to figure if I was crazy. Wambui clutched her baby. The engine roared as we climbed toward the plateau.

We drove on like that for a minute or two without speaking. I was racking my brains trying to think of a way I could get away from Morgan. I thought about jumping from the Land Rover and telling Nguji to keep driving, but there was no cover along the road, only short brown grass and small stones, and I was certain Morgan would see me. I was getting frantic, when the front end of the Peugeot appeared through Nguji's window, overtaking us.

Morgan slowly pulled up even with us. I slouched down in the seat so he couldn't see me, but I could see Nguji glancing nervously out his window. He still wasn't sure how seriously to take what I had said.

Suddenly I heard a gunshot over the engine and wind noise, and the windshield in front of us cracked. Wambui screamed, and Nguji swung the steering wheel to the right. I felt the Land Rover crash into the side of the Peugeot, and heard glass breaking. Nguji swung the wheel back to the left and floored the accelerator. The pitch of the engine noise rose a bit.

I ventured a look out Nguji's window, but there was nothing but road and grass, moving by very fast. Morgan must have dropped back behind us. Nguji was weaving back and forth, trying to keep him from overtaking us again. He bent over and reached under the seat with one hand between his legs. I expected him to come up with a tire iron or something else we could throw at the Peugeot. Anything, no matter how puny, was better than nothing.

Instead, he pulled out an old sawed-off shotgun. Both barrels and the stock had been shortened considerably, and the whole thing was only about two feet long. We heard the blast of an air horn ahead, and Nguji swerved back to our side of the road just in time for a big Mercedes truck to roar past in a cloud of diesel smoke.

Nguji looked at me doubtfully. He handed the shotgun across Wambui to me. "I will make him overtake us on your side."

I took off my hat and looked for someplace to put it. Wambui was looking at me, terror-stricken. Absurdly, I put the hat on her head and smiled at her. She didn't move. Her baby drooled on my trouser leg.

I turned back to the window and cocked both barrels with my thumb, but kept the shotgun out of sight below the sill. Nguji had pulled back out into the oncoming lane, and had stopped weaving. I tried to look to the rear without leaning out the window, but as soon as I caught sight of the front end of the Peugeot gaining on us, Nguji had to swerve to the left again to avoid another truck.

As soon as we moved back to the right, the front of the Peugeot appeared again. Its left headlight was broken from our sideswipe. Morgan started to move up on us.

When the front of the car was about eight feet behind my window, I raised the shotgun and leaned as far out as I could. The wind buffeted the back of my head. I caught a momentary glimpse of Morgan behind the wheel before I let go with one barrel into the windshield. It imploded in a cloud of broken glass. He swerved sharply to the left and I lost sight of the car in a swirl of dust behind us as Nguji swung back to miss another truck.

I settled back into the seat and exhaled slowly, staring straight ahead. After a moment I noticed Nguji glancing in his rear view mirror.

"Is he there?"

"No. I think you gave him a good fright."

I handed the shotgun back to him. My hands were shaking. Nguji deftly reloaded the spent barrel while continuing to drive, throwing the empty shell out the window. The thought occurred to me that fish salesmen generally don't carry firearms.

But there was one trade which immediately came to mind, and which seemed to fit. "Which is it, Nguji, ivory or rhino horn?"

He looked askance at me as he had in Kilifi. A smile flickered across his broad sweaty face.

LORESHO   8

It was well past midnight when Nguji dropped me near my house in Nairobi. We had turned off the main road as soon as we could after our encounter with Morgan, and taken a longer route to the capital. Swinging to the east, we drove through the towns of Mutomo and Kitui, and finally approached Nairobi from Thika, from the northeast. That wide loop had been safer, but had meant more hours of bone-jarring, dusty driving on unsurfaced roads. By the time we regained the tarmac east of Thika I was stiff and the inside of my mouth felt gritty.

I lived on Loresho Ridge, northwest of the city center. We skirted around the northern periphery, through Muthaiga, where the ambassadors and millionaires lived, to Spring Valley. There, heading away from town, I asked Nguji to drop me off on Lower Kabete Road.

We hadn't spoken much during the trip, but I was pretty sure he would want to renegotiate our arrangement in light of the unexpected events after Voi. So when he commented that the whole affair had turned out to be more expensive than he had figured, I didn't argue. I gave him all the money I had with me and thanked him for his help. There's no question I got fair value.

Wambui and her baby were both asleep, so Nguji and I parted quietly with a quick handshake. The Land Rover bounced through a couple of potholes before pulling back out onto the tarmac. I stood at the side of the road for a few moments and watched the small red tail lights disappear to the sound of shifting gears.

I turned and entered a path which I knew led uphill to Loresho Ridge Road. I wanted to approach my house from the end of the street it was on, just in case anyone was watching. I didn't think the police would have a stakeout, since they presumably thought I had been kidnapped, but I didn't want to take any chances.

The bright moon was there in the clear sky again that night, and a light breeze, and I thought of dinner on the patio at the Coriander. That had been only two days earlier, as best as I could recall. It seemed like a month.

Walking as quietly as I could so not to arouse the neighborhood dogs, I brushed past tall grass and bushes fringing the path. After about five minutes of climbing I found myself at the dead end of my street. I stood behind a small stand of sugarcane where the path opened onto the street and looked out into the moonlight. A Peugeot sedan was parked about halfway between where I stood and the gate to my driveway. I couldn't make out the color in the moonlight, but I didn't think I needed to. I wondered how he had discovered my address so quickly.

I turned back onto the path and spent the next half hour carefully working my way around to the rear of my property. At that point I was thankful that I had no dog, and that my *askari*, my guard, wasn't Masai. That tribe prided itself on its warlike heritage, and had given it up much more recently than the other tribes in Kenya. They made excellent and very lethal *askaris*. Mine, however, was a Kalenjin. He normally fell asleep on the wood pile shortly after midnight, and there had been times when I had been nearly unable to awaken him with my car horn down at the gate.

The most remote corner of my fence was invisible from the road. I climbed over it, using a compost heap and a small tree for footing. Once inside my garden I made my way directly to the front door, where my key worked silently.

The hours spent bouncing next to Wambui had given me plenty of time to plan exactly what to take. I packed a small canvas duffel bag with some clean clothes and toilet articles. From my wall safe I took my tourist passport, not the black diplomatic one, and all the money I had there. It would be enough to get me out of Kenya, but I was still thankful for credit cards.

I think I was in the house less than ten minutes before I was ready to go. On my way out I stopped for a moment at the bathroom door and gazed longingly at the bathtub, faint in the moonlight. On several occasions I had luxuriated in that tub after a few days in the bush. I smelled strongly of fish and sweat. But this time a bath would have to wait.

Before opening the front door, I stepped into the kitchen and hid an unmarked envelope filled with shilling notes in a place where I knew only Kami would find it. That would hold him for quite a while; severance pay, I guess.

Standing just inside the door, I scanned the house in my mind to make certain I had left everything apparently as I had found it. I cracked the door, looked outside for a minute, and stepped out into the shadows.

This time I made for a different corner of the garden, next to the road, but out of sight around a curve from where the Peugeot was parked. I dropped the bag over the fence and it landed on the grass with a faint thud. I climbed over after it and bent over to pick it up.

When I stood up, warm hands closed around my neck from behind.

Gunnery Sergeant Murphy. My first thought was of the Marine drill instructor who had taught me as a midshipman that the worst possible way to attack anyone is to grab them around the neck. I had never before had occasion to use that knowledge, but Gunny Murphy had taught his lessons well.

Reflexively, I raised my left arm and spun in that direction, using the back of my upper arm to break the grip. As soon as I felt the fingers slip on my throat, I brought my arm down to pin his wrists in my armpit. I only needed a fraction of a second. I bent over into a crouch and there in front of me, with his hands momentarily immobilized, was my target. I punched as hard as I could with my right fist and connected with his groin.

The animal growl in my ear coalesced into a grunt. His wrists slipped out from under my arm, and I saw in the moonlight that it was Morgan. I kicked him and he went down. A kick in the head and he lay still.

I stood over him, breathing heavily and feeling sick from the surprise and the adrenalin. Dogs were barking from several houses. I couldn't be sure how much noise we had made, but I thought it wasn't enough to raise human interest. I felt in Morgan's coat pockets and pulled out his Browning. I put it in my bag, under the clothes, and turned back to take one last look at him before leaving. A trickle of blood from one corner of his mouth shone black in the moonlight. He must have bitten his tongue. I rolled him onto his stomach to keep him from bleeding into his lungs.

KABETE   9

I walked westward, through the remnants of the old Loresho coffee estate, across the fields of the agricultural research station, and past the barns of the veterinary labs, all washed and colorless under the moon. The cool highland breeze made me shiver for the first time I could remember. I realized I was still tense, and I hoped walking would help me to relax.

But my reaction was the opposite. For the first time I started to feel the real gravity of what I was doing. I felt panic begin to creep over me with the same effect of helpless urgency I used to feel as a child when I heard a train approaching. I was overwhelmed by what seemed to be imminent doom, and I had a sudden impression that each step would bring immediate catastrophe.

The more I thought about it, the more surprised I became at my commitment to the vague plan I had begun in the Nyali underbrush. It had seemed natural to me then. I thought back to the half-formed words and I kept walking. I picked my way over the rutted road, past looming colorless trees casting stark shadows across my path.

I tried to concentrate on the words. Fear and excitement washed back and forth over me until I couldn't distinguish between them. I tightened my stomach muscles to help keep myself under control. All at once I realized I could have turned Morgan over to the police. I might still be able to do it. But the thought hadn't even occurred to me when I had stood over him a few minutes earlier.

I shivered again, and this time I knew it was more from excitement than from the chill. My intellect was telling me I was being foolish. But my gut was telling me to take the gamble. It wasn't the first time in my life I had been faced with that kind of struggle. To hell with it, I thought.

The words tailed off. I increased my pace.

There was still plenty of night remaining when I arrived at the main road to Nakuru. Heavy trucks use that road carrying cargo up from the port at Mombasa and on to Kampala, Kigali, and Bujumbura. They lug slowly up the hills, and it was easy to hop one of them as the driver was downshifting. I sat next to some kind of machinery, unidentifiable under a heavy tarpaulin, and watched the moonlit scenery unfold.

We had only other trucks for companions on the road at that time of night. I nestled comfortably in the folds of the tarpaulin and let the vibrations from the big diesel soothe my aching muscles. It was very pleasant in spite of an occasional whiff of exhaust on the crisp air. I laid my head back against the rough canvas and watched the stars and the tops of the trees moving by.

After about an hour the driver downshifted two or three times, and I leaned forward to see what was coming. We had reached the eastern escarpment of the Rift Valley. Starting down, the trees gave way to a magnificent panorama. In surreal moonlit tones it looked to me as if a great inland sea had opened up in front of me. From two or three thousand feet above the grassy plains of the valley floor the widely scattered lights of farmsteads could have been ships, and the two volcanoes, Susua and Longonot, islands. I leaned forward, hugging my knees, and grinned into the breeze as the truck headed down the steep cut in the side of the cliff.

I have read that Nairobi owes its existence to the Rift Valley. The British engineers building the Uganda Railway at the end of the nineteenth century had to hold up construction while they figured out how to lay a roadbed down the escarpment. A few months earlier Rebecca and I had driven to the top of the Ngong Hills with a bottle of Champagne to celebrate New Year's dawn. As the sun had risen behind us and warmed our backs, the shadows on the valley floor far below had shrunk toward us and finally disappeared.

I stopped thinking for a moment and Rebecca filled my brain. I missed her already, and I didn't think it was just the thought of her in the candlelight two nights before which made me feel that way. I felt the guilt again, but faintly now, coiling and stretching farther under the surface. I forced it from my mind. I leaned back into the folds of the canvas, closed my eyes, and imagined us, our limbs entwined as we had been so many times in the past.

GILGIL 10

The truck bounced through a bad section of road, and I knew that I had fallen asleep. I sat upright and looked to the east. The sky above the escarpment was streaked with rose-colored light. My immediate goal was a collection of roadside buildings called Gilgil, and I hoped we would arrive there before dawn. I knew truckers stopped there for breakfast and to refuel. It was also the junction for a smaller road which headed due north to Lake Turkana.

In those days, there wasn't much traffic on that road, at least not past Thompson's Falls, but there was one way I was fairly confident I could reach the lake. Once a week an ice truck drove from Nairobi to Turkana to buy perch from the fishermen at Loyangalani. More fish, I thought, as if I hadn't had enough of that already. But it was the only regular transportation I had heard of on that route, and I thought I could probably persuade the driver to let me ride along.

At Loyangalani, aside from the fishing cooperative, there was also a safari camp and airstrip. I wanted to catch a northbound flight into the Sudan.

I didn't know how long I would have to wait for a plane, or whether I would be able to catch a ride when one came. At some point I might have to give up and get one of the fishermen to take me to the other side of the lake where I could continue overland or try the airstrips at Eliye Springs or Ferguson's Gulf. There were fishing lodges at both places. I decided to face that problem when I came to it.

In the meantime, I thought I remembered a small police post at Loyangalani. It would have radio communications with Nairobi. I hoped the sergeant there hadn't been notified about me because it would be impossible to avoid the police in such a small place.

The truck slowed to negotiate another bad section, and I took the opportunity to jump off onto the road. It was lighter, but not yet full daylight. The traffic was still limited to trucks and I felt I could risk walking in the open. It seemed unlikely that anyone would be looking for me west of Nairobi.

Someone had shot holes in the sign which announced Gilgil. The buildings of the town are interspersed among trees, and it looked like an oasis in the middle of the brown grass of the valley. I couldn't see it, but I knew Lake Elmenteita, one of the saline Rift Valley lakes, lay just northwest of the town.

As I walked past the sign and toward the edge of town, a freight train emerged on the single tracks to my right from behind some small buildings. An engine and eight or ten boxcars, it creaked and squealed its way slowly back in the direction of Nairobi.

The sun was getting strong when I reached the shade of the trees. My shirt already clung to me in the increasing heat, and I began to notice the variegated smells released again from my clothes. I didn't know what I could do about that right away. I fished in my bag for my hat and my fingers brushed the cool steel of Morgan's Browning. I put on the hat to cover the bandages on my forehead and walked into town.

As I had remembered, there were two or three garages and an equal number of eating places on the main road. In front of each of the garages, in addition to the gas pumps, were vehicles under repair. They were mostly large diesel trucks, their bonnets up or a wheel off. I noticed the truck which had brought me from Nairobi in front of one of the eateries, where I had once stopped for a beer on the way to Kisumu.

I went in. I remembered the owner seemed to be friendly. Several truckers sat at tables and drank coffee or tea. I sat down and ordered coffee and something to eat. The aroma of the coffee made me ravenous.

I lingered over breakfast until all the truckers left. Then I got up to pay my bill and managed to engage the owner in conversation as he made change for me. He reminded me a bit of Kami. Yes, he knew the fish trucks from Nairobi. There were actually two of them. The round trip to Turkana took more than a week, including three or four days loading at the lake. Northbound, they stopped in Gilgil on Fridays. Yes, this was Wednesday.

I asked if they stopped in Thompson's Falls, to the north. He said he thought they did, but he wasn't certain. Somehow I had to kill two days, and I decided to do it there. Gilgil was no place to spend any time.

The owner directed me across the road to one of the garages, where a *matatu* was loading. This was a light pickup truck with a sheet metal body fitted on the rear to cover a bench on each side. In Nairobi, there wasn't enough bus transport and people packed into matatus until they sagged on their springs. Matatu accidents were frequent, and they almost always involved fatalities.

Here, however, there were only two other passengers enroute to Thompson's Falls. I paid a few shillings to the driver and climbed into the rear. It was hot inside in spite of two small open windows and the rear door held open with a piece of rope. The bench was wooden, which made it bearable.

I smiled across at my fellow travelers, a toothless old woman slumped in a shapeless body wrapped with a colorful khanga, and a little girl, perhaps a granddaughter. The old woman stared at me with distaste and worked her gums on her tongue. The little girl giggled and moved closer to her grandmother on the bench.

The driver slid the truck into gear and we lurched onto the tarmac. A few minutes later we had turned off the Nakuru road, crossed the railroad tracks, and were heading north. I moved as far to the rear as I could in order to be next to the open door, and put my feet on the bench across from me. The little girl looked at me and wrinkled her nose. She said something to her grandmother in a language I didn't recognize. I leaned back, pulled my hat over my eyes, and scratched at some sand fly bites on my elbow.

It was impossible to sleep in that oven, quite aside from being thrown off balance at irregular intervals as the matatu hit ruts and potholes in the gravel road. The most I could do was to hold myself upright on the bench. I couldn't see anything out the tiny side windows, which looked like they had never been washed, so I entertained myself with the view out the open door in the rear.

We climbed gradually as we drove to the north, actually moving out of the Rift Valley, although there was no dramatic escarpment here. I began to see more trees, and the brown background wash of the landscape gained tinges of green. I watched dust from the road filter through the door and settle lightly on my legs stretched out in front of me.

As we swayed along I unbuttoned my shirt pocket and pulled out Haverton's coordinates. I unrolled the paper and stared at the numbers for a long time, wondering what I would find when I got there. Then I had a vision of the paper blowing out the door, and I quickly put it back in my pocket. I made sure the button was well fastened over it.

The trip didn't take long, and soon the driver started to slow down as we pulled into Nyahururu. That was the new name for the town built where the British explorer Joseph Thompson named a waterfall after himself in 1883. I could hear the roar of the falls as I got out of the matatu and stretched. The old woman and her granddaughter got out after me and hurried away, the little girl looking at me over her shoulder.

I picked up my bag and walked slowly to a game lodge I knew not far from the falls. Checked in under a false name, I followed the instructions of the manager to find my room. After opening the door I stood just inside the room for a moment and took it all in: stone walls, wooden floor and ceiling, large window open to the garden. The bed was large, and I knew it would be too soft, probably with noisy springs—the kind which embarrassed Rebecca. But that didn't dampen my enthusiasm for trying it out.

Dumping my bag on a chair, it took only a few seconds to get out of my clothes. I left them in a small odoriferous pile in the middle of the floor. Every muscle and joint in my body ached. Surprisingly, my head felt pretty good; maybe only by comparison to the rest of me, I thought.

It felt good to be naked. I walked to the window and leaned out, sniffing the quiet scents of the garden. After a few minutes I turned and shambled to the bathroom. Almost as large as the bedroom, it was dominated by an old cast iron bathtub which I filled with hot water, as hot as I could stand it. I slipped slowly into the water, wincing as it covered my loins, and settled in up to my neck.

I lay there for some time, feeling stunned and letting the stiffness melt away before starting to scrub. Once I had finished, I walked back into the bedroom, still naked, and tried the bed. I lay on the clean sheets, savoring their roughness against my skin, and contemplated the next day and a half.

That room in the lodge at Thompson's Falls seemed as much like home as any place I had ever been.

NYAHURURU 11

Scrambled eggs and kippers lay invitingly on my breakfast plate. It was another beautiful morning, as they all seem to be in Kenya that time of year, the soft yellow sunlight playing on the chintz curtains hanging next to me, and I was rested and refreshed after a good night's sleep. The morning breeze washed into the dining room through open double doors leading to the patio, and garden smells mingled with the Earl Grey steeping in a teapot in front of me.

I had dreamed very pleasant dreams of Rebecca. I stabbed at my eggs with my fork. Feelings of guilt and regret rose within me, coiling and stretching just beneath the surface. I hoped she wasn't worried, yet I knew she would be, and I wanted to think she would be. I hadn't expected to miss her.

I had lost my appetite, and pushed my chair away from the table. I got up and walked out onto the patio, my hands deep in my pockets. At least it felt good to wear clean clothes again. I raised my face to the sun, closed my eyes, and took three or four deep breaths. The roar of the falls filtered faintly through the trees at the foot of the garden.

I decided to walk there. I had gone to the falls the day before, after lunch, and found them strangely reassuring. The cascade and the noise—the unremitting overwhelming violence of the falling water—blotted everything else out. It was a primal feeling, like staring into the depths of a log fire. I could sit very close to the water, feel the spray on me, and it made me feel secure.

I left the garden and entered a small lane which led under tall trees down to the river. The lodge was on the north side of town, at the beginning of the Turkana road. Just before turning down the lane I looked over to the road and stopped in my tracks.

A truck had emerged from the trees that blocked the town from view, and was heading up the road toward me, in the direction of Turkana. It was a blue Mercedes with a big square white body bolted to the chassis behind the cab. That was my goddamn truck; and a day earlier than I was expecting it.

I started to run up the lane to my right, past the side of the lodge and toward the road. It didn't look as if I would be able to intercept him before he passed the lane, and I began to shout and wave my arms as I ran. I didn't want to be so obvious, but I didn't see what choice I had. I couldn't lose that truck.

The driver reached the lane when I was still a good fifty yards from the road. To my immense relief he slowed and then actually turned onto the lane. The truck rocked heavily as it left the camber of the gravel road and started down the parallel tracks of the lane. The most I had hoped was that he would stop and wait for me on the road when he saw me running and waving like a madman.

I stopped running and tried to regain my breath so I wouldn't appear an idiot when I tried to talk him into taking me north as a passenger. I put my hands on my hips and tried to look nonchalant. The truck rolled slowly down the lane toward me.

When he reached me he kept on driving. I raised a hand in greeting and smiled nicely. The driver, a small African who seemed almost lost in the large cab, stared at me with a frown as he drove by without stopping. He rolled up to the side of the lodge, stopped the truck, and switched off the engine. The natural sounds of the place flooded back—the breeze in the leaves and the muted roar of the falls—but faintly in comparison to the engine. He climbed down from the cab and entered the lodge through the kitchen door.

I started to walk back toward the lodge, feeling very foolish. He was probably having a good laugh with the cook about this crazy *muzungu* out front. Very funny. Why the hell was he a day early? I hadn't asked anyone at the lodge where he normally stopped before continuing north.

When I reached the truck I walked around it once, in a sort of inspection. I was certain it was the truck I was looking for. The cargo body was insulated and fitted with a large freezer-type door at the rear. I knew it would be filled with ice. I had once gotten some ice for my camp cooler from another fish truck which was waiting to load perch at Loyangalani.

I sat on the front bumper, leaned back against the radiator grille, and waited for the driver to come out of the lodge. The metal was warm from the drive and from the sun, and the engine ticked slowly as it cooled. As my breathing returned to normal, the sound of the falls on the far side of the trees seemed to grow louder.

After a few minutes the driver came out. He shouted a last comment to the cook in a language I didn't recognize, and backed down the two or three steps to the ground. The cook's muffled reply shot back, and the driver turned on his heel to walk back to the truck.

He saw me sitting on the bumper and the smile on his face disappeared as if someone had slapped him. I stood up and waited for him to come closer. He eyed me suspiciously.

"Jambo," I said, hands in pockets and smiling.

"Jambo," he said, obviously not meaning it.

"Are you on your way to Turkana?"

He hesitated a moment, then nodded twice, still frowning.

"The reason I was running like a madman and trying to catch your attention is that I very much need a lift up to Loyangalani."

He stared at me.

"I would appreciate it if I could ride along with you."

He frowned at me without any indication he would respond.

"I won't be any problem for you." I began to feel like I was repeating my half of my earlier conversation with Nguji. This fellow, however, wasn't holding up his half of the dialogue.

"I can take care of some of the expenses of the trip as well."

He blinked. Maybe I was getting somewhere.

The cook was standing in the kitchen doorway, wiping his hands on a cloth and watching us. He called over to the driver in the language they had been using.

"How much?" The driver opened his side of the conversation seemingly without moving a muscle in his face.

I thought for a moment because this was also an issue I had planned to consider later in the day. I offered him the equivalent of about twenty dollars in shillings.

He didn't say anything, but the cook called something else to him. I didn't like this form of negotiation at all. I knew I was being whipsawed, but I couldn't tell what the cook was saying or what the driver was thinking.

"All right," he accepted, much more readily than I had expected.

I asked him to wait while I collected my things. He motioned assent.

I walked around to the front entrance of the lodge to ask for my bill. The driver still had uttered only three words to me. I was beginning to think he didn't speak English. Just as well, I thought, I didn't feel much like conversation during the ride anyway.

Once in my room, I threw my bag on the bed and knelt down to retrieve Morgan's pistol from under the mattress. I knew I wasn't being original, but I hadn't been able to think of anyplace else to hide it. I was in that position, arm extended far under the mattress, when a young maid walked briskly into the room.

She had the clothes I had sent to be washed the previous afternoon, folded neatly into a small stack. She stopped and looked at me for a moment. I slowly pulled my arm out, minus the pistol, and stood up. I was getting tired of feeling stupid.

"Jambo," she said sweetly.

I smiled thinly.

"I have the gentleman's laundry." She held it out to me.

"Thank you very much." I tossed the stack onto the bed, letting it fall to one side on the mattress.

She hesitated before leaving. "I thought the gentleman would like to know that Daniel Mungai always takes people to Loyangalani for no money."

"Daniel Mungai?"

"Yes, the one who is driving you there in his truck."

MARALAL   12

The drive as far as Maralal is an easy one which I had done several times in my car. Emerging from the forests at Rumuruti, the gravel road winds across the wide Lerochi Plateau, crossing rivers and lazily circumventing grass-covered hills which dot the plain.

Then the road begins to climb again, and the forests start again, and there is the town of Maralal. I knew this would be the last real town I would see in Kenya. Maralal is mostly a government administrative outpost. The district commissioner was there, and there was a police barracks, and a hospital of sorts along with offices of the forest, game, and veterinary services.

Mungai and I hadn't said anything to each other since we left Thompson's Falls. I would pay him the price we had agreed upon, but I didn't have to like being taken for a sucker. I just wanted to get to Loyangalani.

Outside Maralal there was another game lodge. This one consisted of a string of bungalows arranged in a pleasing arc, with the main lodge at one end. The rough log buildings sat on a slope with a good view of the Karisia Hills in the distance and enough grassy open space before the forest began so that herds of antelope and zebra moved freely by. Each bungalow had a small veranda and a large fireplace. Rebecca and I had taken our drinks to our veranda at sunset, to watch the animals graze and move around playfully in the cool of the early evening. I think it was the Thompson's Gazelles that pleased us the most, and the big graceful oryx. Later, after dinner in the lodge, we had started a fire in our fireplace and pulled the bed over near the hearth.

Mungai stopped the truck behind the main lodge building. I looked over at him as he wiped his face with a handkerchief. He was skinny as well as small, with close-cropped hair. He could barely see over the steering wheel.

He stuffed his handkerchief back in his hip pocket and looked at me. "Time for lunch," he said.

"Do you stop at all the lodges on the way up to the lake?"

"Unfortunately, there aren't any more between here and the lake. But I stop here and in Nyahururu. I let the cooks have a few fish on the way down, and they give me the hospitality of their kitchens in return. I would say it's a most convenient arrangement from my standpoint."

He spoke impeccably, with what sounded to my ear like an Oxbridge accent. I nodded and opened the door to climb down. He said he wanted to get going again in about an hour, implying that I was not to follow him into the kitchen. That was just as well as far as I was concerned. I wouldn't have been comfortable trying to fit into his arrangement anyway.

I walked around to the main entrance and went in. It was a little early for lunch and only one or two tables were being used in the dining room. I sat at a table in the shade of the veranda, as far away from the enclosed part of the building as I could. The grassy expanse in front of the lodge sloped downward toward the dark greens of the forest and the lighter bluish-brown hills beyond. I ordered a beer and something to eat, and while I was waiting a pair of dik-diks came around the corner of the building.

The tiny antelope, not much more than knee high, always travel in pairs—male and female. They moved carefully, alternately grazing and sniffing the air. When they saw me they froze, and we stayed that way for perhaps a full minute. The only sounds I could hear were the buzzing of flies and faint kitchen noises. The waiter came with my beer and the dik diks started, then bounded off and out of sight.

I was beginning to feel in a better mood, and ordered a second beer as I was still pouring the first. It was cold, and I gulped it until my throat hurt. I remembered that the only other time I had traveled north of Maralal I had taken with me a large camp cooler filled with beer. I was going to miss that amenity on this trip.

By the time we started again, with a reasonably good lunch and two beers in me I felt more like talking.

"How long have you been doing this run up to Turkana?" I asked him.

He glanced at me briefly, no expression on his face. "Ever since I finished university, about three years now."

"You studied at the University of Nairobi?"

"Yes, Literature."

"And now you've been driving a fish truck for three years?" I hesitated, thinking perhaps I had been undiplomatic.

He shrugged and smiled. It was the first humor I had seen in him. "Unfortunately, the Kenyan economy doesn't have a great many uses for experts in literature."

"Um, I suppose not. Did you concentrate on any particular area?"

He smiled again, looking through the windshield at the slowly unfolding road ahead of us. "American Literature. I did a dissertation on William Faulkner."

"William Faulkner?"

"I was interested in the American South. I wanted to learn more about the aftermath of slavery, and I think literature is a less distorted window than history."

"I suppose even novelists have their prejudices."

"Yes, but they tend to be expressed through the behavior of the individual characters, not the broad situations. Too much history has been written by people who select their facts to help them prove a point."

"I think you're right about that." I thought for a moment. "I'm afraid 'Absalom, Absalom!' is the only one of his works I've ever read."

"I liked that, but 'Light in August' was Faulkner's high point. I focused my arguments on that book."

"Why?"

He glanced at me as if to ask if I really wanted to know. "Because in that book, Faulkner transcends the limits of the American South. Joe Christmas and Lena Grove together define the Southern situation, but in the final analysis the story is universal. I don't think Faulkner ever reached that level in another novel."

I tried to remember the details of the book I had read years earlier. "I don't know. It seems to me that 'Absalom, Absalom!' had a pretty universal theme."

"I disagree. In my opinion, that book represents the reason I turned to the study of Faulkner in the first place: it is a finely crafted work, but it is essentially a treatise on the bitter fruits of slavery."

"You mean the tragedy of the family—Sutpen, wasn't it?—was a direct result of the system of slavery in the South?"

"Yes. Thomas Sutpen arrives in the 1830s with a wagonload of slaves and carves his fortune out of the swamps. But that fortune doesn't even last a generation. It is obliterated before his own eyes by the shock waves from the explosion of the corrupt and immoral system he used to build it."

"Well, I certainly don't deny that slavery was a corrupt and immoral system. I've heard people argue that it was a necessary evil in its time, necessary for the economic development of the South, but I don't buy that argument. It's clear to me that we would be much better off today had it never existed. We're still paying the price for it."

Mungai downshifted for a small hill. "But you said you thought 'Absalom, Absalom!' had a universal theme."

"Yes, it seems to me that the tragedy of the Sutpens stems from the character of Thomas Sutpen in the same sort of way the Greek tragedies hinge on the foibles of individuals. Sutpen carries with him throughout his life a crystal clear picture of what he wants for himself, along with a firm and inflexible view of society."

The outlines of the story began to return to me. "He plants the seeds of his own destruction when he rejects his first wife and their son because they don't fit into that picture, into that view. He treats them in a way he believes to be honorable, since he thinks he is the one who has been misled. But he fails to understand that in human terms he is behaving abominably."

Mungai glanced at me. "And so, what is his sin, if not the perpetration of slavery? Isn't that inhumanity?"

"Of course. Owning slaves was certainly his greatest sin, no doubt. But I think that sin was the result of a fundamental flaw in his character."

I hesitated for a moment, and Mungai looked at me again. "And what is that?"

"Selfishness. Thomas Sutpen is guilty of a colossal selfishness which allows him not only to own slaves, which after all wasn't uncommon at that time, but to treat his own wife and child like slaves when he discovers they have Black blood in their veins. They don't fit into his plan and he disposes of them. It's that simple. It's that selfishness which makes inevitable the destruction of everything he touches. In fact it goes beyond what he touches. Not only his own family suffers, and his friends and acquaintances, but even the grandson of his friend, fifty years later, is not safe from it."

We rode in silence for several minutes, thinking our own thoughts. Mine touched on Rebecca. I recognized the old feeling again, the coiling and stretching, but far beneath the surface this time.

"But there is something else I wonder about," he said after a few minutes.

"What is that?"

"Women are the truly tragic figures in Faulkner's story because they feel the full weight of the curse without any freedom of choice. And the weight they bear is an endless hopeless unendurable weight. The men make their decisions and pay the price, usually in a fairly quick reckoning when the time comes. The women make no decisions and yet have the price extracted from them, drop by drop, in a kind of Chinese water torture. Why is it that it's the women who suffer the most?"

He glanced at me and a few moments elapsed in silence. "I guess because the women had no power in that society," I finally replied. "And without power, no agency beyond what they could claim from the force of their own personality. I think it's better now. I hope so. No one should have to bear all the consequences of someone else's bad actions."

And with that, we rode in silence for a while, each again lost in his own thoughts.

MOUNT NYIRU 13

Mungai had never been outside Kenya, but he was well educated, starting with a Methodist mission school. He not only spoke impressively, but knew what he was talking about. He spoke for some time about Faulkner, and then asked me about the South and about politics in the United States. The time passed quickly.

From Maralal the road, dirt now instead of gravel, climbs through broken, forested country to a ridgeline. There a tiny hamlet named Poror marks the lip of another section of Rift Valley escarpment and the threshold to the remote northwestern region of Kenya. We broke out of the trees and Mungai stopped the truck just where the road starts its long descent.

"I always like to stop here for a minute or two," he said, as if he had to explain.

The wide flat valley floor stretched out in front of us, in varying shades of brown, with dried lakes in its center and the crater of an extinct volcano to our left. To the north, the general direction the road pointed as it looped down the escarpment, lay the Samburu Hills. Still farther north I could see Mount Nyiru in the distance, low and blue, and I knew we would pass close by it on our way to the lake.

Mungai put the truck in gear and we started down into the valley. He stayed in low gear, but still had to brake frequently, scattering loose pebbles on the curves where the road had been graded recently.

After the green of the forest the mountainside here looked very brown, with occasional brush and short grass the only vegetation. The road reaches the valley floor in the basin of a dried lake bed, and Mungai took advantage of the smooth going to accelerate through the gears. The big diesel roared beneath us, and I stuck my head out the window to feel the hot wind. After hours of slow progress, it seemed like we were rocketing.

Soon after that in those days the road gave out almost completely. It became twin ruts through the grass, without benefit of any kind of maintenance. During the rains it disappeared in streams and mud, but now it was dry and hard, cracked in places from the heat.

The Ndoto Mountains had come into view, far to the east. As we bounced and rocked our way northward along the rutted track, the valley narrowed imperceptibly, the Samburu Hills and the Ndoto funneling us to the north. All the while, Mount Nyiru, dark under its thick forest cover, loomed nearer.

The going was slow across country which wasn't nearly as flat as it had looked from the ridge at Poror. In fact, we moved over the surface of a plain which was serrated by dried stream beds. Between streams, where the land was high and the only vegetation was brown grass and scrub, we could see the mountains and hills in all directions. In those sections the track was relatively clear and hard.

But then the land would dip through scattered boulders and loose rocks, and the scrub would become trees on the banks of a swath of naked sand. Sometimes it was rough going to maneuver the truck, which wasn't four-wheel-drive, down one crumbling bank, across the shifting sand, and up the opposite side. Mungai grappled with the big wheel and the gearshift masterfully, from much practice, and the truck lumbered out of each successive ravine like some determined beast, belching black smoke and roaring from the effort.

Neither of us spoke much after descending into the valley because of the heat and the effort of holding oneself inside the lurching vehicle. The afternoon sun scorched my left arm and that side of my face, and the metal on the outside of the door burned to the touch through a fine coat of dust. On the smooth high sections I could sit back and watch the dark mountains in the distance or the cloud of dust we left in the rear view mirror, or lean out the window to feel the hot wind in my face and look up into the pure blue sky. But in the ravines I had to brace myself to keep from being thrown into the dashboard or the side of the cab as the truck rocked through ruts and over rocks.

Mungai wrestled his beast and sweated freely. So did I. The heavy dust on the seat soon became a kind of thin mud which added to our discomfort. After several hours I lost count of the number of streams we had crossed. They became a regular cadence, and I looked back on my trip through Tsavo in Nguji's Land Rover as effortless by comparison.

By five o'clock we had almost reached Mount Nyiru. We had passed between two steep hills on the valley floor, outliers to the mountain, and had started down into yet another gully. But before heading down the dry bank into the sand, Mungai pulled off the track under two thorn trees and stopped the truck. He set the brake, switched off the engine, and leaned his head back against the seat with his eyes closed.

The silence was deafening. My ears rang from the noise of the diesel, and I still felt its vibrations through my whole body. I looked over at Mungai. His face glistened with sweat, his head back, eyes closed, hands in his lap. His Adam's apple moved in his skinny neck as he swallowed what saliva he could suck out of his mouth.

I ran a dry tongue over cracked lips and stretched my arms out in front of me. "That it for today?" My words sounded strange in my ears.

Mungai pulled himself back to reality from wherever he was. "Yes. It will be dark in about an hour, and the lake is less than a day's drive from here. I usually stop around this time to get a fire going before it gets too dark to collect wood."

I noticed the sound of birds in the trees above us, and opened the door to lean out and have a look. Bright yellow swallow-like birds flitted among wattle nests hanging from the branches. I looked back at Mungai, who was observing me.

"Let me know what I can do to help," I said, starting to slide myself off the seat and down out of the cab.

"You can start by gathering some firewood while I get the camp equipment out. Dinner will be simple, but then I don't suppose you expected anything posh."

"What, you mean to say for the fare I'm paying I won't get caviar?"

He smiled but didn't say anything.

I jumped to the ground and felt a bit uneasy standing on firm soil, much as if I had been at sea for a while. I started off slowly in search of fallen branches and dead trees. What firewood I could find was thinly scattered among the trees on the stream bank, and some in the bed itself, perhaps carried there in the torrents after the last rains.

I had gathered about half an armload of branches when I came to a column of ants. I had seen these ants before and they fascinated me. Large, as ants go, but not particularly impressive individually, they travel in a numberless horde. The column was several ants wide, maybe an inch and a half, and snaked across the ground in front of me. I could see neither its beginning nor its end, simply a constant stream of black scrambling insects. I remembered seeing the beginning of such a column once. It moved inexorably over anything placed in its path. It moved as if seeking a specific goal, without ever indicating what it might be. I kicked sand across the column. The ants recovered their momentum immediately and continued onward. I decided I would sleep in the truck that night.

I stepped over the column and resumed my search for wood. Standing on the edge of the bank I noticed a good piece in the stream bed and climbed down to get it. When I stood up, holding my bundle of twigs in front of me, my heart stopped.

A naked African lay sprawled in the sand at the edge of the stream bed about twenty feet from me.

Still clutching the wood I had gathered, I ran over to the prone figure. He was lying on his stomach in the sand, and was either unconscious or dead. I dropped the wood to the side and squatted next to him.

The tribespeople of that arid and inhospitable region are tall and lean. They are herders, and rely on their cattle and goats for most of their needs. This was a young moran, a warrior, I guessed from his age and appearance. His ochre-greased hair was parted across the top, from ear to ear, and plaited forward and back from the part. The ear I could see was decorated with two metal clips and a bone ring inserted into the distended lobe. He wore several necklaces of red and black beads and small cowrie shells, and decorative wire encircled his waist and his ankles. His only garment was a dark cloak which normally hung from his shoulders, but now lay crumpled under his inert body.

I squatted next to him for a few seconds, wondering what to do. From the little I knew, I thought he was probably a Samburu, Turkana, or Rendille. Because of their remoteness and their semi-nomadic cultures those tribes have remained relatively isolated from modern society. I was more than a little apprehensive about touching him.

I remembered once breaking down in my car on a dirt track between Maralal and Wamba. I had been driving toward Archer's Post and Isiolo with Rebecca, on the same trip I had remembered in Maralal earlier that day. It seemed a long time ago.

We had driven through a dry stream bed, smaller than the ones Mungai and I had crossed in the truck, and I had been driving a bit too fast. We bottomed on a rock, and snapped the drive belt in the fuel injection system. During eight hours of tinkering in the blazing sun, under the car and leaning over the engine, I had isolated the problem and concluded there was nothing I could do about it. During that time a number of Samburu moran had emerged soundlessly from the bush to lean on their long spears and observe me in my work.

We had been unable to communicate verbally, but I remembered well how a couple of them had come forward to touch various parts of the engine. They pointed and spoke to me in their language as if offering suggestions for its repair. I nodded and responded politely in English or fragmentary Kiswahili.

I had watched them carefully out of the corner of my eye as I continued to work, but they nonetheless managed to take some of my tools with them when they moved on. I sometimes imagine two or three metric sockets now composing a bright chrome Samburu necklace somewhere in that region. Rebecca and I spent a day and a night at that breakdown before the first truck came by and picked us up.

Some of that same apprehension had returned to me now as I looked down at this man. His spear lay beside him where it looked like he had started to dig into the stream bed for water. He hadn't moved since I had been watching him, and I reached out and lay a hand on his hot shoulder. There was no response. I shifted my position and with some effort rolled him over.

Sand stuck to his skin on one side of his face and down his torso and legs. But across his chest and one arm it wasn't smooth black skin the sand clung to. There he was a mass of blood and ooze through the sand and dirt. I had no way to tell what had happened to him, but it was obvious he had lost a lot of blood. The sand where he had been lying was dark from it. Flies buzzed. I pressed three fingers to the side of his neck and felt a faint pulse. I started to feel dizzy.

"Mungai!" I shouted as loudly as I could. I stood up too quickly, and had to bend over for a moment to clear my head. I looked up, but couldn't see the truck from where I was, and Mungai evidently hadn't heard me. I stumbled off down the stream bed as fast as I could. "Mungai! Bring some water! Quick!"

The truck came into view from behind a rock outcropping and some brush. Mungai was digging in a camp box bolted to the chassis. He looked up when he heard me yelling at him, grabbed a canteen, and came running.

I waited for him to run up to me, then turned and led him back to where the moran lay. Mungai stood and looked at him for a moment.

"Samburu," he said. "He has been mauled, probably by a lion."

He knelt down in the sand and opened the canteen. Pouring a little water into the palm of his hand, he let some dribble onto the Samburu's lips. At first there was no reaction, but eventually there was a slight flutter of the eyelids and the lips worked a little. After a few minutes of this treatment there were definite signs of life.

"Let's move him back to the truck," he said. "We have less than an hour of daylight, and if he remains out here tonight some animal will have him for supper."

The Samburu was lighter than he looked, and Mungai was strong in spite of his small size. Nevertheless, we ended up half carrying, half dragging the man along the sand and up the bank. We laid him on the ground next to the truck. The movement had opened his wounds, and blood dripped onto the dirt next to him. Mungai pulled the handkerchief out of his pocket and wet it from the canteen. I did the same with mine, and we did the best we could to clean the sand from the deep gashes and stanch the blood.

By the time we had finished and I was pressing the two handkerchiefs against the worst of the wounds, the Samburu was fully conscious. He was looking at me with doubt in his eyes, but he didn't flinch in spite of what must have been great pain. When Mungai returned from the truck's water tank with a refilled canteen, the moran shifted his eyes to him. He didn't move, but drank thankfully when the canteen was held to his lips.

There ensued a short conversation between the two in Kiswahili. After a half dozen exchanges Mungai turned to me and the Samburu closed his eyes to rest.

"I don't understand Samburu," Mungai said, "but he speaks enough Kiswahili of a sort for us to communicate. My guess was correct. He and another moran went out after a lion which has been attacking their livestock. This was their chance to prove their prowess against a lion. Those chances don't come very often anymore.

"They found their lion not far from here earlier today, somewhere over in that direction," he pointed to the southwest. "His companion took the lion's charge on his spearpoint but was badly mauled, as was this one when he ran in from the side. He is certain they killed the lion, and he is very proud, but he is worried about his friend."

"Maybe I should go see if I can find him," I said.

"Perhaps. But if they didn't kill that lion he is out there in the bush, wounded. In that case I wouldn't want to go out there unarmed."

I got up, leaving the makeshift bandages in place, and walked around to the passenger side of the truck. I opened the door and reached up into my bag for Morgan's pistol. The blued metal felt cool to the touch. I worked the slide once to chamber a round, and flicked on the safety. When I turned around, Mungai was watching me. He wore the same frown he had when he first saw me in Nyahururu.

"That isn't going to be much use against a lion," he said.

"Maybe not, but it's better than nothing. A few nine millimeter rounds in the head might discourage a lion, especially one weak from loss of blood. Anyway, we've only got about a half hour left before dark. It seems the least I can do is have a quick look over that hill. Let me have a canteen in case I find his friend."

I left Mungai to tend the Samburu and start a fire, and set off for a low hill just south of where the sun was fast going down. I was tense and gripped the pistol too tightly, with my thumb on the safety, and I had to tell myself to loosen up. All the same, I walked as quietly as I could, all my senses straining ahead. The full canteen hung on a strap from my shoulder and bounced lightly against my back as I walked. For once there seemed to be no flies to bat away as the shadows lengthened and joined and the air cooled.

Looking down from the crest of the hill, I saw broken terrain with a fair amount of heavy brush. It was all in shadow now, and I noticed it would be a beautiful sunset over the northern end of the Samburu hills. I started down the slope and into an open space in the brush. I decided I would give myself about fifteen minutes before turning back to camp.

The vultures first drew my attention. I was about to turn more to the south when I saw one of the big birds fly in and land over to my right. I turned and threaded my way in that direction, never able to see through the brush more than fifteen or twenty yards ahead. When I did see them there were about a dozen, hopping in their peculiar way, balancing with half-open wings, and plucking with their beaks at some carrion.

At the time I couldn't identify their victim, but the sight of feeding vultures always disgusted me. This time I was able to do something about it. I put three shots into the flapping group. One of them crumpled to the ground with a strange sort of squawk, a pile of lifeless feathers, and the others exploded into the air.

I walked toward the pile of torn flesh, but didn't have to go very far before I realized it wasn't the lion. I didn't get closer than ten feet from the corpse of our Samburu's unlucky friend. It was obvious he was beyond caring. The bile started to rise in my throat as I looked at his ruined body, a mass of blood and exposed bone, and I turned quickly away.

His spear lay on the ground at some distance. I walked toward it, and noticed that its oval blade, metal shaft and wooden handle were all stained dark. A few feet away the dusty ground was similarly stained. I looked ahead and started to walk again, very carefully.

Again the vultures marked the scene. But this time they were early. Five or six stood on the ground around the lion, a large male lying under a bush, panting. He could hardly move. His stomach, legs, and the ground around him were dark from his blood. The vultures, sensing his helplessness, made sharp little attacks on his hindquarters, retreating out of range when he turned his head with bared fangs and lashed weakly with huge claws. He was bleeding from the small wounds made from their plucking beaks.

This time with sadness rather than anger I raised the Browning and laid out one of the birds, sending the others away in a rush. The lion didn't seem to notice. I walked closer. He looked at me with large red unfocused eyes filled with pain. He, too, had proven his courage, but would be carrion for the vultures anyway.

I picked a spot two inches behind his right eye and from a distance of about ten feet, feeling sad and unworthy and angry, put two bullets into the great beast's brain.

JAMBA   14

Morgan scrutinizes me with his dry blue eyes as he drains the last of his warm beer. His look has a chill to it which contrasts with the oppressive heat in the hut. When he lowers the bottle a drop runs through the slight stubble from lower lip to chin. Beer or sweat, I can't say. He wipes it away with the back of his hand.

"It seems you've come here to start a row," he says, still eyeing me carefully. "I don't know what your game is, but I've played fair with you. I've answered your questions, although I'll be damned if I know why I've gone to the trouble. You've evidently made your judgments about me, I'd say long before you came to Jamba.

"But that doesn't matter," he continues to speak as he sets his bottle down again on the map in front of him. "I frankly don't care what you think about me. I've been honest with you, and, more importantly, honest with myself from the beginning. I make no pretensions that I'm doing anything more than looking out for myself.

"So now it's my turn to ask you a question."

"All right," I answer carefully. Our eyes haven't broken contact in a long time.

He stands up, pushing his chair away from the table, and walks slowly to one of the windows. There he stands with his hands clasped behind his back, surveying the scene outside. About twenty yards away three or four African troops, dressed in the khaki and blue of UNITA, train and elevate a Bofors anti-aircraft gun in a sandbagged emplacement. The sun reflects off their shining sweating faces as they move around the gun. Morgan watches them appraisingly for a few moments before turning back to me.

"You can talk all you want about climbing mountains, or however you want to call it. You can think you're not being selfish. How very admirable." His voice takes on a dry edge.

"My question is this, and the answer is for you, not me, because I really don't give a damn: Can you be absolutely certain that's true? Because if it isn't, you're standing on very shaky ground. I may not have the morals you hold so dear, your upright ethics, but if you ask me, you are a hypocrite."

He turns on his heel and walks the few steps to the open door and disappears out into the bright sunlight.

LAKE TURKANA

The lake below us reflected the afternoon sun like a vast sheet of metal foil, shimmering in the heat and blinding us. Mungai and I sat in the truck on the lip of the escarpment at the southern end of Lake Turkana. He was wiping his face with a handkerchief again, and taking in another sight which he must have seen dozens of times before. It seemed to refresh him nonetheless.

We had dropped the Samburu and the remains of his friend at a cluster of small buildings called South Horr, where he could be helped by a government medic before returning to his *manyatta*. I had heard of the remarkable recuperative powers of the Samburu and others like them, and the medic had said this one would be fit in no time. Maulings usually cause blood poisoning, he told us, because of the rotten meat which clings to a predator's claws. But the Samburu and their kin, like the Masai, seem to be immune to it, and if they don't bleed to death right away, they recover. I guessed our friend would tell stories for the rest of his life about those scars.

We sat squinting into the sunlight, with the engine idling under us, and neither said a word. A camel appeared from behind a cluster of large boulders, gazed passively at us for several seconds, and disappeared. Eventually Mungai took a deep breath and put the truck into gear. We started down the long rocky incline to the lake.

The terrain had turned volcanic. Pumice in shades of grey and black extended in all directions, and very little seemed to grow there. Right after the rains a sort of green haze covers the ground and softens the harshness of the place, but there was no sign of that now. It was a land which seemed utterly barren and which carried the aspect of another geological age.

In the distance to our left as we descended, the crater of an extinct volcano rose at the south end of the lake. Those slopes were colored in tones of brown and purple which seemed all the more intense for the lack of color close around us. We rolled slowly down the rough track toward the shore, the truck in low gear and Mungai braking frequently as the wheels rose and fell over large rocks.

When we reached the shoreline the track turned to the north and became much smoother on its lava bed. We picked up speed, and I watched the small waves breaking on the gravel beach as the hot wind washed into the cab and stirred up the dust. I put one foot on the dashboard and pushed my back into the seat to ease the ache. The rigors of the trip had started to wear on me, and I looked at the lake and wanted to have a swim. I knew the water was heavily salted, hot, and infested with crocodiles. I had also heard stories of six hundred pound Nile perch which could swallow a swimmer without thinking twice about it. But after all the dust I had eaten during the past few days none of that seemed very important.

I realized I couldn't remember how long I had been traveling, how long it had been since my last dinner at the Coriander. And I was too tired to figure it out. My previous life was growing paler and more unreal by the day. I didn't care. I was feeling good in spite of the aches and pains, and I reveled in my escape.

Eventually we drove up onto a small promontory. From there we could see the trees and some of the small buildings at Loyangalani. It seemed strange to me, so close to a large body of water, but Loyangalani is really an oasis. To humans, the alkaline lake to its west is as much a desert as are the barren mountains and sand wastes to the east.

As we drove into the village, children came out of the tiny mud huts and trotted alongside the truck. They knew Mungai and waved and laughed. The ones on my side were more subdued, but answered with smiles when I waved. Mungai chose a spot under a cluster of palms, not far from the small pier where the fishermen of the cooperative brought in their catch, and braked to a stop. During the heat of the day the trees would offer some protection from the scorching sun.

I hesitated a moment before getting out. "I'm afraid I didn't hold up my end of the conversation, but I enjoyed it. Where do you stay while you're here?"

"In the truck. That way I can keep an eye on things, and I'm right here when the fishermen come in. But you know there is a lodge here." He pointed to a low hill overlooking the village and the spring.

"Yes, thanks, I'll be heading up there." I opened the door.

"How long will you be staying in Loyangalani?"

I hesitated again because I hadn't told him anything of my plans beyond that spot. What the hell. "Not long, I hope. I want to catch a flight north if I can."

He looked at me carefully, his hands still on the steering wheel. "If I were you, I would discard that pistol you're carrying before I go. The

Sudanese authorities don't like them any more than do the Kenyan." He nodded past me, and I turned to look.

The sergeant from the Loyangalani police post was walking toward the truck. I knew the village was too small and remote to have a police or district officer in residence, so this man would be the senior government authority there. He looked very colonial in his grey uniform with pressed shorts, knee socks, and chevrons on his sleeves. His face glistened under the brim of his cap.

It wasn't possible for me to sweat more than I already was, but my pulse quickened. I think Mungai noticed the tension in me, and I realized I wasn't putting anything past him.

We climbed down from the cab and walked out in front of the truck to meet the policeman. He and Mungai conversed happily in Kiswahili like two friends who hadn't seen each other in a while. I stood beside them with my hands on my hips, feeling uncomfortable.

Mungai eventually introduced me to the sergeant, and he greeted me pleasantly. But they soon lapsed back into their own language, and I shifted my weight uneasily before interrupting.

"Thanks for the lift," I said, extending my hand to Mungai. "I think I'll be heading up to the lodge."

He turned and looked up at me before taking my hand. "Remember what I just told you," he said. "It could save you a lot of trouble."

The sergeant looked on innocently.

"Yes, I will. Thank you." I turned to walk back to the truck and half expected to hear the sergeant call to stop me. But he didn't. I reached up into the cab and pulled down my hat and bag, and started off toward the lodge.

The bandages had come off my forehead. As I walked past the children and the huts and the palm trees I ran my fingers up under the brim of my hat and lightly over the hot smooth skin covered in sweat and dust.

The walk to the lodge took me past the Loyangalani airstrip, a wide black volcanic swath cut between the village and the palms which stood over the spring. It was empty. A small group of children played in the blazing sun at one edge, and an old man with a staff, naked except for a cloak hanging from his shoulders, made his slow way toward the village.

I stopped at the foot of the hill where the lodge was and turned to scan the skies. There were a few birds circling high in the clear blue, but no sign of any aircraft. I turned and started up the hill, badly wanting a cold beer. My clothes were thoroughly damp and fairly steamed in the heat of the sun, but it felt good to walk after so many miles of riding in the big truck.

The lodge faced to the west, toward the lake. There were two Land Rovers parked in front of the veranda, I thought like horses tethered in front of a frontier saloon. But when I stepped up the flagstone steps and through the open door the similarity faded. The sitting room was spacious and open, with a stone floor, woven rugs, and wicker furniture. The dry hot breeze rippled through the door and open windows. As I looked around me I caught a glimpse of the green lake in the distance below.

No one was in the room, but over on the other side, where a closed doorway led to the rear of the building, stood a side table with a lamp, a registry book, and a bell. I threaded my way past sofas and chairs, dropped my bag on the flagstones next to the table, and slapped the bell sharply.

The building was quiet except for some stray kitchen noises coming from the rear of the dining room. I heard a door close somewhere, and I waited. In a moment the rear door opened and a sandy-haired European man dressed in khaki shirt and shorts and low boots appeared. I judged him to be in his late forties or early fifties. His complexion was painfully ruddy, and I hoped he wore a hat when he went out into that sun.

"Hullo," he said. "Sorry, I didn't hear you drive up." His accent was English.

"That's because I walked up from the village. I'm wondering if you've got a room I could have for a few days."

"You come in with a group from Nairobi, then?"

"No, I caught a lift up from Thompson's Falls by truck."

His eyebrows went up. "You mean the fish truck?"

Lately it seemed I was always surprising people. "Yes, that's the one. I guess that's the only regular transport up here. Anyway, it got me here and I saw a lot on the way up."

"I suppose so. If it works, do it, that's what I always say. In any case I admit it's not the most bloody unusual thing I've seen in the years I've been up here. I've seen some odd ones. You'll be fishing, then?"

"No, I'm just passing through. I hope I can catch a northbound flight out of here soon. What are my chances this time of year?"

"Not bloody wonderful, I'll warrant you. You'd stand a better chance looking for a lift overland from the west side of the lake. People with airplanes don't generally give lifts to strangers."

"If I have to, I'll do that. But I'd rather try it by air first. I thought maybe I could catch a ferry job or a cargo flight up toward Juba. In the meantime I could use a cold beer and a room, in that order."

He looked at me and then down at my bag, both covered with dust and looking more than a little the worse for wear. I was certainly traveling light, it was true.

"I'd be happy to pay in advance if it would be simpler."

He looked back up at me and made his decision. "That won't be necessary, but I will ask you to sign the book."

He opened the registry for me and as I signed he rang the bell twice. When I finished he turned the book to read my name.

"Thank you, Mr. Morrison. Now we'll get you that beer as soon as I can find the bloody help." He walked over to the archway leading to the dining room and shouted toward the kitchen in Kiswahili. I caught the words *pombe* and *baridi* which covered both the substance and the desired temperature of my order very nicely.

Without another word he came back to the table and pulled the drawer open. He rummaged among a number of keys before pulling one out and scrutinizing the number on it.

"I don't think I caught your name," I said, trying to fill the silence.

"Falkland," he said over his shoulder as he walked toward the rear corridor. "Roger Falkland. Your room is this way. Your beer will be here when we get back."

LOYANGALANI 16

Five days later I gave the bell on the side table two rings and walked out onto the veranda. The wicker chairs there had good, comfortable cushions, and I liked to sit with my feet up, look down at the lake and the village, and drink a couple of beers during the peaceful time before dinner.

Not long after I'd settled myself the waiter was at my elbow with a cold Tusker. I thanked him, took the bottle, and let the cold liquid slide down my throat, chilling me all the way down. I kicked off my shoes, wiggled my toes in the hot air, and ran a hand down my shirt-front. Crisp, clean cotton; it is amazing what clean laundry can do for one's attitude.

I was happy in spite of having failed to find transport out of Loyangalani. Two planes had stopped since I had been there, but one was southbound, and the other was piloted by a Frenchman who was taking his African girlfriend back to Nice.

But I was not all that anxious to leave, not just yet. I had developed a very comfortable routine, and I almost felt like I was on holiday. My room was bright and airy, with a view of the lake, and I allowed myself to sleep in every morning. I awoke to a light breeze through the mosquito netting at about nine o'clock, and had a leisurely breakfast there in the room. Later, I would walk down to the beach near the village and swim and lie on the sand. At first I had been nervous about the crocodiles, but I relaxed after I found some enterprising boys about ten years old who agreed to be my lookouts. They kept watch from a small stone breakwater, and they knew if the *muzungu* got eaten they'd never get paid.

In the meantime, my suntan had a new depth to it, I was well rested for the first time in days, and the food wasn't as bad as I had expected. Falkland turned out to be friendly enough, and a fanatic for cards. His game was Hearts, and every evening after dinner he would badger the guests until he got a game going. As long as I was there he was sure to have at least one ready player aside from himself. We would stay at it until about midnight, working on his stock of brandy as we talked and played. Sometimes, when no other guest could be found to play, his wife joined us for a few hands, but I could see they had played so much over the years that they knew each other's styles instinctively, which robbed them of some of the enjoyment. She was a hard worker, thin and quiet. But he talked enough for the both of them, particularly after a brandy or two. Her name was Olivia.

That evening I felt more restless than I had before, and I decided it was time to take Mungai's advice. I set down the sweating empty beer bottle, got up, and walked back to my room. There I dropped down to my knees, reached far under the mattress, and pulled out Morgan's Browning. I released the magazine and counted only three rounds. After rechecking that the chamber was empty I reinserted the magazine and hid the pistol in my bag.

The only sounds on my walk down the hill were the early evening breeze in my ears and my footsteps on the pebble-covered ground. Even the village seemed to be deserted for once. Mungai's parking spot was empty. The fishing boats were pulled up on the rocky beach, and the small opaque green waves rushed toward land under what had become a light wind, freshening as the sun set.

I looked around to confirm that no one was watching me, and took the pistol from my bag. I balanced its smooth dark weight in my hand, and it seemed a shame what I was about to do. I leaned back and threw it as far as I could out over the lake. Squinting after it into the last rays of the sun, I watched it tumble slowly end over end until suddenly swallowed with a small, disembodied plop. The rushing wavelets covered the spot in an instant.

I stood there on the beach for several minutes with my hands in my pockets, letting the wind and the gathering dusk envelop me. Then, like some mythical beast conjured from my offering to the lake, an old DC-3 leapt from the palmtops to the south and roared low over the village. It continued about a mile to the north, its navigation lights blazing, banked a sharp 180 degree turn to the right, and disappeared down behind the village, where the airstrip was.

I had turned to watch it, and the wind now pressed my back. Slowly, I picked up my bag and allowed myself to be pushed back into the village and toward the lodge.

When I passed the airstrip the plane was parked at the near end, its familiar rounded, nose-up shape recognizable in the gloom. The two big radial engines were still hot and ticked loudly as they cooled. The moon hadn't yet risen, and I picked my way carefully up the hill toward the lights of the lodge.

The pilot was sitting with Falkland at a table in a corner of the dining room. He was a big man with a booming voice, which rose often into a laugh. Whatever they were talking about, they clearly were enjoying themselves. I chose a table near a window on the other side of the room and had dinner along with the four or five other guests scattered at other tables.

When I had finished, Falkland and the pilot were still hard at it, so I took a brandy into the sitting room and waited. A couple of other guests were there, fishermen up from Nairobi, and we exchanged pleasantries, but I held myself apart from them.

After about a half hour Falkland emerged and called over to me. "How about a hand or two, Morrison? Your dumb luck is about to change, I figure. You've got real competition tonight."

His name was Guy Brooks, and he had a firm grip, steady if slightly watery eyes, and a big grin. He looked about the same age as our host. Falkland went for the cards and a bottle.

"Cut it a bit fine tonight, didn't you," I said. "Another twenty minutes and you'd have had a hell of a time finding that airstrip."

"Observant fellow, you are," he replied dryly. His accent sounded to me like Morgan's. "Had a bit of a problem in Nairobi today, and got a late start. My copilot quit, the bastard, and left me in the lurch." Falkland came back to the table and sat down. Brooks addressed us both. "He said I wasn't paying him enough, when all he had to do was sit there and look pretty. I was doing all the fucking work anyway. I told him to bugger off." He took a swig of beer, swallowed and laughed.

"I always thought he was a bit of an ass," Falkland said. "You'll find someone better quickly enough."

"I'd better. I don't like doing my own preflight checks. That and filing flight plans is a pain in the arse."

Falkland shuffled and dealt. "Shilling a point, as usual?"

I swallowed some brandy and picked up my cards. "Great plane you've got, anyway," I said to Brooks. "How long have you had it?"

"Ah, the Dakota, she's a beaut, she is. Doesn't look like much, but she flies like a dream. I picked her up for next to nothing in Beira three years ago after the Portuguese flew the coop. Was Portuguese air force, but they left her for junk, and our Frelimo friends were only too happy to accept a little hard cash, especially since they never believed I could get her flying again. A few days of TLC, though, and she was turning over nicely. I heard they were going to renege on the deal, so I had to fly her out in the middle of the night. A little work back in Salisbury and she's been purring like a kitten ever since."

I passed Falkland three assorted clubs, voiding myself in that suit. "So you've been operating up here since then?" Brooks passed me the queen of spades and two low hearts. He grinned at me and took a swig of beer.

"Nope," he answered absently while checking the cards Falkland had passed him and inserting them into his hand. "I made some runs into southern Angola with fuel and ammunition for Jonas Savimbi. Not bad work, and I don't mind telling you I rather liked helping him beat up on Neto and the other Marxist bastards in Luanda. But he's a little low on the folding stuff these days, and the SADF has a monopoly on his supplies, at least since you Yanks cut him off in '76."

My pulse quickened a little at the mention of Savimbi. Haverton had said something in his rambling monologue to me about UNITA, Savimbi's revolutionary army in Angola.

Falkland opened with the deuce of clubs. "What's the latest from down there?" he asked Brooks. "I haven't heard anything for a while."

"Not much to report," Brooks played a card. "The MPLA is consolidating itself in Luanda. Savimbi is regrouping in the southeast, and Roberto is farting around in Kinshasa, as usual."

I threw the ten of diamonds on the trick. Brooks looked at me as he pulled the cards in. "No clubs, eh?" He looked through his hand and led with the five of spades. He smiled at me and swallowed some more beer.

I played a low spade and sat back in my chair. Falkland picked through his cards. "Two years ago Roberto looked pretty good," he said. "What happened to him?"

Brooks snorted. "Holden Roberto hasn't figured much since those bloody North Korean cannon of his blew up outside Luanda in November '75. In five years he won't be in the picture at all, mark my words."

Falkland took the trick with a high spade. "What about Savimbi?"

Brooks watched his friend play another low spade. "Savimbi. Now he's another case altogether; a smart bastard, and tough, and with enough charisma to fill a whole politburo. That's part of the problem. He's a threat to any Angolan politician who has ambitions. He's got problems now, but the Boers will keep him going, and I wouldn't be surprised to see him in power in ten years. He's got staying power, that one." He played the jack of spades and looked at me.

I took the trick with the ace, and led in diamonds. I wanted to take all the hearts if I could, but I needed to dump some useless cards first, as well as pick up some key hearts before the others suspected anything. "So what brought you up here?"

Brooks ran a hand through his dark hair and scratched the back of his head as he looked at his cards. "Oil. I thank the good Lord every day for the Arabs and their fucking OPEC. I've got a contract with one of the oil companies drilling up in the southern Sudan, and it pays well. Niceties and necessities for the troops, you know; sometimes it seems like it's mostly shitpaper and beer, but there's other things as well—fuel and machinery and supplies. It's easier to bring it up from Nairobi and Mombasa than it is to get it down to Juba through Khartoum."

He took the trick and led another low spade, damn him. "Someday the bloom will go off oil, but maybe then Savimbi will have some money and I'll go back to flying bullets for him. In the meantime, I'm happy to let the oil companies pay me exorbitant charter rates while I enjoy myself setting up Yanks to lose games of Hearts." He laughed heartily and took another swig from his bottle.

I played my last backer to the queen of spades and decided to take a chance. "I wonder, then, you may know a fellow I met a few days ago in Mombasa: a Thomas Morgan. I think he said he'd done some work for UNITA as well."

Brooks looked at me as if I had broken wind in the presence of the Queen. "Bloody hell. *Morgan*! I'll say that bastard has done some work for UNITA! If they or the SADF could ever get their hands on him, they'd flay him alive. Mombasa you said?" He stared at me from under raised eyebrows.

Falkland looked at his friend, and I could see he was surprised by the vehemence of his response. "Who is this bloke?"

"Ex-South African military intelligence." The pilot glanced at Falkland, then turned his stare back to me. "I say 'ex' although I doubt he ever formally resigned. Morgan was one of the SADF's liaison officers to UNITA for a while, back when I was flying for them. We all thought he was a good man. But he took the wind out of one of Savimbi's biggest successes back when UNITA needed anything it could get."

He licked his lips, took a pull from his bottle, and leaned back in his chair. His stare changed to a thoughtful look, but his eyes stayed on me. Neither Falkland nor I said a word, waiting for him to continue.

"The MPLA took control of the gold mines in the northeast about the same time they took over in Luanda. A Portuguese company, I think, was still doing the work for them, but the revenues went to the party and from there to the war effort—assuming not too much of it ended up in Swiss bank accounts. They pulled a fair amount of money out of those mines, too; not like the oil up in Cabinda, of course, but some tidy sums just the same.

"Well, Savimbi and his SADF advisors decided one of the gold convoys would make a good target. They put together a couple of companies of Savimbi's best, under six or seven SADF regulars. Nobody in Luanda thought at that time that UNITA could carry off a long range operation like that—so far north of the Benguela. But they did it. They spent about six weeks behind the MPLA lines, dodging Cuban regiments the whole time, and came out with all the gold they could carry—and only three casualties."

He took another drink. I noticed we still held our cards in front of us, but none of us had looked at them since Brooks had started talking about Morgan. The two spades of the uncompleted trick still lay in the center of the table.

"That's when our bloke Morgan enters the story. Savimbi wanted to use the gold to buy arms. It was important to him to show some financial independence from the Boers. That was fine with them too—anything that added to UNITA's credibility as an independent force was in line with their plans.

"So Morgan and one of Savimbi's blokes took the gold down to Cape Town to wave it in front of some international arms types. That's the last anybody's ever seen of Morgan. Savimbi's man turned up dead a few days later, but Morgan—and the gold—disappeared without a trace. Until now."

"How long ago was all this?" Falkland asked him.

"Two years, more or less. But what really interests me," Brooks closed his hand and leaned toward me, "is what Morgan might be doing in Mombasa. We all thought with that gold he'd be in Tahiti by now, with some bare-breasted beauty fanning him in the shade." He looked at me expectantly. The perspiration on his forehead glistened in the soft dining room lamplight.

"He didn't say," I answered. "I met him only briefly in a bar in the old city, down by Fort Jesus. Like I said, he made some noises about being an old UNITA hand, and I bought him a drink. One thing's for sure, though, he didn't look like he was sitting on any gold. I'd have guessed it had been some time since he'd drawn a wage." I wondered if I was laying it on a bit too thick.

But Brooks ate it up. "Ain't that rich! The arsehole must've lost the damn hoard." He looked at Falkland. "Or maybe he was robbed in Cape Town, and was too scared to show his face to Savimbi." He threw his head back and boomed his big laugh.

"How much gold was there?" This was the only other question I wanted to ask. Nothing Brooks had said so far made me want to change my plans.

"A shitload. The exact amount wasn't advertised, but it was all those two companies of troops could carry, and there must've been over a hundred of 'em."

"More money than I'd know what to do with, anyway." I turned my attention back to my cards.

Brooks fanned his hand again and leaned back in his chair, checking his cards. "I can tell you one thing, I wouldn't be flying to dung heaps like Juba. Whose play?"

"Mine." Falkland took the trick and led a diamond. I decided Brooks must have the other spades, but I was finding it difficult to concentrate on the game. "Speaking of that," Falkland said to Brooks, "our friend Morrison, here, is looking for a lift to Juba."

Brooks played the ace of diamonds, and I swallowed some brandy before letting him have the trick. "Well, I just might be able to work something out there," Brooks said slowly as he appeared to concentrate on his cards. He pulled one out of his hand and scratched his chin with it, face down.

"As I said, I'm temporarily in need of a copilot, and you might be able to help me out." He threw the card out onto the table, but it wasn't the low spade I had expected. It was the king of diamonds.

"But I'm not a pilot," I said, surprised on both counts. I played a low diamond.

"That doesn't make any difference. All you have to do is fly when I have to take a leak."

Falkland dumped a heart on Brooks' trick. Brooks scraped in the cards and arranged them neatly in front of himself, grinning broadly. "In fact, I have a proposition for you," he said. "If you win tonight, you've got your flight for nothing. If I win, you can give me a hundred of those green folding notes of yours in return for your passage. Deal?"

I smiled grimly and nodded. Falkland poured some more brandy into my glass.

Brooks surveyed his hand and selected a card. "I do believe most of the rest of this hand is yours," he said to me as he played a low spade and sat back in his chair.

TO JUBA   17

We left the lodge early the next morning. Brooks explained that he
wanted to get off before the air got hot enough to rob him of his takeoff
lift, so I downed some hot coffee to try to clear my throbbing head.
Falkland was nowhere to be seen, but I thanked Olivia when I paid my
bill. Brooks planted a big wet kiss in the middle of her forehead, gave
her a hug, and we started off down the hill.

A small circle of naked children was squatting under one wing of
the DC-3 as we approached. Brooks began checking the oil-streaked
engine cowlings and the landing gear, and I walked over to see what
the children were looking at. They had sticks, and they were poking at
something. When I got close enough I could see it was a scorpion. The
little insect looked strangely translucent in the early light, and waved
its claws and tail defiantly against its tormentors.

One of the children soon managed to pin the scorpion with his
stick, and the others smashed it as best they could. Finally, one of them
dropped a rock on it and the battle was over. I didn't wait for them to
inspect the goo, but walked out from under the wing and took a look
at Brooks' Dakota.

He was right about one thing: it didn't look like much. Oil-streaked and mud-spattered, it still wore its original olive drab military paint and many of the old Portuguese air force markings showed through fading spraypainted coverups. On the tail, the white initials FAP had never been painted out.

I walked around to the other side. Brooks had already boarded, so I threw my bag through the door and climbed up.

"Close up back there, will you?" he called back from the cockpit, over piles of boxes and crates lashed to the floor.

It took me a minute, but I figured out how to get the door closed and latched, and pulled myself up the inclined cargo space to the cockpit. Brooks was starting one of the big radial engines. I seated myself on the right and strapped myself in. The first engine coughed to life, sputtered a few times and roared smoothly. Brooks turned his attention to the other.

"Not bad this morning," he shouted over the din. "We didn't lose much oil during the night."

The second engine caught and the stuttering propeller outside my window disappeared in a whirl. Brooks let the engines warm up a little while he checked the gauges in front of us. He leaned forward and looked across me to a panel on the right side of the cockpit.

"Tap that gauge for me, will you?" he shouted over the engines, pointing to one of two next to me. The needle pointed at zero.

I tapped it and it didn't move.

"Harder."

I tapped it until I thought I might break the glass. The needle didn't move. "What's that?"

"Hydraulic pressure. But the bloody thing only works about half the time. No trouble."

He throttled forward on one engine and swung the plane around to face the length of the airstrip, which looked awfully short to me.

"You want to take her off?" His hair ruffled from the propwash through the open cockpit window next to him.

I shook my head and tried to look calm.

Brooks reached down with his right hand and jammed both throttles forward. The Dakota strained as the engine pitch rose, and when he released the brakes we lurched ahead.

"That's the trouble with you Yanks," he shouted above the din. We picked up speed and the tail rose up off the ground. "You've lost your sense of adventure!" He pulled hard back against the yoke and the big plane lifted slowly off the ground and slewed into the crosswind. He retracted the landing gear, and some tall palms spun by under us in a blur.

We flew out across the lake, gaining altitude as we went, and I watched the green water and the purple hills fall away beneath us.

BAHIA

Iemanjá is Bahia.

She is the goddess of the sea, and she is known by seven names:
Iemowô, Oxalá's wife; *Iamassê*, Xangô's mother; *Euá*, sister to
Ògùn; *Olossá*, the mouths of the rivers; *Ogunté*, wife to Ogum
Alagbedé; *Assabá*, the spinster; and *Assessu*, the respectable one.
These names are spoken on both sides of her sea, and those who
utter them know that her name and her form will vary with the
circumstances of her appearance. She was born of the Yoruba
and she crossed from Africa to the West, to Macúmba and
Candomblê and Voodoo, and there she remains to this day.

PRAIA DA BARRA 18

I was balanced on the slack line which separates thought from dream, the hot sand pressing my back. The tropical sun basted my skin and worked its fingers into the deepest of my muscles. And the surf washed faintly in the recesses of my hearing. But I became aware that a shadow had moved over me, and when fine droplets of cool seawater scattered on my hot skin I pulled myself awake.

When I opened my eyes I saw a young woman standing above me, arching her back and wringing water from her hair. Droplets beaded on her and caught the flashing rays of the sun on her slender curves. She held her head back, face up to the sky, eyes closed, and her stomach stretched taut from under her breasts until it disappeared into the bottom of her tiny black tanga. The sheer fabric clung to her by strings looping high over her slim hips. From where I lay her legs seemed impossibly long, and gracefully curved. As I felt my blood surge I brought myself up onto my elbows.

"Oh, perdão, estou no seu sol, me desculpe." Her voice flowed in the honeyed tones of her Brazilian Portuguese.

"No, that's all right, don't go away," I said as she started to move off.

"Oh, you are American," it was a statement rather than a question. "I'm sorry I got you wet, I wasn't thinking. Did I wake you up?" She spoke perfect English, but I was pleased it still held her accent.

"Yes, but I really didn't want to sleep anyway. I'd much rather talk."

"Então, fala português?"

"Não, desculpe, eu não falo português. I've only been here three days. I'm trying to learn it, though."

"Very good. Your grammar is fine, but you need work on your pronunciation. Just the same, I think that's very impressive for only three days." She dropped her towel on the sand and knelt on it. Her skin was well oiled, and thoroughly bronzed from the sun.

"Thanks, I'll keep working on it. Are you a Bahiana?"

She laughed. "No, I'm from Rio de Janeiro."

"Oh. What are you doing up here, then?"

"I'm supposed to ask you that, you're the foreigner."

"That's right, I forgot." We exchanged smiles. "I'm here on vacation. I've always heard Bahia was beautiful and I decided to come see for myself."

"How long will you be staying?"

I hesitated a moment and shrugged. "I don't know yet. Probably a month, at least. It depends on how much I like it."

"Well, that's a good long vacation. But I predict you'll want to stay longer."

"Perhaps you're right. And you?"

"I come up to Salvador quite often. I have relatives here, but the real reason is that I love the place. This is the real Brazil as far as I'm concerned. Here you feel you're in a unique place, and it hasn't been spoiled by tourism like Rio has."

I noticed she wore a fine gold chain around one ankle. "Well, I'll do my best not to spoil it with my tourism. Where did you learn your English? It's perfect."

"Here in Brazil, but I also try to get to New York and London whenever I can, so I manage to keep in fair practice. Thanks."

I thought for a moment, wondering what stroke of luck this was. If I had seen her lying on the beach I might have sat down near her, and she probably would have moved away. The small black triangles of her tanga obscured nothing of the form and outline of her body.

"What's your name?" I asked.

"Cristina Campos," she answered. I thought she raised her chin just a little as she said it.

She smiled again. "And what's yours?"

"Argus. Argus Morrison."

"Angus? That sounds like a good Scottish name."

"No, Argus. Like the hundred-eyed monster in Greek mythology. My parents liked mythology."

"You don't look like a monster to me."

"You don't know me. But I guess it's true my parents meant to name me after the hundred-eyed part, not the monster part. I guess." We both smiled.

"Well, Argus Morrison, I have to go. It's been nice to talk with you." She got up and picked up her towel.

I jumped up as well. "Are you staying around here? Would you like to have a drink later?"

"I can't, I'm having dinner with my family." She hesitated. "But I'll be back here again tomorrow. Perhaps I'll see you then. Goodbye."

She turned and walked up the beach toward the sea wall. Her bikini was all but invisible from behind. Now that her hair was drying I could see it was light brown, and it fell below her shoulders. I watched her small suntanned buttocks move firmly as she walked across the sand.

ITAPUÃ 19

When I had arrived at the airport in Salvador I had rented a car and driven down the coast road to the city. My map named the towns and districts: Itapuã, Pituba, Amaralina, Rio Vermelho, Ondina. Each one was a little more built-up than the last; Itapuã really just a fishing village, Ondina a well-established neighborhood. But all along the drive there stretched on my left a series of beautiful beaches and the bright blue water of the South Atlantic. The intensity of the blue reminded me of the Indian Ocean, along with the clear sky and the tropical vegetation. There was also the red clay soil which is so common in Africa.

But there were obvious differences, too. In Kenya the beaches are for fishermen and tourists. The average Kenyan spends his time elsewhere. The Brazilians, however, clearly spend a great deal of time on the beach. My arrival happened to be on a Sunday morning, and the beaches were thronged, cars parked haphazardly under the tall palms and people walking in all directions. On the beaches there were thatched huts selling food and drink to a brisk trade. The traffic was heavy, almost everyone going to the beach. Some cars had windsurfboards lashed to their roofs.

The slow pace gave me a chance to absorb the atmosphere. It was only ten thirty, but the sun was already strong. I had all the windows open in the car, and leaning against the sill as I drove, I caught an occasional breeze off the beach laden with smells of fish and cooking oil. And along with the traffic noise moving slowly along the hot asphalt, there was the constant hubbub of Portuguese from the pedestrians walking on the sand at the side of the road or weaving their way through the sometimes stationary cars. Most of the men wore only shorts. The women wore tiny bikinis, sometimes with a t-shirt over the top.

By the time I reached Rio Vermelho I started to see some large hotels on the coast. These would be the luxury tourist accommodations, and not what I was looking for. Not that I had anything against luxury, but I wanted to stay away from the obvious places where someone might be looking for me.

What I wanted was a small hotel on a back street in a part of town where foreign tourists were not uncommon, but where they didn't dominate. I wanted someplace where I could come and go at odd hours without drawing attention to myself.

The coast road ends at the lighthouse, the *farol*, in Barra. That district sits at the tip of the peninsula which forms the east side of All Saints Bay. It is the Bay which gives Bahia its name.

I drove through some of the back streets of Barra, and it looked good. There were restaurants, small shops, inconspicuous hotels, and apartment buildings. And while most of the people were locals, there were some tourists as well.

But I didn't want to decide too quickly. I had most of the day ahead of me, and I wanted to see what the rest of the city looked like. So I worked my way northward along the bay, checking the map as I went: Graça, Vitoria, Canela. All were too thoroughly residential, with tree-lined streets and houses and apartment buildings.

From the large park square called Campo Grande the surroundings became more commercial, and slowly evolved into the old city, the *Cidade Velha* the map called it. The terrain was much more rugged than I had imagined, and it became obvious why certain parts of the map showed no roads. The city was crisscrossed with steep hills and escarpments, the most extreme of which held the old city high above the level of the bay.

I thought I had probably seen as much as I needed to, but my curiosity led me on. I drove down to the new commercial part of the city, built on landfill below the escarpment. There I saw the new port facilities and modern office buildings. I kept driving, past the markets at São Joaquim, and past the railroad station to Monte Serrat and Bonfim.

I ate lunch at a small cafe overlooking the beach at Monte Serrat. Pulled up on the sand were well-used fishing boats which at one time had been painted in bright colors. Most of them were now a chalky pastel, but in the bright sunlight they made for a picturesque scene nonetheless. The bay water lacked the intense blue of the ocean, and it looked to me almost like a postcard scene which had faded a little in the strong sun. But the sky was the same clear light blue I had seen along the coast, and the green of the palm fronds was reflected in the hills on the far side of the bay.

As I ate I watched the people in the street and on the beach. The real color of the place, I decided, was in the people. Sitting there in Monte Serrat drinking my Brazilian beer I watched people of every shade from almost-pale to as black as I had ever seen in Kenya. But there were very few there who looked like tourists. I decided I would blend in better in Barra.

The walk back to where I had parked the car led past an old fort, sixteenth century by the look of it. Like most of the buildings I had seen, it wasn't in good repair. It looked well-weathered, but pleasing all the same. I smiled to myself as I strolled along the cobbled street with my hands in my pockets and the sun pressing on my face. I thought I was going to like Bahia.

BARRA   20

I walked toward my hotel after that first encounter with Cristina on the beach, passing the farol out on the grassy headland overlooking the ocean, and continuing on along the seawall toward another old fort. It was built out on the rocks, and waves broke and washed in white foam around its feet. I had stayed late on the beach after Cristina had left, and I was among the last stragglers to head off for home. The sun was low in the sky out over the bay, and the palms which lined the road cast long shadows across the black and white mosaic sidewalk and out onto the asphalt.

Before I reached the fort I crossed the road and entered the maze of backstreets in Barra. My hotel was just a block from the bay in an old building wedged into an area of shops and bars and restaurants. From the outside it wasn't immediately apparent there was a hotel there at all. Only a small sign hanging over the sidewalk announced the 'Hotêl do Sete Voltas,' and marked an open entrance to a narrow staircase leading upstairs into the building.

The staircase was old wood, polished smooth over the years from thousands of feet, and it creaked as I climbed it. The walls were rough whitewashed plaster. When I reached the landing at the top of the stairs I pulled open a door which had old glass panels in it, almost too thick to see through, and entered the reception area.

This was a long, narrow room which extended from the front of the building, with two windows overlooking the street, back to a balcony on a courtyard dominated by one huge tree. The clerk had told me it was a *sucupira*, a tropical oak. The lower branches of the tree were about at the level of the balcony, and from them hung several large cages with colorful birds. Some of them were parrots, others songbirds. During the day the reception area was filled with resonant chirps and screeches.

Here, and throughout the hotel, the atmosphere was of whitewashed walls and polished dark wooden floors, wide planks slightly warped from age. The furniture was cane or wicker, with old cushions, lumpy and worn, but clean.

I stepped over to the desk and asked for the key to number eight. The clerk reached into the last slot behind him and pulled out the key on its heavy wooden tag. I thanked him and walked to the street end of the room, where a second staircase began above the first.

At the top the stairs opened onto a narrow corridor which wound around out of sight to the right. All eight rooms in the hotel were off that corridor, but from the staircase I could see the doors of only three. Number eight was across to my left, where the room occupied the rear part of the building. I unlocked the door and went in.

Here were more whitewashed walls and polished floors. There was also a big bed with carved wooden head and foot boards, wicker chairs, a chest of drawers, and a round table in one corner. The only things on the walls were a mirror over the dresser and a small nondescript oil painting hanging over the bed.

I threw my beach towel on one of the chairs and walked over to the windows. When I opened the shutters onto the courtyard a view of bright green leaves flooded into the room. I leaned out one window and looked up into the late afternoon sky; still a clear blue, but speckled here and there with a few puffy white cumulus. The sounds of the caged birds drifted up to me through the leaves.

When I emerged from the shower, wrapped in a towel and flushed from the day's sun, I walked over to the dresser and pulled one of my nautical charts out of the top drawer. I unfolded it fully and laid it out on the table

The wooden floor felt smooth and warm under my bare feet. I leaned over the chart with both hands stretched flat on the thick paper, and my eye ran down the coast from Salvador to the south. Across the bay was the island of Itaparica. I had seen the island's hills from Monte Serrat the day before.

For about fifty miles south of Itaparica the coast was broken by irregular islands and inlets. Some of them were navigable, others not. Farther south the shoreline became more even, although punctuated by numerous rivers and streams. Towns marked where the most notable joined the ocean: Itacaré, Ilheus, Canavieiras, Santa Cruz Cabrália, and Porto Seguro. The names looked exotic to me and I tried to imagine how they were pronounced.

But out of habit my eye stopped at Porto Seguro. It stopped there because it was drawn to an irregular kidney shaped reef about a half dozen miles northeast of the town, and barely three miles off the coast. It was there, on the southeastern edge of the reef, that Haverton's coordinates had crossed.

A breeze came through the open windows and cooled my hot damp skin. I hadn't made any mark on the chart, another of my precautions, but I knew I didn't need to. I would never forget that spot. My only worry was that after two years the wreck might not be there.

After several minutes I unrolled one last time Haverton's greasy scrap of paper. I had long since memorized the numbers, and had kept it more as a talisman than for any other reason. I dropped it into the ashtray and struck a match. The flame spread to the paper immediately, and in seconds all that was left was a little ash.

PORTO SEGURO 21

The electronic tones of my alarm clock awoke me in the next day's predawn darkness. Before driving off I opened the trunk of my rental car to check the scuba gear I had rented in Pituba the day before. It was all there: the single tank, regulator, vest, weight belt, mask, and fins. I had told the dive shop owner that I was an experienced diver. In fact, I had only done some orientation dives a few years before. But I didn't plan to spend much time in the water. If the boat wasn't where it was supposed to be I would have to rethink my strategy. I put that thought out of my mind.

I threw my old canvas bag in on top of the diving equipment and closed the trunk. The street at that hour was perfectly still. The upstairs bar across from the hotel was dark and quiet, potted plants hanging in the still air over the balcony railings, illuminated only dimly by the light of the streetlamps. I could see no sign of dawn in the eastern sky.

The drive to the lower city took only a few minutes on the empty streets, but by the time I reached São Joaquim there were streaks of grey in the east, and a number of people were already opening their stalls in the market. I was able to drive directly onboard the ferryboat moored at the pier.

A LESSON IN GEOGRAPHY

Dawn came in its quick tropical way while we were making the crossing to Itaparica. I stood at the steel railing and watched the sun rise from behind the city skyline and remembered the dawn I had watched from the beach at Nyali. That was a different kind of dawn, a less refined kind, breaking the clean rim of the Indian Ocean horizon and enveloping me suddenly in its light. I thought of that dawn as the catalyst which had set everything in motion for me, a sort of unforeseen actor in a play, who steps onto the stage in the blaze of his character and galvanizes the audience in a second; the kind of experience which causes the viewer to awaken in the middle of the night and relive the impressions of the actor's entrance. That dawn had erupted from nowhere, up over the edge of the earth, and had sent out waves of energy which had carried me this far on their crests.

But this dawn I watched with the engines of the ferry throbbing under my feet, sending vibrations through the deckplates to my bones and into my brain. I gripped the railing and the rough steel felt good under my palms. The steel and the engines somehow made real what I was doing. I grinned at the new day and watched the wake of the ferry churn away astern.

The drive across the island went quickly, and soon I had crossed the causeway on the far side and was climbing hills on the mainland again, heading west to pick up the main road. I passed fields of oil palms and pepper plants and clove trees. These things I had seen in Africa, and they brought back more good memories.

I picked up the main road in a small town called São Antonio de Jesus and turned south. I drove fast and although there was truck traffic on the main road I was able to pass most of it without slowing down.

The small scattered hamlets came and went and by midmorning I had passed through the only sizable city I would see, a place called Itabuna.

By then I was well into *cacau* country. I drove by groves of the large trees which stretched away from the road until lost from sight in valleys and amongst other vegetation. I also saw piles of husks and the old stone drying kilns used by the farmers in the processing of the beans.

But all this passed with a regular beat, accompanied by the diesel harmonies of the trucks. About four hours after leaving Itaparica I crossed a broad river and soon after entered a strange desolate area. The thick forest cover had been stripped and splintered off the hillsides. I was reminded of photographs of First World War battlefields, and it was only the bulldozers and the timber trucks which kept the image of war from coming fully alive.

After several miles of destroyed landscape I wanted relief, and as I rounded a curve I was pleased to see the battered sign for Porto Seguro. I turned off to the left and drove toward the coast. The timbering operations continued for a few miles, but then gave way to untouched trees, thick and green and seemingly permanent, immovable and unre-movable. The road began to descend, and soon I caught occasional glimpses of the ocean, still pristine and blue in the distance.

I dropped the final couple of hundred feet to sea level through a narrow cut in the coastal escarpment. Porto Seguro came into view when I was about halfway down, below me and to my right. It was a pleasant looking village built on a small peninsula extending south-ward into a bend of the Rio Buranhém at a point just before the river flows into the sea. About half a dozen blocks of one and two story buildings stretched across the peninsula from the beach back to quiet mangrove waters on the inland side. There the river widened and slowed behind the town before winding around it and on out to open water. In those days, from its northern outskirts to the tip of the peninsula the town couldn't have been more than twice as long as it was wide. Altogether it was a quiet and unimposing cluster of little buildings drowsing under the midday sun. The ocean stretched bright blue out to the horizon.

After the fast drive down from Itaparica it was refreshing to roll slowly into the town, one elbow out the window, listening to the faint sounds of the ocean. The sea breeze blew in from my left and washed through the car. An old pickup truck left the main square just as I entered, but otherwise I could see no movement. I drove down the ocean side of town, between whitewashed one storey houses with brightly painted doors and shutters to my right, and beached fishing boats, equally colorful, to my left. I drove through patches of small shells and the tires made crunching noises on the asphalt.

At the tip of the peninsula, across from the channel sandbar which extended from the south side of the river and offered some protection from the open sea, there was a quaywall, and a number of boats moored to buoys out in the estuary. I turned right and drove slowly along the quay. It led back around to the inland side of the peninsula, where small neat houses like those on the ocean side looked out over dark quiet water to a dense tangle of mangroves on the far side of the river. A few boats were moored to the quaywall, but mostly it was empty.

In all of this I saw only half a dozen children and adults in the streets. I turned right again and drove slowly through the town back toward the beach. Some of the houses had tiny gardens in front, filled with weeds and flowers, and guarded by low walls and small iron gates. I closed the circuit at the beach and turned right again. There were some restaurants on that side of town, and I thought I might as well have lunch and ask a few questions.

About halfway down the length of the village I drove into a small square, with low buildings on two sides, the other two open to the beach. I remembered seeing two restaurants there, and I headed toward them. Two cars were parked on the square, both of them in front of the same building. I pulled in between them.

The quiet embraced me when I stopped the car and switched off the engine. I got out to stretch in the sun and listen to the wind. Some seagulls called to each other out over the channel. Then I heard the thrumming of an engine and a boat broke into view from behind the last building at the end of the square. It was headed out the channel, running northward parallel to the beach until it reached the end of the channel bar. When the boat reached a small buoy, it turned away and chugged out to sea, a small swell catching it by the starboard bow and rolling it gently. I could see only a single fisherman at the wheel. The gulls circled above him as the boat moved through the swells.

I turned and walked through the open door into the restaurant. It seemed sheltered inside after the breeze and sunshine of the open square. I blinked a few times and looked around. The room was filled with rough wooden tables and chairs, and potted plants hung in the open windows in place of curtains. The ceiling was draped with fish netting and assorted weatherbeaten flotsam. Thanks to the open windows and the whitewashed walls it was fairly bright inside. I picked a table and sat next to a window where I could see the ocean on the far side of the square.

"Boa tarde, senhor. O que é que o senhor quer hoje a tarde?"

I suddenly felt a bit overwhelmed linguistically. But I had been studying during the past few weeks, and my university Spanish helped. I smiled up at the young man in blue jeans and white t-shirt who was being so polite. When in doubt, order a beer. "Uma cerveja, por favor." I tried to make my Portuguese sound suitably nasal.

"Certo." He disappeared into the rear of the restaurant and reemerged almost instantaneously with a large bottle and a small glass. He poured. "O senhor é americano?"

Four words out of my mouth and he had me pegged. On second thought he probably knew before I ever opened my mouth. "Sim. E o senhor é brasileiro?" I might as well play it back at him.

He laughed. "Sim, Bahiano mesmo." He put the bottle down on the table and stepped back. "Se quer almoçar, temos uma moqueca de siri mole hoje que faz milagres na lingua."

I looked at him stupidly. "Como?"

He leaned forward earnestly, hands outstretched, eyebrows raised. "Uma moqueca, sabe? Moqueca de siri mole, sem duvida a melhor na Bahia."

This was definitely beyond me. "Desculpe, eu não entendo. Que é uma moqueca?"

He looked at me, shocked. Without a word he turned and walked to one of the other tables where a man and a woman were eating. He said something to them, jabbing a thumb over his shoulder in my direction by way of explanation. They leaned around him to look at me and nodded. The waiter picked up a double earthenware bowl on their table and carried it over to me in both hands. He held it out for my inspection. "Moqueca de siri mole." He said the words slowly, in a tone reserved for idiots and tourists who didn't know what a moqueca was. "Very good."

The inner bowl was very hot, and in it sizzled a kind of stew, creamy yellow, with onions and tomatoes and small soft shell crabs. It smelled wonderful and I was suddenly very hungry. I learned later that the magic lies in its coconut purée and dendê palm oil, but then all I knew was that I would give it a try. "Bom; quero uma moqueca."

He smiled, vindicated, and returned the bowls to the other table. The five or six other people in the small restaurant all peered at me curiously. I reflected that this was not the best way to go unnoticed. I raised my beer glass and smiled a silent toast to my fellow diners. They smiled back and shifted their attention back to their lunches.

I lingered over the meal, which included rice and manioc meal which had been toasted in dendê oil and was sprinkled on the moqueca the way parmesan cheese is sprinkled on pasta. Its attraction was not so much its flavor as the textural contrast it offered to the smooth and slightly oily moqueca. I was well into my second large beer when the last of the other diners pushed himself away from his table and walked slowly outside.

The young waiter appeared at my side. "Quer mais uma cerveja?"

But I had already had more than enough beer. "Não, obrigado, mas a moqueca foi muito boa." It had, indeed, been a delicious lunch.

He smiled. "Café?"

"Por favor."

He returned shortly with a small cup of coffee, and I decided to ask him to recommend a place to stay.

"Você pode recomendar um hotel aqui em Porto Seguro?"

He hesitated, an empty beer bottle and glass in one hand, and looked at me. "Com certeza. A Pousada Cabrália, aqui mesmo."

He pointed at the building next door. I thanked him, paid the bill, and left, feeling well-fed and a little lightheaded from the beer.

The inn next door was simple but clean. A little old lady with wrinkled brown skin and greying black hair in a bun showed me upstairs to a room which had the minimum of furnishings. A small crucifix over the bed was the only decoration on the whitewashed walls. But there was a window with a view of the sea past a corner of the restaurant where I had just eaten. The room was scrubbed by the sea breeze, and the curtains moved constantly at the window.

I asked her several questions as she showed me the room and the bath down the hall, all clean and spare, but she never acknowledged anything I said. Either she couldn't understand my Portuguese or she wasn't in a conversational mood. I accepted the room and went back to the restaurant next door.

The front door was closed now, so I walked around to the rear of the small building. The sandy soil was hard underfoot and covered sparsely with grass. I felt the warmth of the sun more fully as soon as I stepped between the buildings and out of the breeze. When I reached the rear I saw that the kitchen door was open and I leaned inside. I wanted to ask my friend the waiter where I might find a boat to use for a day or two.

I expected to see someone washing dishes. Instead, I saw a lithe young woman with long flowing black hair. She was leaning against some cabinets, her head back and her eyes closed. Her white shirt was open and pushed off her shoulders, and her fingers were buried in the dark hair of the waiter, who was on his knees, kissing her passionately while gripping the seat of her jeans with both hands.

She moved slowly against her lover and moaned softly. Her breasts moved under the pressure of his mouth. I swallowed hard and tried to withdraw quietly, but I heard her exclaim sharply the moment I pulled myself back out the door.

I stood in the sun, bracing for an unpleasant confrontation. I was trying to be inconspicuous in this town, damn it.

My pulse had quickened, and I realized that when I saw those two a picture of Cristina had flashed through my mind.

There was some movement in the kitchen and the waiter was standing in the door facing me. I looked at him blankly, and became aware that I should say something. I half expected him to take a swing at me.

"I'm sorry, I didn't mean to interrupt you, I mean, I apologize for intruding. Sorry."

It was far beyond my ability to say anything in my shaky Portuguese, but I held out my hands in a placating gesture, and he must have understood my meaning. He gave me a very thin smile.

"Minha namorada," he said, as if he had to justify himself by telling me she was his girlfriend. I nodded and he disappeared back into the kitchen.

Back out in the square, I closed my eyes and took several deep breaths of the fresh breeze. A great start I was getting. I walked to the corner of the square and down the street toward the southern end of town, toward the tip of the peninsula.

I passed houses and shops and a few more restaurants. Even in those years Porto Seguro was more a tourist town than a real fishing village, although it was far from the resort it would later become. I smiled to an elderly woman who was sitting in a chair in front of her open door. She was holding a lighted cigarette with knobby brown nicotine fingers and watching me closely as I approached. She blinked at the sun and the rising smoke and nodded back at me with great dignity.

It was about three o'clock and there were a few more people in the streets than there had been earlier, but still not many. I walked down to the end of the street, to where it widened into an open space by the quay, and where I could look out over the protected estuary and the moored boats there. The tide was flooding, and the boats trailed upstream from their mooring buoys.

The riverbank across from me was the dense mangrove thicket I had seen earlier. To the left, near the beach on the other side of the river, was a small cluster of buildings. They were apparently reached from the town by means of a powered raft, just large enough to ferry a single car across. And in the distance down the coast, looming above the tops of the trees, was a high section of the coastal escarpment. I remembered that my chart noted those cliffs were visible from twenty five miles out at sea. A small church sat on one of the hills between the town and the cliffs, and caught the afternoon sun in its whiteness.

"A very peaceful place, is it not?"

I started and looked down toward the voice. An old man was standing on the deck of a boat tied up about twenty feet down the quay. He was shirtless, wearing a dirty pair of khaki shorts, and he was looking up at me. He had a hairy chest and a large pot belly, and the skin on his arms was wrinkled where he had lost the strength of his youth. He looked like he spent a lot of time out in the strong sun.

"Yes, it is," I replied simply.

"Unfortunately, the tourists will start arriving in a few days, and much of that peacefulness will be lost. You are an American." He was the third person to remind me of that in two days.

"Yes, just visiting. Do you live here?"

"I live here and in Rio and in Belém, depending upon the time of the year."

"What do you do that allows you such freedom?"

"I paint."

I moved toward him along the edge of the quay. As I approached him I noticed the dirt on his shorts was multicolored, in spatters. He held a wooden paintbox up to me. I hesitated for a moment and then understood that he wanted me to help him. I took the box and set it on the stone quay. A canvas about three feet square followed, and after I took it from him I turned it to look at it.

The style looked somewhat primitive to my eye, but with a sophisticated use of colors and textures. The old man was climbing a wooden ladder bolted to the face of the quaywall.

"I like this very much," I said.

He stood next to me and surveyed his work. He smelled of oil paints and sweat. "I'm not certain it is yet complete," he said in his precise English. "But if you like it there are others similar to it presently showing in New York." He looked at me from under bushy grey eyebrows, clear brown eyes half buried in creased leathery flesh. "My agent in Rio tells me I should go to New York to promote my work. Tell me, do you think I should go to New York?"

"If you like Porto Seguro, probably not."

"That is what I think. And the last time I was in New York a bicycle messenger ran into me on Seventh Avenue. Now, if it were London I would perhaps feel differently. To hell with her."

I decided he was speaking of his agent.

"Do you paint from your boat?"

"I paint in my boat, not from it. You will notice it is not a seascape." The painting was of the sun, a fish, and a nude woman, arranged arbitrarily on the canvas. I decided I would call the style allegorical rather than primitive.

"That's true. Then why do you paint in your boat?"

"The sea feeds the soul, and I need that when I paint. The soul is very important, is it not?"

I didn't think he was speaking of religion. "Yes, I agree. And I think I know what you are saying about the ocean. I was six years at sea and I often felt that."

He scratched his chest with bony painted fingers, and looked thoughtfully at the canvas again. "I believe perhaps it is finished," he said. He looked at me again. "Come have a drink with me to celebrate the birth of a new painting."

"All right." This old man put me at ease.

He turned and picked up his paint box and started off along the quay, upriver. I walked next to him, carrying the painting. "So now

I will have a drink with the harbinger of the tourist horde," he said, reprimanding himself. "Why have you come to Porto Seguro?"

I slipped into my prepared explanation. "I'm looking for a good place to do some diving."

"There is no good diving here. The bottom is sandy and too turbulent."

"I've heard that, but I'd like to give it a try anyway."

We turned down one of the side streets and walked past several small houses before stopping at a large wooden door in a high white-washed wall. The handle on the door was a carved wooden mermaid, the varnish worn where hands gripped her torso. He opened the door and we entered a walled garden, a few feet lower than the street level, green and shaded from the afternoon sun. It was bounded on the far side by the house, about fifty feet away. The house evidently faced the street on the other side of the block.

I latched the door and followed him down wooden steps to the grass, moist and soft after the dry dustiness of the street. We moved under two large Jacaranda trees which together nearly filled the garden, and past several small palms to the tiled veranda. He called into the house.

"Olá, Lourdes, estou aqui com um amigo americano que tem sede. Um pouco de rum sem mais nada, por favor."

I heard a woman's voice from inside, but I couldn't hear what she said to his request for rum. He walked to the end of the veranda, shoeless and silent on the smooth brown tiles, and entered the house through open double doors. I followed him into what was obviously his studio.

There was a large workbench against one wall with brushes and tins and tubes of paint, and in the center of the room was a hand press with a large cylinder and cast iron handwheels, the kind used for printing with plates or woodcuts. And everywhere there were leaning stacks of canvases, some clean and some painted. He motioned to one stack and I added my charge to it.

We hadn't spoken for several minutes, but it hadn't been an uncomfortable silence. I looked through some of the other paintings while he cleaned his hands with turpentine. His other works were all of the same general allegorical style, but each quite different in its colors and composition. I found most of them very pleasing.

"I like these very much," I said, and then, to save him from having to answer, "They seem almost allegorical, the way you use the different figures. It seems very symbolic."

"One thing I do not consider myself responsible for is the interpretation of my paintings. That is the task of the viewer. Feel free to do so as you please." He finished cleaning his hands, threw the rag down on the workbench, and stepped over to a sink to wash with soap and water.

While he was washing, I turned to look out the door into the garden. Framed in the varnished woodwork, with the tropical foliage in the background, was a teenage girl. She was barefoot, wearing a long cotton print skirt and tight fitting white tank top which contrasted with her dark hair and skin.

"My daughter, Janine," the old man came from behind me, buttoning a khaki shirt which was only slightly less paint-ridden than his shorts. He kissed the girl on the forehead as he passed her on his way out onto the veranda. She never took her eyes off me.

"Oi," I said, in my most avuncular manner. She turned slowly, and floated after her father, shoulders back and hands clasped behind her.

I followed them out onto the veranda. The old man was seating himself in a chair in the garden. Next to it was another chair and a small table laden with a bottle and two glasses. I joined him. The girl had disappeared.

"My name is Argus Morrison. I just realized I hadn't introduced myself."

"Anísio Dantas. I see Lourdes has put ice in your glass, no doubt because I said you are an American."

"That's fine, thanks."

He poured the rum and handed me a glass.

"Saúde."

I raised my glass in acknowledgement and took a sip. The breeze dipped into the garden and ruffled some of the leaves around us. A bird chattered in one of the jacarandas.

"So how do you find our Brasil?" he asked after he had finished swallowing.

"Very much to my liking. I have never been anywhere so sensual before." I watched Janine approach from the house. "Since I've been here I've been awash in sensuality; the tropical heat and humidity. Even for a hedonist like me it's a bit unsettling."

"Yes, I suppose so. Those of us who have spent our lives here are convinced this is the way life was meant to be lived. It is difficult to realize that not everyone knows that. But you will become accustomed to it. You may not want to leave."

Janine sat on the grass, took one of her father's feet onto her lap, and began to massage his toes.

"You may be right." I thought a second time that day of Cristina, nearly naked on the Salvador beach. I took another sip of rum and felt it warm my throat and stomach.

So we talked into the evening, mostly of art and how he translated the sensuality of his life into the sensuality of the images he painted. The daylight slowly faded and before long the only light in the garden came from the house, although it remained warm. I could see stars in the clear sky through the leaves above me.

I got the impression that he didn't often have the opportunity to talk at length with someone he didn't know well. As the conversation moved from art to politics to philosophy Janine brought plates of oysters and shrimp and chunks of fried coconut. We ate as we talked, and the rum lubricated our words and our thoughts. And always she watched me. Her father said she didn't understand English.

"The key," he said at one point after a few seconds of silence, "is in the feeling, not in the thinking." He picked something out of a bowl on the table and chewed on it thoughtfully.

"You mean if you tried to analyze your painting intellectually you would rob it of its energy, its pungency?"

"My painting, yes. But more importantly, my life. As I have been saying, the one flows from the other. It bubbles up from my loins and my guts and through my arm and out the end of my brush onto the canvas. Once it starts I cannot stop it. It has a life of its own, and like a well-drawn character in a play it begins to take on responsibility for its own actions. The playwright loses control."

"But what makes it start in the first place?"

He looked at me for a moment. "That comes from within. It must come from within. And it must be strong enough to prevail over anything in its path. Otherwise the beginning will never come, and there will be nothing."

"And what happens when that thing which stands in its path is something, or someone, also very important to you? How do you decide? To follow your inner compass you risk a kind of overwhelming selfishness, the kind which eventually dominates your life and keeps you forever from happiness."

"But we are not speaking of happiness," he replied. "It is impossible to plan one's life for happiness in any case. If it comes, it is as the fruit of other things. And the most important of those other things is your 'inner compass,' as you call it. To follow it is not selfishness. Far from it. It is necessity. If you do not follow it you lose your humanity. Then you have nothing. And the one you love has nothing as well, even if she has you. No, it is not selfishness. It is life itself."

There was an awkward silence and I looked at my wristwatch. I saw that I had been there for more than six hours. It was getting late, and Janine had been absent for some time. Anísio explained that she was his youngest child, the youngest of fifteen from his relations with several women over the years. Some fifty or sixty years must have separated them in age, but they seemed very close.

I decided it was time to go. "I wonder," I said, "if you would know where I might charter a boat for a day or two."

A LESSON IN GEOGRAPHY

"Well, if you will not take my advice about the poor quality of the diving here, I would be happy to give you the use of my boat. I will not need it tomorrow. It is old but seaworthy and reliable."

"Are you sure that wouldn't be an inconvenience to you?"

He dismissed my question with a wave of his hand.

"Thank you very much. I'll take good care of it."

"I think after six years at sea you should know how to do that. And if you don't, I will take your car in trade for it." He smiled. "Also, if the diving is no good you can buy me a drink."

"Agreed." I thought the terms sounded good, especially since the car wasn't mine.

RECIFE DE FORA   22

The early morning sun felt good on my skin. I had stripped down to swimming trunks, and was standing on the quay, looking down at Anísio's boat. The town was awakening in its own characteristic way. I could hear voices and shutters opening and doors closing from behind me. And the onshore breeze had started already, and brought with it the faint sound of the surf.

The boat was not a yacht. It had been built with work in mind. Wooden lap-strake construction about twenty-five feet long, it showed the scars of years of service on its faded blue paintwork. There was a half cabin forward, with two small portholes for light, and a stand-up pilothouse of sorts, at least a windshield and small protective roof, but open to the afterdeck without side or rear bulkheads.

But there was plenty of deckspace aft, which was the important thing. Bounded by sturdy bulwarks about two feet high, the only interruption to its smooth camber was a raised engine hatch, about five feet by three. Altogether over half the boat's length was devoted to the open deck, and there was plenty of space for equipment. I hoped I would reach the point where I could use that.

I lowered my gear onto the boat and climbed down the ladder on the quaywall. The smooth wooden deck was cool under my bare feet. I set about looking around. Anísio had a good selection of mooring lines and ground tackle stowed forward, including a second anchor which would come in handy if I wanted to set a two point moor out at the reef. There were also a couple of folding chairs and Anísio's easel.

The pilothouse was pretty straightforward: spoked wheel, engine controls, gauges for fuel and temperature and oil pressure, and a compass. The starboard half of the windshield was propped open a few inches to let the breeze through.

I walked back to the engine hatch, and slid it off its coaming. The bilges were oily, but the engine itself didn't look too bad. I had expected a diesel, but it was an old inline six cylinder Ford gasoline engine. Its critical points showed signs of attention, and the oil level was right at the mark.

I stood up and walked the few steps back to the transom. The bulwark where I rested my palms was rubbed smooth and the natural wood tones showed through the old blue. I peered over into the water. In weathered white letters hand painted with an artistic touch I read upside down "Rosa Janine." I wondered if the girl I had met had been named after the boat.

The tide was ebbing now, which was good. I wanted to arrive at the reef for low tide in order to see as much of it as I could without diving. Another boat puttered past, heading out, and its wake snubbed the Rosa Janine gently against the old tires hanging from the quay. The man in the other boat turned to watch me, and I lifted a hand in greeting. He acknowledged and turned back to his wheel.

There were switches for the battery and an engine compartment ventilator as Anísio had described the night before. I set the choke and the engine started on the second try. I let it warm up while I replaced the engine hatch, switched off the ventilator, and pulled my chart out of my canvas bag.

The engine vibrations and the sun massaged me while I sat cross-legged on the smooth wooden deck and studied the chart for the hundredth time. I doubted that I really needed it anymore, but my navy training would have made me uncomfortable in unfamiliar waters without a chart in front of me. There were, in fact, plenty of navigational hazards noted along that section of coast, and I knew I would have to be careful, particularly since I would be approaching the reef closely.

Another boat passed by on its way out to sea, and I stood up before its wake reached us. The mooring lines were fixed permanently to small bollards on the quay. I let them go, forward and aft, and pushed Rosa Janine's stern away from the stone wall. She clunked gently into reverse, and backed smoothly out into the river. I swung the wheel around and moved the throttle forward. The rudder was like silk and the boat came around nicely with the tidal flow in the estuary.

I couldn't stifle a smile as I chugged slowly out toward the open sea. I swung around to the north, the estuary narrowing and the channel bar coming up on the starboard side, sheltering the moorings in the river. The buildings of the town passed gradually on the left. I watched a couple of small children playing on the beach, and they waved as I passed. Their high pitched voices barely reached me against the breeze.

A minute or two farther on I passed the small square where my hotel was, next to the restaurant where I had tasted moqueca and witnessed passion the day before. The wind kicked up a plume of dust in the square and danced it across into the buildings.

I traced the same path as the boat I had seen the day before. On my right hand the channel bar tapered into the sea, washed by the surge and sending an occasional wave spewing whitely into the air. I continued to parallel the beach until the channel buoy bobbed past to starboard, about fifty feet away. Rosa Janine had started to roll in the swells as soon as we had left the lee of the sandbar, and I was glad to bring her around into the wind.

Once on course to the east, I took the swells on the starboard bow and rode over them comfortably, twisting slightly as they passed beneath us and out under the port quarter. The light wind whipped through the open windshield and gulls circled above us and called out. I turned to watch the town, one hand gripping a spoke of the wheel and feet braced against the motion of the deck.

I had forgotten the feeling I always had when getting underway. For all the pleasures of the land, and I could think of many, the sea offered a welcome change. It cleansed everything, inside and out. I took a deep breath and blew it all out in a rush. And again. And a third time. Then I grinned and laughed. I laughed into the wind with an unwinding tension which seemed to spring from the soles of my feet and force its way up through my stomach and into my lungs and out my gaping mouth.

Eventually I calmed down and steered quietly, squinting into the wind and feeling subdued, and glancing at the chart every few minutes to gauge my progress. I guessed I was making eight or ten knots through the water. Anísio had said there would be a northerly current of three or four knots that time of year, so I set a course to take that into account.

After not much more than a half hour the reef was plainly in view, ahead and to the left. It was large, and a fairly smooth shape according to the chart. Even now, at low tide, it didn't extend much above water. It would be nearly invisible at high tide. The sea surged around its edges and broke over the rough shapes formed by the coral.

I adjusted course and wished there was a depth sounder onboard. Lacking that, I would have to trust the chart and be very careful. At about two hundred yards I slowed, and at a hundred I brought Rosa Janine down to idle speed. There weren't supposed to be any irregular projections from the reef or outlying rocks, and the water all around us was a dark opaque blue beneath the chop and the swells, absorbing the hazy light blue of the sky. All the same, I was going to get to know that reef as carefully as possible.

I kept a close watch on the water ahead as I idled along the reef at a distance of about a hundred yards. I also searched the water toward the reef for any sign of rocks. Occasionally I glanced at the reef itself in the vague hope that I might spot signs of a wreck. But it had been two years, if Haverton had been telling the truth, and the chances were slim that any wreck would remain in plain view through two seasons of storms.

The coordinates had crossed on the southeast edge of the reef. So when I was well up on the eastern side I reversed course, closing to about fifty yards, to cover that quarter a second time. I looked up from the water for a few moments as I made the turn. The coast stretched about three miles distant at its closest point, and while I couldn't see the beach at that range, I could make out the fringe of palms at the base of the escarpment. Rosa Janine idled smoothly and I noticed both the wind and the swells, which hadn't been bad to begin with, were abating. The sun was climbing in the sky, and bore heavily on my shoulders and back as we swung through the turn. A lone gull still circled above us, but quietly.

Again we idled along, my attention to starboard now, divided between the water ahead and the edge of the reef. The time passed slowly until we had covered the entire section back to the point at the southwest corner where I had arrived. Again I reversed course, but this time I didn't close on the reef. Fifty yards was already too close for comfort, and close enough for me to know there was no wreck visible from the surface.

So I would have to dive to find it. While I wasn't surprised, I was disappointed. It would have been so much easier if I had been able to spot it from the surface. It might take a long time to find it underwater if the visibility was as bad as Anísio said it was.

I idled back to a point along the southeast face of the reef which was marked by an unusual coral formation. I had decided I would use that point as a reference mark in organizing my search. I pulled back on the throttle and it clicked into neutral. I had been a little worried that with all the idling the engine might overheat, but the temperature and oil gauges read well into their normal ranges.

By now the morning breeze had died away almost entirely. Rosa Janine rocked gently and swung a little to port as we sat off the reef, but there was no sign of a current, and after five minutes I couldn't see that we had drifted at all. For the first time I noticed the sound of the breaking waves over the regular rhythm of the engine noise.

I backed her down a little, swinging the bow back to starboard, and then moved the throttle to slow ahead. The wheel spun smoothly under my hand and the bow swung around until we were headed directly away from the reef. I waited until we had moved back out to about a hundred yards from the reef face, stopped our momentum with a short throttle astern, and left it in neutral again.

The anchor was stowed in brackets on the cambered foredeck, just forward of the windshield. I swung around the side of the wheelhouse and out onto the deck, using the edge of the wheelhouse roof for a grip. It was a good modern lightweight anchor, with long flukes which would work well in the sandy bottom. There was six feet of chain followed by fairly new nylon line, which disappeared through a fairlead in the deck. I pulled about a hundred and twenty feet up and secured it to a bowcleat before heaving the anchor overboard. About a third of it paid out after the anchor.

Looking back over the wheelhouse roof, I judged we had drifted a little back down on the reef, but not much. I swung back behind the wheel and backed down slowly to pay out the rest of the line and set the anchor.

As I laid my gear out on deck I was reassured by the large coil of light nylon line which I had bought in Salvador. I had serious misgivings about diving alone, particularly since I had very little experience. There was three hundred feet of the line. I tied one end securely to my weight belt, and the other to one of the cleats on Rosa Janine's afterdeck.

I put on my wetsuit vest and pulled myself into the tank harness. By now the sun was directly overhead and there was no breeze. I was already dripping with perspiration, and the weight of the tank added considerably to my discomfort. I realized with some chagrin that I had only thirty minutes of air, and that if I didn't find Haverton's boat in that amount of time I would have to go back to Porto Seguro to recharge the tank. That would mean coming back tomorrow to resume the search. I should have rented two tanks.

Before putting on my fins and mask, I scanned the horizon in all directions. Brown dust stained the sky over land, but there were no signs anywhere of a change in the weather. The anchor also seemed to be holding well, so I switched off the engine. The stillness flooded around me in the heat and my ears throbbed a little from the memory of the engine vibrations. I listened carefully and the sound of the small waves on the reef came to me across the fifty or sixty yards which separated us.

The Atlantic Ocean was surprisingly cold when it enveloped me. But it was a welcome relief from the heat on deck. After hitting the water on my tank I rolled over and kicked toward the reef, angling deeper as I went. Down at about ten feet the visibility was not very good; I estimated about fifteen feet in every direction through the fine sand suspended in the water. Scattered rocks and weed were just visible on the sandy bottom beneath me. I checked the line tied to my belt, and was pleased to see that it was light enough not to hinder my movement.

I bore to the left as I approached the reef face, since my intention was to cover that section from left to right. I was kicking strongly and my first notion of the reef was a darkening of the water ahead which turned quickly to seaweed, strangely colorless in the filtered light. I stopped my forward motion and swiveled around to look behind me, always a little paranoid in the restricted vision of the facemask. The open sea was a blank featureless mist.

I turned back to the reef and kicked for the surface to check my position. I was well to the left of my reference mark, which was about where I wanted to be. Toward open water, Rosa Janine sat motionless, her anchor line sagging into the water. She looked small in the distance in spite of the angle of my view. I dove again, feeling clumsy when my flippers broke the surface for a moment.

This time I went down a little farther before leveling off. At about fifteen feet the light was good, but the fine sand kept the visibility below what I had hoped for. Anísio had been right. The diving here was lousy.

As nearly as I could tell, the reef reached the sand bottom at a depth of about twenty-five feet, among small outcroppings of coral and irregular stands of seaweed. The face was also irregular, with sizable indentations every few yards. But none of this was significant enough to hide a wreck.

I kicked rapidly along the reef, keeping both the coral face and the bottom within reasonable view. I know I was able to survey a fair distance in a short period of time, but all the same it was a distinct disadvantage to be able to see only about fifteen feet to either side. A good storm easily could have knocked the wreck more than thirty feet from the reef.

But in the end, as I should have anticipated, my tether was the greatest limiting factor in the search. After a very few minutes my weight belt tugged firmly from the point where I had tied the line. I surfaced to check my position, and saw that I had covered about five hundred feet of the reef.

Back on the boat I did some calculations. The southeastern quadrant of the reef had an arc of about two miles. By simple trigonometry, the most I could cover with a three hundred foot tether would be about five hundred feet. That meant shifting moorings more than twenty times to cover the quadrant. I thought I could do three such short dives on one tank of air, but I was still looking at a long search.

I would have liked to have done away with the tether altogether. That would have simplified things enormously. But I didn't have enough confidence in my diving abilities, especially in an area where I didn't know the currents. I would just have to be patient. Besides, I might get lucky and find it on the next dive.

I didn't. I did two more dives that afternoon; first to the right of the section I had covered, then to the left. Each time I had to motor up to the anchor, haul it and the line onboard, shift Rosa Janine's position along the reef, and reset the anchor. After the third time I tossed my fins onboard and pulled myself up the jacobs ladder with the tank on my back. I was exhausted. I shrugged off the tank and belt and lay on my back on the hard wooden deck, savoring its support and trying to let my breathing return to normal.

By that time it was midafternoon and the sun had lost some of its sting. After a while I got up, slipped out of the wetsuit vest, and started the engine. It was still almost a dead calm, but occasionally a random breeze ruffled the surface of the water and passed across the deck. I weighed anchor for the last time that day and set a course for Porto Seguro.

On the way in my thoughts were anything but confident. I had come a long way and I intended to find that boat. But what were the chances that it was still within thirty feet of the reef? I wished I had a high-resolution side-scanning sonar like the one I had used for locating wrecks in the navy. But I didn't. And what if Haverton's coordinates were screwed up? What if there wasn't a wreck at all?

But I couldn't believe that. If Haverton had double-crossed Morgan and taken the gold for himself he wouldn't have been tramping around the Indian Ocean like he was. And Morgan clearly believed there was a wreck. And he was willing to kill for those coordinates. Even though Haverton had obviously dropped a bit off the deep end, Morgan must have had confidence in his technical competence to have hired him in the first place.

So there had to be a wreck out there, and perhaps some gold. And it had to be somewhere near where I was looking. I hoped.

Anísio was on the beach when we rounded the channel buoy. He waved in a leisurely way and I waved back. He must have been more concerned about Rosa Janine than he had thought he would be the night before.

I had tied up and shut down the engine when he ambled up to the edge of the quaywall, hands stuffed into the pockets of his shorts. He was wearing sandals now, but otherwise was dressed as he had been when I had last seen him.

"So, how was the diving?"

It occurred to me that I had seen nothing of interest out there, not even many fish. "Not bad. Not the greatest I've seen, but worth sticking around a while."

His eyebrows bounced up. "That is indeed bad news! The last thing we need here is reason for more tourists to plague us."

I laughed as I finished packing my gear into the duffel bag. "Well, don't worry, I'll keep it a secret, just for your sake."

"I would be grateful for that favor. But of course, my real disappointment is that I have lost our wager and will not have the pleasure of accepting a drink from you."

"Not so fast. I may not have lost the bet, but you've got a drink coming. I want to thank you for letting me use Rosa Janine today. And I don't know about you, but I could use a few drinks. And some food. I'm starving."

He made some noises about going back to his house for that, but I insisted. After dropping my equipment in the trunk of my car we walked over to a bar facing the estuary. We sat at a table outside where we could watch the boats moored out in the river.

It was starting to be that peaceful time in late afternoon when everything quiets down in preparation for the evening. I felt better for talking with him. And I felt better for eating something as well. In my excitement I had forgotten to take food out with me, and I hadn't eaten since breakfast.

We sat out there until well after the bartender had hung a kerosene lantern from the veranda to push the darkness back a little. Anísio said he was going to Rio the next day and wouldn't be back for two or three days. He was going to meet with his agent who lived there. I hesitated, not wanting to abuse his hospitality, but eventually asked him if I could continue to borrow Rosa Janine. He agreed readily, and he seemed sincere when he said he was glad to let me use her.

After a while I nodded off a few times and decided I should head for my hotel. We walked back to my car together, and I only remembered at the last minute to ask him where I could recharge my air tank the next morning. I bid him a good trip and we went our separate ways.

The staircase at the little inn seemed much steeper than it had the day before. When I reached my room I had time only to strip off my clothes and fall naked onto the bed before sleep washed over me.

RIO BURANHÉM   23

The next morning I was up early to get a good start on what promised to be a long day. After breakfast I drove to a small beach hotel
on the outskirts of town. There I was able to recharge my tank and
rent a second one. Evidently there was some scuba diving going on
in those parts, but the man at the hotel echoed Anísio's comment that
he didn't think it was worth my time. He asked if I didn't want to rent
a sailboat instead.

The weather was a carbon copy of the day before. I was later
in getting started from the quay, and the brisk morning breeze was
already moderating when I rounded the buoy at the end of the sandbar.
But I saved time in not having to do an initial survey of the reef. I set an
anchorage off a new section, to the right of my reference point, which
showed clearly although the tide was higher than it had been before.

Three dives and two anchorages later, I pulled myself out of the
water and climbed up on deck. I let my tank down by its harness, and
took off the vest. I still hadn't seen anything of interest: no boat, no
junk which might have scattered from a nearby wreck, not even any
remarkable fish. I was pretty depressed as I sat down on the hot deck
to eat my lunch. Two gulls circled lazily above me and caught breadcrumbs I tossed up at them.

While I was sitting there digesting my meal another boat chugged by, coming from the northeast and heading for Porto Seguro. I followed it for a while with my binoculars. The man who stood at the wheel was bearded and wore a large straw hat. He waved when he was close enough to see me watching him, and I waved back. He continued on without slowing.

I used the second tank during the afternoon, and covered four more sections. That meant I had scanned almost half the southeast quadrant, almost a mile of reef. Another six dives would just about finish up the most likely part. If I hadn't found it by then I would have to decide whether to expand the search along the reef or out into open water. But I wasn't sure I could run a decent search pattern without the reef face for reference.

I made those six dives on the third day, and still didn't see anything. On the way back in I consoled myself with the thought that at least the weather was cooperating. It could have been fairly nasty that time of year. The man who recharged my tanks had told me that the wet season should still have a few weeks in it before we could expect several unbroken months of hot sun.

I moored Rosa Janine at the quay, dumped my gear in the car, and drove back to the hotel. After showering I lay on clean sheets and let the fitful early evening breeze play over my skin. I throbbed a little from the sun.

Later, after another good meal next door, I walked through the darkened streets to the bar by the river where Anísio and I had gone two days earlier. A couple of drinks on top of a full stomach left me in a relaxed mood. I sat outside in a comfortable wicker chair, watched the moored boats swinging with the tide in the dark water, and tried to decide what to do.

Eventually I noticed a figure in white approaching from the other side of the square. It was a girl, and as she drew closer I recognized Janine. She was dressed much more modestly now, in a long, loose cotton dress with a high neck and short sleeves edged in lace.

She was going to pass the spot where I was sitting, but she noticed me in the light of the lantern and shifted course a little to approach me.

She walked up to my table and smiled back at me in that heavy-lid-ded way of hers. "Oi."

"Boa noite," I said. "Como vai? O seu pai já voltou do Rio?" I wondered if Anísio had returned from his trip.

"Ainda não." Not yet. "Tudo bem com você? Como vai o seu scuba?" She wanted to know how my diving was going.

"Mais ou menos." Not bad, but I didn't want to talk about it. "Onde você vai?" Where are you going?

As nearly as I could understand she was on her way to some kind of religious ceremony. She used the word Candomblé, which I had heard before. I knew it was one of the African spiritist cults which had come to Brazil and other parts of the New World along with slavery. Beyond that I didn't know anything about it.

Janine wanted to know if I cared to come along. My first impulse was to decline, but the more I thought about it the more I was attracted by the idea. I needed a little diversion. Three days of anticipation and disappointment were beginning to have an effect on me. So I accepted, downed the last of my drink, and went along with her.

We walked past the open square where my hotel sat and on to the outskirts of town. In the darkness before the moonrise the stars were splayed across the sky in a shimmering profusion. Looking north, I could see the lights of the beach hotel where I recharged my diving tanks. Janine led the way first along unsurfaced roads, then on a path which led back toward the river.

As the scrub thickened closer to the riverbank, we passed a few small houses along the path, illuminated by lantern light from their open windows and the bright starlight from above. Eventually I realized that I had been hearing drums for some time as we had been walking. The rhythmic beating came in surges and stopped altogether every once in a while, then started up again. Soon I could distinguish voices as well, and then the path broke free from a thicket of mangroves to reveal the river shining a faint silver.

The mangroves had been cleared along the river to make room for several buildings in a small compound ringed by a rough picket fence. Janine called it the *terreno*. It was a colorless picture under the stars except for the strong yellow light streaming from the windows and door of the largest of the buildings, set in the middle. The others were all dark, but this one was crowded with people and voices and the pounding of the drums.

We stood in the doorway and looked over shoulders into the room. I found an old packing crate next to the wall which Janine stood on in order to see. The light came from a number of kerosene lanterns hanging from ceiling beams and from candles placed on the dirt floor among leaves which had been scattered there. Palm fronds hung from the walls. Most of the people wore white, which contrasted sharply with their dark skins. The two long sides of the room were lined with small bleachers of sorts, and I noticed that one side was filled with women, the other with men. But the sexes commingled among the latecomers who had no place to sit and who crowded the near end around the door.

At the far end of the room on a low dais sat a heavy Black woman in a heavy wooden armchair. She was dressed in a white blouse with puffed sleeves and lace trimmings and full skirts and a light blue head wrap like a turban. She held a ceremonial staff in one hand, and was clearly presiding. We arrived during a short lull in the drumming, and Janine whispered in my ear that the woman was the *Mãe-de-santo* for this terreno. Around her moved a number of participants, several of whom were dressed in African-style khangas. The men who were drumming sat off to one side, naked above the waist.

The ceremony had clearly been underway for some time. It was hot inside, and most of the people were sweating profusely. Their faces shone in the light, and some of the women fanned themselves. No one took any particular notice of us.

We waited for several minutes, and while there was rustling and movement in the crowd, no one spoke except in whispers. A faltering breeze passed through the windows and fanned the sweating congregation, flickering the candles on the open floor.

Then, without warning or apparent provocation, the drummers started up again, this time with a rhythm different from what I had heard as we had approached the terreno. The Mãe-de-santo sat impassively, gazing out over the room. After several minutes there was a movement in the curtains hanging to one side of the dais and a dancer appeared.

She was a young Black woman dressed in a full satin gown, light blue with silver trim. A white crocheted shawl covered her shoulders, and around her neck she wore a long fringed scarf in the same material as her gown. She had a tall silver hat with stones set into it which sparkled in the lamplight, and strings of blue beads hung from it across her face.

She danced with her head back and her eyes closed, and she made unusual undulating motions with her arms and body as she moved barefoot across the leaf-strewn floor. She wore metal bracelets and held in her right hand a round silver disk embossed with symbols. I noticed when she danced closer to us that cowrie shells dangled from the fringe of her shawl, and a picture of the Samburu I had found with Mungai flashed through my mind.

As soon as the dancer appeared the congregation came alive. Men and women clapped their hands and called out, not in song, but in encouragement to the dancer. I heard many shout "Odo Iya!" and I didn't understand what they were saying. Speaking louder over the noise of the crowd and the drums, Janine explained that we had arrived in time for the main event of the evening.

The terreno would honor several Orixás during the course of a single evening. But this one was a favorite of this terreno, and of many Bahianos. She was the goddess of the sea, Iemanjá. I could see that the dancer's movements recalled the wash of the waves. Janine said that much of what was being said by the crowd was in Yoruba. I recognized that by name as one of the main languages of West Africa. I learned later that almost none of the people using the words actually spoke Yoruba, but the Candomblê chants and songs had been passed down from one generation to the next accurately enough that a modern Yoruba-speaker would understand them.

After several minutes of the undulating dance and the pounding drums and the cries of the crowd, I felt a self-sustaining momentum developing. The dancer moved as if in a trance, her eyes still closed, among the flickering candles. The drummers bent over their instruments, the muscles straining in their arms and shoulders and sweat glistening on their skin. And the crowd swayed in the heat, many also with their heads back and eyes closed. The noise and the heat and the vibrations seemed to build in intensity and wash over everyone in the room.

Then I noticed a woman in the seats who had stood up suddenly. She moved spasmodically, and those sitting next to her tried to help her and stay out of her way at the same time. An old woman moved to take her arm, and led her out of the seats and out onto the floor. Janine said this meant that they had been successful in conjuring Iemanjá, and that the Orixá had possessed that woman's body. She danced with the same general movements as the dancer in blue, but in short spasms rather than smooth undulations.

I smiled to myself. It seemed to me that in this group there must be real social prestige connected with being "possessed." And by the same token, anyone who had never been the chosen vessel of the gods must be looked down upon by those who had. I was surprised it had taken so long for someone to jump into it. I wiped the sweat from my face with my handkerchief, and the man standing next to me shouted something in Yoruba.

The dancer and the woman continued to move sinuously around the floor, each oblivious of the other, and the drummers continued in the same beat. After a few minutes the woman's dance had brought her near us at the end of the room. The nearest to her moved away a little and she danced into the crowd. As she approached I could see that she was in her forties or fifties, her hair streaked with grey and her face crossed with deep lines from a lifetime of working under the tropical sun. The crowd parted before her and she danced slowly toward the door.

I was standing in the opening and backed away to one side, pressing myself against those next to me to open a path for her. It looked like she was going to go outside. Janine got down from the crate and moved it out into the darkness. I stood with my back pressed against the rough wall and feeling the man next to me and watched the woman move past, eyes closed and head back.

But before she passed through the door she turned and opened her eyes. The crowd gasped and a shudder went through me. She was looking at me, I was certain, but only the whites of her eyes showed. It was a blind stare and it scared the hell out of me.

She moved close to me and the others around me backed away in fear. I tried to move but couldn't seem to gather the strength. She reached up and put her hands on either side of my head. They were rough, and clammy in spite of the heat. My eyes were locked on hers, rolled back in her head. Sweat ran down me under my shirt. The drums pounded insistently. Her mouth worked but no sound came from it. A stream of saliva escaped from one corner and fell to her dress. The drums pounded and the voices rose and the sweat fell into my eyes and stung. The pressure on my head built and my vision narrowed until all I could see was the blurred image of her unseeing white eyes in her black face. My heart pounded with the drums and the voices combined into a great rushing in my ears, and my vision narrowed further and there was only blackness.

BAÍA DE PORTO SEGURO 24

Janine sat crosslegged in the early morning light. Her eyes were closed and she was leaning back against an unpainted wooden wall. I stretched and every muscle in my body ached, and when I looked around I saw that we were on the veranda of one of the smaller buildings in the terreno. It was perfectly still in the dawn light and I couldn't see anyone else. When I sat up Janine opened her eyes and looked at me.

In fractured Portuguese I asked her what the hell had happened the night before. I didn't know whether I should be embarrassed or angry. But she didn't answer me. She moved over to me and, putting a soft hand on my cheek, looked carefully into my eyes. Then she stood up and helped me to my feet.

I felt a bit wobbly but followed well enough when she turned and headed down the steps and on through the gate. She led the way along the path we had taken the night before, and when we emerged from the mangroves the new sun struck us in the face. Its warmth felt good to me and seemed to ease the ache in my joints.

When we reached the road I caught up with her and asked her again. She glanced at me quickly and then looked away and began speaking rapidly. I gathered eventually that the Mãe-de-santo had decreed that I had been possessed by the spirit of Iemanjá. We continued to walk and she said that no one had ever seen a visitor so possessed, and that everyone had thought it a rare and remarkable thing. She said the consensus was that I had been blessed by the goddess of the sea, but I could see that she was unsettled and more than a little afraid.

So I tried to put her at ease. I said I thought I had drunk too much the night before, and besides it was probably the old hag's breath that had knocked me out. But she didn't laugh, and I must admit I felt a bit queasy about the whole thing myself. I thanked her for staying with me. She smiled then and we continued to walk in silence.

We walked back into town with the sun warming us and I began to feel better as I started to get hungry. I decided I would ask Anísio about the episode when he came back. In the meantime I simply couldn't accept the explanation Janine had given me. It was preposterous. I wasn't religious, even in an abstract sense, and if I had a hard time processing the metaphysics of the Presbyterian Church I surely wasn't going to buy into African spiritism. But I wanted to talk with Anísio about it.

When we reached my hotel I asked Janine if she was all right. She nodded, and I squeezed her hand and she smiled again before she went off on her own. I went inside, but I didn't feel tired. I put on my bathing trunks and walked down from my room and across the square to the beach. The town was still quiet. I stood on the warming sand and looked out under the rising sun over the ocean. That morning there was no breeze, and the swells came in smoothly and broke on the channel bar. The water looked oily in the slanting rays, and felt warm when I waded into it.

I swam for a while, up and down the beach, and the exercise further eased my muscles. When I came out of the water the town was awake and I was ready for breakfast. While I was still unsettled by my experience at the Candomblé, I felt much better and was eager to get started on another day of diving.

By the time I had eaten and recharged my tanks and gotten Rosa Janine underway the sun was hot in the still air. It felt good on my skin as we chugged out the channel and rounded the buoy. I felt again like I had the first day. It was good to be underway, and the engine vibrations passed pleasantly from the wooden deck to my bare feet. The only air which passed through the open windshield was from Rosa Janine's forward motion.

When I arrived at the reef I set an anchorage immediately, at the nearest point. I had decided on the way out that I would do one last dive, without a tether, along the entire southeastern face of the reef. That decision came partly from impatience with the routine imposed by the tether, and partly from a realization that I might have missed some sections of the reef in my earlier, segmented search. I also felt that the current had not been a problem, and this day was the calmest I had seen.

Looking back on it, I didn't feel any special anticipation as I hit the water that morning. It was stimulating to realize that I wasn't attached to the boat for the first time, but I didn't really expect to come up with anything.

It wasn't until much later that I appreciated my good luck. It was much easier than it could have been. I had only just looked at my watch a second time when I was over it, and I glided past before I realized what I had seen.

A LESSON IN GEOGRAPHY

The boat had slid down the face of the reef and lodged itself between two outcroppings, heeled slightly to port but generally upright. It was a beautiful old-style wooden sloop, about forty feet long. Its single mast was broken three feet above the deck and lay in a tangle of wire rigging. Its bow extended a few feet into a crevice in the reef face.

I hovered motionless above the wreck, all kinds of thoughts racing through my brain. The one image which has stuck, however, was of my finger on the page of my friend's atlas that night in Mombasa. In the pool of light from the desk lamp I had pointed to this spot five thousand miles away. It seemed to me that I had been drawn steadily from that point in time and space to this; from that world to this one. I gazed down at the atomic speck which had lain under my fingertip as it rested on the shiny page of the atlas.

My watch showed another twenty minutes of air. I kicked myself downward until I was level with the wreck and could reach out and touch it. Barnacles had started to grow on the paintwork in small clusters, and fine strands of seaweed floated upward from their footholds on the planking. I moved aft and the reef faded from view. The gunwale where I gripped it at the transom felt smooth, even slippery to the touch.

I looked below my hand to read the painted lettering. Through a veil of fine moss it read clearly "*Bobotie*" with port of registry Durban. Haverton had said he had fitted out in Cape Town. That was close enough.

The hull below looked to be in fair shape. The rudder was pushed all the way to one side. But I couldn't see any major damage, although the port bow was hidden in weeds and I didn't doubt that the seams had opened. I took some time to inspect the keel, which had been kept out of the sand by the outcroppings and looked to be intact. It had been designed with plenty of drag: the point of maximum draft was right at the rudder posts. A good-sized section of the main timber had been replaced with a lead ballast casting. At least it looked like lead when I scraped through the moss and the paint with my knife. But that would be only a portion of the total ballast. Perhaps even the greater part of it would be loaded into the boat and stowed in the bilges from inside. Normal practice would be to coat the inside ballast in hot pitch before stowage to keep it from shifting. The pitch could also serve as effective camouflage.

My watch showed that it was time to return to Rosa Janine. I kicked upward a little until I was level with the gunwales again, and steadied myself on a lifeline which still stretched tautly along the side of the cockpit. If I were Morgan I'd stow gold as inside ballast rather than bolt it to the outside of the keel where it would be vulnerable to groundings and other accidents.

As I stared into the gloom of the open cabin hatch a large eel emerged, swam sinuously past the wheel, and disappeared slowly into the hazy distance.

A LADEIRA DA BARRA

25

"Hello, Argus Morrison. I had begun to think you had decided not to stay in Bahia after all."

"Cristina!" I jumped up from my chair. I had been sitting in the little upstairs bar across the street from my hotel in Barra, thinking about her, wondering if I might run into her again. "Please join me for a drink. I'm afraid I've become addicted to *caipirinhas*; just one of the many things I like about this place." I decided I was babbling and I shut up.

She smiled and looked radiant. "Yes, thank you, I'll have one too; a very nice way to celebrate sunset." She wore a large white blouse which looked like it had been starched. I wondered how it could stay so crisp in the humid heat. Her well-washed blue jeans molded themselves to her hips.

We sat down across from one another at the small table by the balcony railing. I had been daydreaming, watching the pedestrian traffic in the narrow street below. The light was only just beginning to fade, and the early evening breeze set the hanging plants swaying slightly. A samba rhythm and the mixed conversations of the other tables played pleasantly in the background. I motioned to the waitress to order two more drinks.

"So," Cristina continued, "where have you been the past few days? I've been looking for you on the beach."

I smiled at the thought of her in the sun in her tanga. But she was no less appealing now. Her blouse was open at the neck, and her brown hair framed her face and fell loosely in waves back over her shoulders. A topaz pendant hung from a fine gold chain around her neck and reflected the amber tones of her suntan. Her smile was beautiful, just as I had remembered it.

"In that case I'm sorry I wasn't here to be found. I've been south on the coast for the past few days. I think I've found a place where there's reasonably good diving."

"I didn't think there was good diving anywhere around here." She looked surprised and interested.

"That's what everyone says, but there's at least one exception."

"Where did you find this spot?"

I hesitated, annoyed with myself that I had backed into this corner. But it was no real secret where I had been; only what I had been doing there.

"Near Porto Seguro."

"Oh? That's a beautiful little town. One of the reefs down there?"

"No, on the coast. To the south," I lied. It was time to change the subject, and I was happy the waitress arrived with the drinks.

"Here's to our paths crossing a second time," I raised my glass.

"And to caipirinhas at sunset," she raised hers.

The lime and rum mixture tasted good. "You're still enjoying your visit with your family?" I felt a bit awkward, but I wanted to talk about anything but my recent activities.

"Yes. I always enjoy my visits to Bahia. If you've decided to stay a few days you really should let me show you around a bit."

"I'd like that very much. In fact you were right. I've decided to stay in Bahia for a while. I'd like to do some more diving, and it would also be good to get to know Salvador. If you have the time, I can't think of anyone I'd rather have as a guide." I thought I might as well mix pleasure with my business, particularly since I now knew what had to be done. Everything seemed much clearer, and there were a number of arrangements to be made here in the city before I could return to Porto Seguro anyway.

"Wonderful!" She seemed enthusiastic at the prospect, and leaned forward a little, pushing several gold and ivory bracelets up one of her forearms as if rolling up her sleeves before wading into her work. "There's so much to see here. You know, they say there are three hundred and sixty-five churches in Salvador; one for each day of the year. I don't think there are really that many, but there certainly are a number of beautiful old ones. Some of them date from the six-teenth century."

"Uh, that sounds great. I'd like to see a couple of them."

She laughed. "Don't worry, I won't bore you to death with them. Then there's the Mercado Modelo where we can have lunch and look at the handicrafts. And I know you like the beach. There are some fabulous beaches just north of the city where we can get fresh seafood for lunch."

"Ah, the program is definitely picking up."

The light had faded noticeably just since we had started to talk, and the waitress set a candle on the table between us. Cristina sat back in her chair and ran her fingers through her hair, spreading it out over her shoulders. The candlelight caught the highlights of it and the moistness of her skin. The evening was hot in spite of the breeze.

"Speaking of programs," I continued, "are you free for dinner? I drove all the way up the coast this afternoon, and I'm starting to get hungry. Perhaps you could start showing me the city by recommending a good restaurant for tonight."

"Yes, that would be nice." She sipped her drink while she thought for a moment. "I know just the place. You should have good local food tonight. Have you tried a moqueca yet?"

I laughed. "Yes, the best in Bahia, or so I was told. I loved it. That sounds great."

We lingered a while over our drinks and left by way of the narrow staircase which led down to the street. By that time it was fully night, and the street was more crowded than it had been earlier. There were a number of bars and restaurants in that part of Barra, and they all seemed to be doing good business.

We found my car a few blocks away where I had parked it on the sidewalk; a local custom, it seemed. I drove up the long hill known as the *Ladeira*, the lights of Itaparica twinkling at us from the far side of the bay, and on to Campo Grande. Cristina talked about Bahia and Brazil and pointed out sights along the way. Finally we turned up a small street that clung to the side of the steep hill overlooking the bay, and she asked me to stop in front of an old building with a large wooden door. Warm light streamed from the open windows, and cooking smells beckoned.

Cristina said this was one of the most famous restaurants in Bahia. It had been a house, and all of the main rooms were now dining rooms. A woman met us at the door and greeted Cristina warmly, obviously recognizing her. She showed us to a table next to an open window overlooking the lower city and the bay. The place was pleasing in its simplicity. Brightly painted woodwork gave it most of its color, and print curtains hung in the open windows, where the shutters had been thrown wide to admit the warm night breeze.

We spent some time going over the menu, Cristina explaining the various dishes, and I couldn't help remarking how strong the African influence was in the cookery. She agreed, saying that Bahia was culturally more a part of Africa than the rest of Brazil. Most of the slaves brought to Brazil had come through Bahia, and had brought their food and music and religion with them. An image of the possessed woman of two nights earlier passed through my mind and I shuddered a little. But Cristina didn't notice.

We lingered over dinner and coffee, and afterward we went back to Barra and walked along the sidewalk overlooking the beach there. The tall palms rustled in the breeze and the lighthouse on the point swung its beam in a metronomic arc. The wide mosaic sidewalk was filled with other couples walking or sitting on the concrete wall. It was late, but the outdoor tables at the bars across the street were still full.

We walked for quite some time, and when I sought her hand she grasped mine willingly. We talked easily about a lot of things. Cristina liked art and music, and had an interesting point of view. I liked to hear her talk.

Eventually we found ourselves looking at the fort near the beach where we had first met. The moon was up and was full enough to cast shadows where the streetlights weren't too strong. The small surf broke easily on the rocks under the fort. There were few people along that section, and it seemed like the view was ours alone. I put my arm around her and she pressed against my side. Then, almost without realizing it, we were kissing, feeling ourselves touching, caressing through clothing damp from the sea air and the heat of the evening.

Cristina felt as smooth and as taut as she had looked that first day on the beach. She was naked under her blouse and her body pressed against mine as I caressed her back through the cotton cloth. Soon I was leading her by the hand the few steps to my hotel. We walked without speaking, up the two flights of stairs and into my room.

I had left the shutters open, and the lamps in the courtyard gave a warm soft light to the room. Cristina walked to the windows to see the view of the tree and the caged birds while I poured two short glasses from a bottle of rum I had on the table. When I stepped over to her with the glasses she turned to me and her blouse seemed to be open a little more than it had been before. The light from below fell on the curve of one breast and glittered in her topaz pendant.

We drank a silent toast and her eyes seemed large and darkly beautiful in the faint light. She traced the side of my face and neck with her fingertips. Soon the glasses had been set aside and we were both naked, first by the window, then on the bed; exploring, caressing, kissing. I wanted to know every inch of her body, and I wanted to take a long time in the knowing.

There was just enough light to make warm shadows next to the curves of her body. She was deliciously suntanned all over except for a hint of narrow strap marks and the three tiny triangles left by her tanga. Those marks showed faintly, and I traced them lightly with my fingertips. Her stomach was smooth and flat. All the while I could hear only her breathing and the pounding of my heart.

When we made love it was fast and intense for both of us. Afterwards we fell into a dreamless sleep, with the faint strains of a samba playing to us from somewhere in the distance.

BAHÍA DE TODOS OS SANTOS 26

The next days passed for me as if in a dream, beginning with the first dawn when we awoke, still in an embrace. We made love again, more slowly this time. The fragile new light showed the tree outside the windows and brought the gentle sounds of the caged birds to life. Afterwards I buried my face in her hair, which smelled of her perfume and of the sea air and of her, and I slept again.

Cristina took me to churches, as she had promised, and they were beautiful. But I found myself looking at her as she explained their details. We went to the market in the old customs house in the lower city, and we haggled over leathergoods and jewelry, and ate lunch over-looking fishing boats. She also took me to her favorite beach, north of town, where a fisherman and his family had a thatch hut and served fresh fish and shrimp and oysters and cold, cold beer.

Our two anchors were that beach and my hotel room. After we had seen most of the sights in the old city we spent whole days on the beach, swimming and walking and lying on the sand in the hot sun. Cristina would leave me for a while in the late afternoon to meet later for dinner. But aside from that we were together constantly. I truly enjoyed her company, and we developed a closeness which went far beyond the sexual attraction we owned for one another.

I never quite forgot my other purpose, but I found myself thinking that two years had already passed since the wreck and that another few weeks wouldn't matter. And when after some time Cristina asked me if I didn't want to do some more diving, I decided to enlist her assistance in assembling the equipment I needed. I still didn't tell her my true reasons, and I figured my cover story was plausible to explain my need for everything.

"I'd like to find a truck to use for a few weeks."

"A truck? What's wrong with the car you've been renting?"

"Nothing, except that I want to take some gear down with me to make the diving more convenient."

"What kind of gear?"

"Well, an air compressor, for instance. My spot is quite a ways south of the town and it wastes a lot of time to go all that way just to recharge my tank every time I make a dive. And I'd like to get a few empty oil drums, say a dozen, to make a raft."

"What would you do with that?"

"I could anchor it where I wanted, and then just tie up the boat to it whenever I went out there. That would save time, too." That wasn't true either, but I thought it sounded reasonable.

So Cristina helped me find a truck to rent. It was an old red Chevrolet flatbed, rather beat up in the body but in reasonable mechanical shape. We found it with the help of a friend of a friend of her relatives who had a hardware and lumber business in the part of town known as Nazaré, not far from the soccer stadium. I turned in my rental car, and from that time onward we had to park much farther away from my hotel in order to find a space large enough. We started using Cristina's car for most purposes.

I arranged to rent a compressor at the dive shop in Pituba where I had found my other diving equipment, and I paid for various items of cordage, wire rope, and tools at a ship's chandlery in the lower city where I could pick them up later. Finally, we drove the truck one day to a scrap yard in Liberdade where I bought twelve empty fifty-five gallon oil drums in good condition. We lashed them to the bed of the truck, figuring that no one would go to the trouble of stealing them.

I was aware through all of this, of course, that I would sooner or later have to face the possibility that Cristina would want to go diving with me. That was out of the question. But nothing she had said indicated that she wanted to do that, and if necessary I was prepared to come up with some reason she couldn't. I was firmly decided on that point because regardless of how fond of her I had become, I had already been much less discreet than I had intended.

But it seemed natural that she would want to accompany me to Porto Seguro, and I started to feel guilty about disappointing her. The time we had spent together had been wonderful, filled with hot sun and sand and surf and her body stretched almost nude and glistening in the sun's rays at the beach. And the evenings had been long and languorous, spent walking and eating outdoors and making love in the steamy heat. And then, too, there had been the churches and other old buildings and the people of the city: the *acarajé* ladies sitting on the curbstones in their full skirts and cooking in bubbling pots of *dendê* oil, the children playing on cobblestone streets next to faded pastel walls, the sinewy fishermen hanging their nets to dry.

Then one morning it struck me that I had everything I needed and that it was time to get on with it. I was lying in bed watching the leaves on the *sucupira* outside my windows become distinct in the slowly gathering light. Cristina lay beside me, sleeping. She faced me, with one leg across my thigh, a hand on my chest, and her head resting peacefully on my arm. Wherever our skin touched we were slippery with perspiration, and the white sheet molded itself to the curves of our bodies beneath it.

I looked for a long time at her smooth relaxed face and her wild hair spread all around and her suntanned arm lying on the sheet. And I felt her heartbeat soft against my side. Eventually, without stirring, she opened her eyes, as if my watching had awakened her. I looked deeply into those dark brown eyes which were large enough to fall into, and I smiled.

"Bom dia."

She smiled too, and stretched and kissed me in reply. We lay there comfortably and talked for a while. It didn't take long to arrive at the subject I needed to broach.

"I think I have everything I need to do my diving down south. Will you still be here in Salvador when I get back?"

She looked at me silently, but with a little pain in her eyes. "I don't know. That depends on how long you will be away."

"Not more than four or five days."

"Perhaps." Still she didn't ask to come. But the look in her eyes brought a hollow feeling to me. As much for my sake as for hers I wanted to soften her disappointment.

"Let's drive up to Cachoeira today." Cristina had told me about the small village at the head of the bay which dated from the sugarcane days of Bahia in the sixteenth century. She had described it as a place of unspoiled quiet charm. She looked at me thoughtfully for a few moments as I stroked her hair gently back from her temple. Then she seemed to brighten as if a cloud had passed from her thoughts.

"That's a good idea. I've been wanting to show you Cachoeira. But first let's have an early morning swim."

We dressed quickly and walked through the nearly deserted streets to the empty beach. It was a calm morning, much the same as my last day in Porto Seguro, and the sun reflected smoothly off the incoming waves. The saltwater closed warmly around me.

After breakfast we drove north from the city in Cristina's car. She drove and I watched the scenery. The main highway was good and we sped through hilly countryside covered in palms and other tropical vegetation. Occasionally I noticed the red clay soil which I had remarked on the day I arrived in Bahia and which reminded me so much of Africa.

After a while we turned off the highway onto a smaller road which held close to the bay. We drove through small towns, Candeias and Santo Amaro, and vast fields of sisal growing under the sun. Every once in a while Cristina pointed out the ruins of an abandoned sugar refinery, usually first visible by the shaft of its brick smokestack pointing mutely into the sky from a hollow next to a stream. At one point we drove through giant stands of bamboo, large enough to move trucks between the rows.

Then, from the crest of a hill, the town of Cachoeira unfolded below us. Nestled in the valley of a small river, I counted the steeples of six or eight churches interspersed among the tiled roofs of the houses and the tall palms. Cristina drove down the hill and the asphalt soon gave way to cobblestones. She parked the car in the shade of a tree and we got out and stretched. Some people walked through the quiet streets, but there were few cars.

"This is beautiful," I said, meaning it. "But why are there so many churches for such a small village?"

"Three hundred years ago Cachoeira was wealthier than Salvador. In those days sugar was the reason for Bahia, and they used to ship it directly from here to Europe. There were a lot of wealthy merchants and *'fazendeiros'* living here, and they all wanted to sponsor the building of a church. Unfortunately, today there is only one priest here, for eight or more churches, and some of them are falling to pieces."

We walked into several of them and looked at their fading beauty. But I was surprised they had withstood the tropical climate as well as they had. Most had the blue and white Portuguese tilework known as *'azulejos'* which, set together, depicted scenes from history or the Bible. In one remarkably beautiful little church Cristina pointed out some *azulejos* which had been installed randomly, irrespective of the part of the design they represented. Evidently the local masons didn't always pay attention to the numbers put on the backs of the tiles by the artisans in Portugal. Perhaps it was a form of colonial rebellion.

After lunch we climbed one of the steeples, and standing next to the huge bronze bell, close under the sleeping bats, looked out across the river to Cachoeira's twin, São Felix. Later a boatman rowed us across the river and then back again. Before we knew it the sun was low over the hills to the west and it was time to drive back to Salvador.

It had been another day we didn't want to end, like the day we had driven up the coast to Itacimirim to swim in the cold rapids of the Rio Pojuca, or like the day we had sailed to the Ilha dos Frades to picnic on the beach and swim off the boat. The sun set behind the hills on the other side of the bay as we drove back to the city. We arrived in Barra under the bright stars, and Cristina dropped me at my hotel. We agreed to meet for dinner.

It was late when we finally ate, and we were both very hungry. Perhaps for that reason the food tasted even better to me than it usually did. We sat outdoors on a patio overlooking the bay and watched the moonrise near midnight. I thought briefly of the Coriander in Mombasa. But my thoughts were caught by Cristina sitting across from me in the light of the candle. She looked more desirable than ever, her suntanned skin glowing from the sun and her dark eyes and lips shining. Her hair framed her face in a mass of waves, and the dress she wore, with its sheer material and its low neckline, allowed me to appreciate some of the curves I had come to know so well. And she wore the topaz pendant again. It danced lightly against her skin and glittered as she talked.

After dinner we walked down the ladeira, past the yacht club and the boats moored out in the dark bay. When we reached the foot of the hill we walked out onto the beach and almost to the small waves which were washing quietly onto the hard sand. We stood comfortably for a while, her hand in mine as we watched the water and the few lights on Itaparica. Then we decided a nighttime swim would be the perfect end to that day.

Cristina led me by the hand back up to the road and around the point below the little church there. We walked almost around to the yacht club, and down onto the rocks. The night was as still as the day had been, and I heard the rustle of her clothes as they fell to the stone. By that time the moon was high and its light showed her nakedness clearly.

She was eager to swim and stepped into the water while I was still undressing. She swam directly out into the bay using strong athletic strokes. I stood for a moment, enjoying the feel of the night air on my skin and looking up at the moon. It was full, but I noticed only its beauty in the perfectly clear sky.

The warm water rose around me as if the air were thickening, and it felt good. Cristina was about twenty yards ahead of me, swimming out toward the boats moored there, and I put some effort into my strokes in order to catch up with her.

But she heard me and increased her pace, turning it into a race. We swam fifty yards or so like that before I stopped to look around me. When I raised my head I was surprised to see all of the boats off to my right. I had thought we were swimming out among them, but we had both veered off to the left somehow. Just then a spherical object rushed past me low in the water. It hit me in the side and passed under me with a rippling noise before I realized what it was.

Then understanding struck me almost as a physical blow. It had been one of the yacht club mooring buoys, one without a boat moored to it. It wasn't moving, but I surely was, and I was moving fast. With the full moon the tides would be higher than normal, and the tidal currents stronger. And even in the best of times, with the whole gigantic mass of the bay funneled through the opening between Barra and Itaparica, the currents there would be very strong.

Panic welled up inside me and I called out to Cristina. She had stopped swimming as well and was about twenty feet away from me. I think she understood what was happening to us at the same time I did.

We turned back to shore and started to swim. Between strokes I tried to gauge our position, but it was clear that we were well down-current from all of the boats, and our only chance was to make it to the point under the church. I could see the rocks there in the moonlight, and I knew they were the last land before the bay opened into the sea. From there the Atlantic stretched in its infinity to Africa.

I swam for the nearest rocks, knowing that the current would sweep us to the side. It looked to me as though we could intercept the last outcropping with something to spare. The panic seizing me in the stomach abated a little, but I kept up my pace, raising my head every few strokes to look ahead and back to Cristina.

But then I thought I heard something from her, a gargling sort of cry, and I looked back. She was clearly faltering, having swum farther than I had, and the distance between us had widened. I called to her to urge her on, but she seemed to be flailing in the water. I glanced back at the shoreline, which was moving past us, and swam back out to her.

When I reached her I was almost sick with fear. I told her to hang onto my shoulders and kick as hard as she could. I was tiring fast but I tried not to think about it. The only stroke I could do with Cristina on my back was a sort of sidestroke, which I tried to keep long and smooth.

In that stroke I could watch the shore as I swam and the fear rose within me, mixed with bile. As nearly as I could tell, the tide was sweeping us too fast to the side to reach the last of the rocks. I tried to increase my stroke but I felt my limbs starting to fail me. I told myself that this was the most important moment of my life, that everything I had done up until then paled next to this. I willed myself to continue.

I swam and I seemed to be looking down on us from above. I was separate from my body, and my vision narrowed, much as it had at the Candomblê. I saw the rocks sweeping past at least ten yards away and I heard sobbing in my ears, which I realized in a detached sort of way came from me, not from Cristina. By now we were swimming back toward the point, the open sea behind us, and I knew we were lost.

Then my foot slammed into something hard, and then my body, and we had struck an outcropping just under the surface of the water. I scrabbled for the rock, remembering the buoy which had whipped past me before I had known it. But I succeeded in holding onto the slippery surface and Cristina held onto me.

Weakly, I pulled us to a spot where I saw the rock extending a few inches above the small waves. There we clung to each other, sobbing from the exertion and the fear, half unconscious and swaying slightly in the wash. There we lay naked in each other's arms in the ebbing tide, bruised and battered but with the smooth hard rock under our bodies.

PONTA DE SANTO ANTÔNIO 27

We lay for a long time on those rocks, and eventually recovered some of our strength and composure. When the tide had ebbed further we made our way ashore. I led Cristina by the hand, stumbling over the slippery rocks back to where we had left our clothes. As we dressed I thought about what had almost happened to us and I was nearly sick.

We walked slowly back to my hotel, aching from the strain and from bruises from the rocks. By that time the streets were quiet and the bars and restaurants had all closed their shutters. The street lamps cast stark shadows on the pavement.

I locked the door of the room behind us, and it was a matter of only a few moments before we had dropped our clothes to the floor and fallen into bed. We slept as we fell, dreamlessly, with our arms around each other.

When I opened my eyes in the light it was Cristina who was looking at me this time. Her dark eyes were moist in the soft light. I smiled and pulled her closer to me.

We lay like that for a while before speaking. She was stroking my hair and face, and I don't think I have ever felt as close to anyone. We were more truly one than we had ever been before.

"I love you," she said finally. "I didn't realize it, but even before last night I loved you."

I kissed her and told her that I loved her as well, and for the first time in my life I knew it was true. This is the person I've been looking for, I thought. This is the person I love. This is the person I will always love.

Then I wanted Cristina to know everything I had been keeping from her. I told her about the boat. I started in Mombasa and told her about Haverton, and about Morgan, and about my decision and my escape. She listened quietly, still stroking my hair as I spoke.

Then I told her about looking for the boat and not finding it, and about the Candomblé and my success the following day. The more I had thought about it the more I had started to believe perhaps there was a connection after all. She seemed ready to accept that.

"I want you to come with me to raise that boat."

She hesitated a moment. "Only if you really want me to come. You didn't have to tell me all this. I want to come, but only if you want."

"I want you to come. I don't want to leave you now."

"All right; wherever you want."

And we made love, slowly and deeply, with a richness and a satisfaction I had never known before.

ILHA DE ITAPARICA 28

Later that morning Cristina left to make some arrangements for herself and I packed for the trip south. I felt wonderful and refreshed in spite of my aches. The sounds of the birds in the tree came to me sweetly as I ate breakfast on the balcony under my windows. I ate a ripe mango and thought of my garden in Nairobi. It seemed a long time ago. The coffee was hot and rich and good, as good as Kami used to make for me. Probably better, I decided.

Cristina returned after about an hour and a half with a small suitcase, and we moved everything down to the truck. We drove to Pituba first to pick up the compressor, and then back to the chandlery in the lower city where I had bought the other equipment and supplies. By the time we arrived at the ferry slip it was afternoon.

The crossing was as before, except the sun was high. We stood in the stern, above the thrashing propellers, and watched the wake churn away behind us. I felt the press of the sun's rays along with the vibrations of the ferry, and I was happy for the touch of Cristina's hand.

On the other side we stopped along a palm-fringed beach on the southeastern shore of Itaparica. There we ate lunch in the shade looking out over the pure white sand and the bright blue water. There was a bit of a breeze and we heard above the noise of the surf the occasional sound of a coconut crashing to the ground. The beach was deserted except for the two of us.

After lunch we got back on the road, and it felt good to get moving again. Cristina sat next to me wearing white shorts and a knit shirt, and looking relaxed and happy. Her hair blew in the wind from the open window beside her.

The truck was running well, but the front end was pretty loose and we couldn't make nearly as good time as I had in my rental car. But it seemed like a different route, sitting that much higher than I had in the car, and I enjoyed the scenery more this time. We spoke occasionally, raising our voices above the engine and wind noise, but generally we just enjoyed the ride.

It was well after midnight when we arrived in Porto Seguro. We had stopped several times along the way, once to get a quick dinner, but I hadn't wanted to stop for the night because we had no way to secure the equipment on the truck. I was tired from holding the big steering wheel steady on the road and from working the heavy clutch. The aches had returned. Cristina had been dozing for some time, jolted awake whenever we hit a rough patch or a pothole.

I drove slowly into the sleeping village, and noticed immediately that there were more cars than there had been before. I guessed Anísio's dreaded tourist season had finally begun. I parked in the middle of the open square on the beach where the Pousada Cabrália was. The inn was dark, too late to check in, but the little restaurant next door was still open. There were a number of cars parked in the square and I wondered if we would be able to find a room the next day.

When Cristina and I walked into the restaurant the waiter noticed us immediately and happily waved us to the table by the window where I had sat the first day. I had gotten to know him a little better since the time I had interrupted him in the kitchen, and I thought he was a genuinely friendly and hospitable type. He confirmed that the town had filled up considerably during the previous days, but he thought there were still rooms to be had, perhaps even next door.

Cristina and I wanted a cold beer to wash away the dust, and while the waiter was off getting it we looked around the room. There were about a half dozen other couples there, mostly young. There weren't any luxury hotels in Porto Seguro to attract an older crowd, and it was late.

We were ready for sleep long before we finished the beer. For lack of any other options we made a space on the back of the truck, in amongst all the equipment, and padded it as best we could with some blankets. There we slept soundly, in the night breeze and with the bright stars sprayed across the sky above us.

PORTO SEGURO

The next morning we awoke with the sun in our eyes and the sounds of the town growing around us. We rented the last room in the pousada, a small one on the back of the second floor with no view of the ocean. But it was clean and pleasant enough, and we were happy to have it. After a swim and breakfast I felt wonderful.

The first order of business was to go see Anísio. He had still been in Rio when I had last left Porto Seguro. We went to the big front door of his house. The old bronze bell mounted on the whitewashed wall sounded clearly when I pulled the rope. I heard Anísio's voice from within followed by the throwing of a bolt. The heavy wooden door swung inward in a chorus of grinding and creaking.

He held a brush and a rag in one hand, and he smiled broadly when he saw us. We shook hands warmly and he made me feel that he was genuinely happy to see me again. But when he turned to Cristina I could see the appreciation shining in his eyes beyond his friendly greeting. She was much closer to Janine in age than to Anísio, but knowing a little of his background I decided to keep my eye on him when Cristina was around.

Anísio led us across the cool tile floor of the large room, past comfortable-looking leather furniture, and down several steps to the veranda in the rear. The morning sun was beginning to play into the garden through the leaves of the jacarandas. We followed him to his studio where he showed us several paintings he had finished since he had returned from Rio. They were in the same general style I liked so much. Cristina said she liked them too.

Anísio stood behind us cleaning his brush as we bent over to look at the canvases. I turned back to him to make a comment and saw him gazing thoughtfully at the rounded shape of Cristina's white shorts and at her long smooth brown legs. I cleared my throat meaningfully. Anísio broke out of his reverie and grinned broadly at me.

"Yes, life is a wonderful thing, is it not?" he said. Shall we sit in the garden? I have some fresh *suco de caju* which you really should try. It is most refreshing."

We walked back out onto the veranda. Lourdes was evidently not at home, and Anísio went to get the juice. Cristina and I took some chairs from next to the wall and set them up out on the grass, in the speckled shade from the trees. Anísio came out of the house, his knobby brown knees moving under a tray with a pitcher and glasses.

"What kind of juice is this?" I asked as he poured the rather thick yellow liquid.

"Caju, er, cashew you would say."

"But cashew is a nut," I said, a little confused. Cashews were grown in Kenya, but I had never heard of cashew juice.

"Yes, but a fruit as well. And the juice, I think you will agree, is delicious."

It was, and I said so. "I wonder why I've never heard of this before."

"Just one of the many things the so-called advanced nations have missed out on," he said with a grin.

"How was your trip to Rio?" Cristina asked him.

"Ah, mais ou menos," he replied, shrugging a little. Then he switched back to English for my benefit. "My agent, that scheming witch, has talked me into going to New York to promote my show there. She says it is doing well without me but that my presence would make it a grand success. I suspect she is merely flattering me so she can increase her commission. But she was insistent, and I must admit that her saving grace is that she is an excellent agent, the best. So I allowed her to talk me into going.

"In fact, I am leaving next week, so I am very pleased you did not delay your return to Porto Seguro." He took a long draught from his glass. One of the buttons on his old khaki shirt was missing and a portion of his hairy suntanned paunch was visible. He scratched himself contentedly through the gap as he drank.

"So if you want to do some more diving, please use Rosa Janine. I will not be needing her for a few weeks."

I thanked him for his generosity.

He waved my thanks away vaguely and continued. "Which reminds me, Janine tells me you were the center of attention at a Candomblé a few weeks ago."

"Yes," I said, pulling my thoughts back to the Candomblé. "I really owe a debt of gratitude to Janine, who stayed to make sure I was all right. I'm still not certain what happened that night. Janine said I was possessed."

"That was the conclusion of the Mãe-de-santo, who is a well-respected authority on such things," Anísio said, smiling.

"Do you believe it?" I asked him.

"I don't believe it, but then I don't disbelieve it either. I think it is best to keep one's options open whenever possible. In any event, it would seem it was a favorable sign."

"Evidently." I told him about our nearly-disastrous nocturnal swim of two nights before.

"You see," he nodded, "one should never doubt the powers of the gods, whoever they might be. Which reminds me of a story I heard in Rio." He looked as serious as I had ever seen him, and Cristina and I leaned forward a little in our chairs to hear the story.

"It seems there was a man lost in the Sahara, dying of thirst, who came upon a bottle in the sand. When he uncorked it, a genie emerged, and offered him three wishes.

"After thinking a few moments, the man said he wanted as much water as he could obtain; he wanted to be close to a naked lady every day; and he wanted never to leave home again." Anísio paused for effect, looking intently from me to Cristina.

"So the genie turned him into a bidet."

SANTA CRUZ CABRÁLIA   30

We left Anísio with a promise to return for dinner that evening, and spent the rest of the morning loading Rosa Janine with all the equipment and supplies on the truck. It was heavy work in the hot sun, and I stripped off my shirt to do it. Soon my shorts were soaked in sweat.

Cristina was a big help, and I decided I couldn't have done it all by myself. We slid the compressor and the oil drums on planks from the truck bed down to the dirt. Then I backed the rear end of the truck out over the edge of the quaywall, and used it as a sort of gantry. I rigged a small block and tackle to the end of the cargo bed, and we lowered the heavy gear onto the deck. I handled the line from below and Cristina helped guide the loads from above.

We lashed the drums to the after bulwarks, back at the transom, left the compressor forward of the engine hatch, and stowed the rest of the equipment in the cabin. When we had finished it was time for a late lunch and a cold beer. There was no point in going out that day, so we had the rest of the afternoon free.

When I had left Porto Seguro the last time, I had driven up the coast to the end of the road. There was a tiny village there called Santa Cruz Cabrália, which sat on the southern bank of a small estuary. We drove there in the truck after lunch, and on the way I explained to Cristina how I planned to proceed. I told her that the first order of business was to raise the wreck.

"How will you do that?"

"With the oil drums, attached alongside the wreck and filled with air, we can float it to the surface. I think twelve drums will do it. If not, we'll have to find more. Then we tow it where we want to."

She looked at me strangely. "But why are you going to do that? Why do you want the boat?"

At first I didn't understand her question. Then I realized that I had never told her how the gold was hidden in the boat. The wind rushed through the cab and blew her hair around. We had to speak over the noise of the engine, and I watched the faded asphalt disappear under the broad red hood, with its rusty patches from years in the salt air. To our right the tall palms spun by in front of the white beach, and the blue water broke in foam on occasional rocks. The horizon was a crisp line between two shades of clear blue.

"A moment ago I was going to say because the gold is loaded in the boat as ballast. But there are two problems with that answer."

"What problems?"

"First, I'm not certain there *is* any gold. I have to admit I'm working on circumstantial evidence there." Certainly Morgan believed there was gold in that boat. And Brooks had provided some plausible background for it. But who knew what Haverton might have done with it?

Cristina didn't seem too surprised. I supposed she must have guessed something of the sort. "How much gold do you think there is?"

"On that count, I haven't the foggiest notion."

She looked at me, bewildered.

"But that's the second problem with using the gold for an answer. Until this moment I've told myself that I want the boat for the gold. But that's far from the truth. I just haven't made the connection before.

"What I really want is the boat. If there is gold there, so much the better, but it's an extra."

"I don't think I understand." She shifted on the seat to look more directly at me.

"Well, I know it doesn't seem reasonable, but back in Kenya I made that boat a goal, and I've been living for it since then. My life has been focused on finding that boat. I badly needed something to focus on, and that was it."

"And what happens when you raise it?"

"Then I can live the rest of my life."

"Then you will be happy?"

I remembered my conversation with Anísio. "Happy? Perhaps not. But there are more important things than happiness."

She looked ahead, through the windshield, and we were quiet for a few minutes. I was certain it couldn't make much sense to her, but I would try to explain again later. Just then I needed to move on to more mundane matters.

I found her hand on the seat between us, and squeezed it lightly. She squeezed back and smiled at me.

"Anyway," I continued, "I think we can raise that wreck pretty easily and move it someplace where we can work on it more comfortably."

"Where?"

"Last time I was here I found a pretty good spot up ahead. Assuming there is some gold onboard, we'll want someplace where we can leave the boat while we bring out relatively small quantities at a time to sell."

We drove on, past a point where a large cross had been erected high above the surf. Cristina said that was the spot where a Portuguese captain named Cabral discovered South America in 1500. I smiled at her and said that after a few more weeks with her I'd be an expert on Brazilian history. She smiled back and smoothed her blowing hair away from her eyes.

A few minutes later we pulled into Santa Cruz Cabrália. It was a smaller town than Porto Seguro, and evidently not a tourist place. There were no neatly whitewashed inns or restaurants here.

We drove slowly through the potholed dirt streets, looking down on the stained plastered buildings from our perch up in the cab. Children and dogs played in the dirt, and parted to make way for us, looking up and gaping as we passed. Some of the older ones ran alongside for a while, reminding me of my arrival in Loyangalani in Mungai's fish truck.

We were quickly past the few buildings which comprised the town, and at the riverside. Here there were a few fishing boats, most sitting awkwardly in the mud where the tide had left them. A net was spread out over some rocks, and a fisherman worked on it in the afternoon sun.

I stopped the truck, set the brake, and switched off the engine. The doors sounded hollowly when we closed them after climbing down from the cab, and the engine ticked rapidly as it cooled. A little steam wafted through the radiator grille.

We walked a little along the bank, heading upriver, and spoke in low tones against being overheard. "Up this river," I said, "there are mangroves the same as upriver from Porto Seguro. We could tow the wreck upstream and deposit it there, out a little from the bank, among the roots of the trees. It would be pretty much out of sight and inaccessible from land, but we could work on it from a boat without any difficulty. If we don't find what we're looking for inside, we can always careen it someplace to work on the keel."

Cristina responded immediately. "What about secrecy? Everyone in Santa Cruz Cabrália will see us towing the thing upstream and wonder what we're doing."

"That's true, and I don't like it. But one of the advantages to leaving the gold in place is that even if someone finds the boat and ransacks it, they won't recognize the ballast as anything valuable. It's safer as it is than it would be if we took it out and buried it someplace.

"Also, I'm hoping if we time our entry for around dawn we could slip through without attracting too much attention. But I'd want to make a trial run in Rosa Janine before doing it with the tow. What do you think?"

She hesitated a moment. "There is another river to the south of Porto Seguro, the Rio do Frade, which might be better. The town nearby is Itaquena. It's even smaller than Santa Cruz Cabrália, and I think it would be easier to enter unnoticed. The mouth of the river is wider and farther from town than it is here."

"How far south is it?"

"About the same distance from Porto Seguro as we are now."

We walked farther upstream, past the last of the town's buildings and far enough to see a stretch of the river curving between mangrove-covered banks. The water looked motionless. I slapped at an early mosquito.

"We have to remember to get some mosquito netting if we decide to spend the night on any of these rivers."

Cristina smiled and took my arm as we turned back to town. We walked slowly and talked about the next few days. We decided to reconnoiter both rivers by boat the next day. In the meanwhile, it was time to return to Porto Seguro if we wanted to clean up before dinner with Anísio.

BAÍA CABRÁLIA 31

The next morning we were up early, for a swim just after dawn and a good breakfast. We were underway in Rosa Janine shortly after seven. The weather was still clear, and the sun was already starting to have a bite as we rounded the channel buoy and headed into the low swells. As usual, we were accompanied by several gulls, circling and swooping and calling to one another.

When we were a little farther from land Cristina shed her shirt and shorts, clad only in the strings of her tanga. She looked at me and smiled as I steered the boat. She watched me watching her as she spread suntan oil on herself. We both laughed, and I turned back to the wheel.

We ran a course past the reef, to seaward, and north to Santa Cruz Cabrália. There were a number of reefs marked on the chart and I kept a close watch on our position with bearing cuts on some landmarks with a hand alidade. By nine thirty we were entering the estuary. We saw the same boats we had seen the day before, and it didn't look to me like we were attracting much attention. We puttered slowly past the town and on upriver.

I wasn't sure how far inland the river was navigable, so we proceeded slowly. Cristina sat in the bow and watched the water ahead intently. But we were able to follow the river until we were well out of sight of the town before she signaled for me to stop. I backed down a little to stop our forward motion, and left the throttle in neutral. The river flow was minimal and we drifted back downstream very slowly.

Cristina jumped back down behind the wheelhouse and we took a good look at the banks together. We saw several spots which looked promising for our purposes. And the river looked truly remote. We could see no signs of a road or buildings of any kind; nothing to show any human habitation anywhere nearby.

So far, so good. I swung the bow around and we moved downstream past a couple of bends until the town came back into view. It still looked pretty sleepy as we passed it outbound and headed out the channel.

It didn't take long to get back out into open water and for Cristina to return to her preferred state of undress. We headed south, retracing our course back to the reef and onward. We made eight or nine knots through the water, and even though it was against the swells on this course, it wasn't uncomfortable.

I was pleased to see that Cristina didn't mind the motion of the boat. As I steered us southward she opened the basket she had brought and parceled out our lunch: cheese sandwiches accompanied by beer from a small ice chest. It tasted great, hungry as I was. Afterward we had some fruit.

By two thirty or so we were approaching the Rio do Frade. I could see Cristina was probably right. The land was flatter here than it was farther north, and the estuary was much wider. Also, the town wasn't right on the river as Santa Cruz Cabrália was, and it was smaller. The channel was also easier.

Upstream, the river was much the same, however. Either one would suit us. The only thing I didn't like about the Rio do Frade was its distance from the reef. It would be a longer tow than the one to the north, and I was worried about that. Supported by the empty oil drums, the tow would be vulnerable to rough weather. And a tow to the south would be against the prevailing seas. I wanted to minimize that vulnerability.

In the end, we decided to leave the decision up to the weather. The Rio do Frade would be better, provided the tow was secure and the weather was calm. I was glad we had taken a look to the south. It was good to have a choice.

When we reached the buoy off Porto Seguro the sun had already dipped below the escarpment and some of the houses in the town showed lights. Cristina stood next to me, her arm around my waist as I steered. We steadied on course in the channel and I felt the muscles in my stomach tighten with excitement.

We were ready.

RECIFE DE FORA   32

We kept our room in the Pousada Cabrália in case we needed a place to stay ashore, but I expected we would be the next few days aboard Rosa Janine. Once we got started on the salvage I intended to stay at it until the wreck was safely at rest on one of the rivers. So we stocked the boat with food and supplies for three or four days, and by late morning we cast off from the quaywall and backed out into the stream.

As I swung the rudder around and moved the throttle forward, Janine came out of her street and ran down to the quay. When she reached the point opposite us she dropped to a walk and paralleled us for a couple of minutes. I waved and she waved back, then stopped walking and watched us move slowly through the estuary and up into the channel. She was still watching us when I lost sight of her behind a building.

We rounded the channel buoy which by now seemed like an old friend. It bobbed a little in the waves, a fringe of seaweed ringing its waist. The swells were small, as they had been ever since I had been there, and Rosa Janine took on her familiar motion with them under her starboard bow. This time, though, only a single gull circled above us. Its cries seemed a little forlorn, receiving no answer. The breeze through the open windshield was light and gusty.

Cristina stripped down again, as she had the day before. After she had finished spreading suntan lotion on herself she massaged my shoulders and neck and back with it. Then she hugged me from behind as I steered.

"I love you, Argus," she said, and kissed me on the neck.

I turned and gathered her in to me with one arm and kissed her full on the mouth. "And I love you, Cristina Campos." We smiled and I felt for the hundredth time in the past few days that my life was beginning anew.

We reached the spot on the reef where I had mentally placed the wreck in relation to my reference mark. I slowed to idle speed and moved in toward the reef. At about fifty yards I swung the wheel around and the bow came up into the breeze. The engine idled in neutral while I prepared the anchor and scanned the horizon. There were some light clouds low off in the distance to the southeast, but otherwise the weather seemed as fair as it had been all along. By that hour the sun was high and the waistband of my shorts was soaked in sweat.

I heaved the anchor into the water and watched the line pay out after it. Then I jumped back behind the wheel and backed Rosa Janine down until I felt the anchor set. We were a lot closer to the reef than I had anchored before. But I needed to be close to the wreck, and if the spot was correct, I planned to set a second anchor.

Cristina helped me put on my diving gear. She had never dived, so we hadn't rented any for her. But I thought I could do the underwater work by myself. When I thought about it, though, I wondered again how I would have managed everything alone. As she stood in front of me to help fasten the harness I watched a trickle of perspiration run down between her breasts, along the smooth muscles of her stomach, and disappear into the triangle of her tanga.

When I hit the water I had an image through my mask of her standing on deck watching me. The water seemed warmer this time. I flipped over and kicked for the reef about twenty yards away. I wasn't using my tether for this dive, but I intended to for the working dives later on.

The reef came out at me from the haze as it had before, a sudden darkening which focused quickly into rock and waving weed. I turned to my right and kicked along the reef well past where I thought it should be. So I reversed and worked my way back in the other direction. I kicked rapidly and covered ground fast. Just as I was beginning to be concerned, the shape of the wreck loomed out of the murky water below.

I kicked downward and brought myself to the side of it, next to the cockpit. There I reached out and touched the gunwale carefully, just to reassure myself that the boat was really there. I pushed myself down farther and checked the condition of the hull again. I saw the marks on the keel which I had made with my knife the last time I was there.

Nothing seemed to have changed during my absence. I still couldn't see whether there was any damage around the stem or the port bow. But the rest looked all right. I hoped that twelve drums would be enough. But there was only one way to find out.

I kicked directly for the surface, rising at the rate of my bubbles and breathing out as I went, as I had been taught. My head broke the surface before I expected. I swiveled around to mark the wreck relative to my reference point and to Rosa Janine. Cristina was watching and

I wondered if she had been standing in the same spot the whole time. She waved and I raised a hand in reply.

I was farther to the left than I had thought, no question about it. Rosa Janine was about thirty or forty yards away from me. But I was pleased to see that the anchor line was slack, so there was still very little current.

I swam back to the boat and Cristina helped me aboard. After I shrugged off the tank and vest we spent the next hour or so shifting the anchor about thirty yards to the west and setting a stern anchor farther along the reef. So when we were finished Rosa Janine lay parallel to the reef face, about twenty yards off the point where the wreck was. As long as the wind and the seas stayed calm it was a good safe anchorage, and one from which we could manage the salvage work.

We sat on the deck in the small shade of the pilothouse roof and ate our lunch during that hottest part of the day. I rested my back against the cabin bulkhead and watched the light wash of the waves on the reef so close at hand. A gull still sailed on the breeze above us, and I wondered if it was the same one that had come out with us that morning. I tossed some breadcrumbs up at him and we laughed when he succeeded in catching a few.

I thought the next part of the job would be the toughest. It involved moving the empty oil drums over to the wreck and positioning them alongside. I wasn't entirely sure how best to go about this stage of the operation, and I expected we would have to endure some trial and error.

The drums had round openings in one end, with threaded caps. I took one of the lengths of good manila line which I had bought in Salvador and tied it securely around the drum using a double bowline.

I then made sure the cap was on tightly, and we heaved the drum over the side. It floated nicely, bobbing alongside. We did the same with the other eleven drums, securing them to Rosa Janine by their lines.

Then Cristina helped me into my diving gear again. The sun was lower now, and I noticed it wasn't as hot as it had been the last time she had helped me with the tank. I went into the water, and she threw me the line to one of the drums.

I kicked the twenty yards or so over to the reef, towing the floating drum behind me. When I was over the spot, I unscrewed the cap and let some water into the drum, which settled rapidly. As it sank I tried to hold its angle to regulate the amount of air escaping. But that was difficult to do and the drum sank faster than I had intended.

After a few moments it got out of control altogether and I had to let it go. I followed it downward and saw it hit the sandy bottom about ten feet away from the wreck. Not bad, I thought. There was apparently still some air in it, and I was able to move it over alongside and secure its line to a cleat. The drum rested on the hard sand next to the wreck. I screwed the cap back on, but not tightly.

In more or less the same way I managed to position three more drums next to the wreck before I decided it was time to quit for the day. The light was starting to fade down below and I was getting tired. I told myself there was no reason to rush things. We had the whole next day, which would be more than enough time to finish up if all went well.

So I climbed aboard and out of my equipment, and we set about to arrange our housekeeping at the reef. We had a small brazier which hung outboard off the railing, and I started a charcoal fire for dinner. I was hungry after the day's work. Soon the smells of grilling fish were spreading across the deck in the evening breeze.

A LESSON IN GEOGRAPHY

We sat in Anísio's canvas chairs, with our feet propped on the engine hatch, and watched the sun go down over the coastal escarpment. Venus stood out brightly even before the last rays were gone, and the stars followed shortly in their own time. The breeze picked up a little as the darkness gathered around us, and Rosa Janine rocked pleasantly on the swells. We talked easily over the lapping of the small waves against the hull, the faint sound of the sea on the reef, and the occasional creaking of the anchor lines.

Later we lay on blankets on the deck, feeling our nakedness next to one another and perspiring lightly. I kissed Cristina and she murmured softly before we were both carried off on the smooth currents of sleep.

RECIFE DE FORA   33

After a swim we cooked breakfast on the brazier, with eggs and bread and fruit and coffee. While we were waiting for the coals to heat I surveyed the weather. The breeze was still light, but steadier than it had been the day before, and the sea was still nearly calm. But for the first time since my arrival in Brazil there were signs of a shift in the weather.

There had been fair weather cumulus from time to time, scattered pleasantly around the sky. But mostly there had been nothing, a perfectly clear light blue stretching overhead day after day, allowing the sun to sear everything below it with the full force of its energy.

But today, high fingers of cirrus stretched into the sky from the southeast. It was a thin cover, but I knew it would thicken as it approached us. We would have to be prepared for an increase in the wind and seas, but I wasn't sure how long it would take to develop. All we needed was another twenty-four hours of good weather.

"I thought we were into the dry season, now," I said.

Cristina followed my gaze upward. "We should be, but you can never tell for sure around this time of year. There could be a late storm any time through the next few weeks. Do those clouds mean anything?"

"They mean we might not want to wait until tomorrow morning to move the wreck upriver. If the wind starts to pick up this afternoon and we're ready to go, we should move right into Santa Cruz Cabrália. Even if that means people seeing us."

She nodded and looked a little worried.

But the sun's rays passed under the high clouds as it rose into the sky. It looked like it would be another hot day. We got organized as quickly as we could, and I had the remaining eight drums alongside the wreck by ten o'clock.

Then I went down with some more line and spent quite a while rigging the drums into a kind of harness. First I used the lines already secured to them to connect them in pairs under the boat. It would have been impossible to do that had the wreck not been suspended by the coral and stone outcroppings as it was. But there were sizable areas open under the keel where I could connect the lines.

I passed the lines to the aftermost drums between the rudder and the keel, under the upper rudder post. I did the same with the second pair, but under the lower rudder post. The four other pairs took a bit longer to pass under the keel.

The line I had taken down with me connected the pairs, horizontally around the hull. I wanted to make sure they didn't shift forward or aft and allow the wreck to slip out of the cradle. I couldn't get around the bow since it was wedged into the reef, so I passed the line through a fairlead up forward, across the deck, and back out the other side.

When I was finished I moved back to look at what I had done. The drums still rested on the sand, but they were securely connected together in a way I hoped would be strong enough to bear the weight of the wreck. I had left enough slacked line on each drum so that when it became buoyant it would rise to the level of the deck, and I intended to add another line around at that level to give some more strength to the makeshift cradle.

By that time I was getting low on air in that tank and I kicked back to Rosa Janine. When I surfaced, I threw my fins onboard and Cristina helped me up as she had each time before. But I immediately noticed some tension in her.

"What's wrong?"

She pointed to the west, and I saw that we had neighbors for the first time. There was another boat a little more than a mile down the reefline. It wasn't moving, but I couldn't see at that distance whether it was anchored.

Cristina handed me the binoculars. "They arrived about twenty minutes ago. It looks like they're fishing."

"If they are, I don't think they'll catch much. I haven't seen more than a dozen fish in all the dives I've done out here." Through the glasses I could see that it was a modern fiberglass sport fisherman. Its high bow pointed away from the reef, into the breeze, and I thought I could make out an anchor line curving down from the stem. "It's definitely not from Porto Seguro." I thought at first it might be some nosy bastard who'd seen us coming and going and wanted to know what we were up to. "That boat's come in from someplace else."

"Yes, it came up from the south."

Cristina looked worried by it, and though I didn't like it much myself, I wanted to put her at ease. "Well, let's keep an eye on it. I suppose they'll get tired of not catching anything pretty soon and move on."

She nodded and helped me out of the wetsuit vest. When she turned to lay it out on the engine hatch I grabbed her from behind and kissed her on the side of the neck. She laughed a little and squirmed, but not with her usual spirit. I let her go and looked up at the weather.

The late morning sun was hot and strong, but it shone through a very high veil of light haze. The cirrus was thickening a little. I wouldn't yet call it cirrostratus, the next stage of an approaching front, but it looked that way down by the horizon. At least the breeze was still light. I couldn't see any change in that or in the size of the small waves lapping around us. The swells might have increased a bit, but I decided it was my imagination. Rosa Janine still rocked comfortably between her two anchor lines.

We prepared our equipment for the next part of the operation. I had been using the compressor only to recharge my tanks, but now I pulled a coil of small rubber tubing out of the cabin and connected it to the output valve. There were thirty-five meters of the tubing, which was another reason we had to anchor so close to the wreck.

I weighted the end of the hose with a small bag of old bolts which I found in the cabin. Most of its length would float on the surface, but I needed to be able to control the end without difficulty. I added a short length of light line which I could use to secure the hose to anything close at hand.

The final thing I wanted to do before going back into the water was to adjust our anchorage again. We brought in the stern anchor, and let Rosa Janine drift down a little closer to the reef. We also brought the towline out from the cabin and faked it out on the deck between the engine hatch and the transom.

We were ready shortly after noon, and I climbed back into my diving paraphernalia. I told Cristina I felt like a knight being screwed into his armor before going off for a joust. She smiled.

I held onto the end of the hose as I fell backwards into the water. As soon as I had arranged myself, Cristina lowered a new coil of manila line to me, and I kicked back to the reef. The hose was much more of an encumbrance than my tether, and with the coil of line made for slow going. But Cristina helped it pay out over the transom, and I was down at the wreck in a few minutes.

I secured the end of the hose to the lifeline which still ran alongside the cockpit. Then I left the coil next to the wheel, and surfaced slowly. Cristina was watching carefully, and when she saw me wave, she went to start up the compressor. I heard the clatter of the small gasoline engine reach me across the surface of the water.

By the time I had flipped over and kicked back down to the wreck there was an increasing stream of bubbles coming out of the tubing. The buoyancy from the air inside made it a little difficult to maneuver, and I was glad to have the weight of the bolts to help me. I took the hose down to the nearest drum. There I unscrewed the cap and pushed the end of the hose through the opening. The stream of bubbles which had been churning to the surface was immediately cut off. I looked upward after the last of them as they rose toward the light.

After a few minutes the drum started to shift a little on the sand as the air built up inside. I continued to fill it until it had very weak positive buoyancy. The drum rose very slowly until it was alongside the wreck, a little above deck level. I replaced the cap and moved over to its counterpart drum on the other side.

Alternating that way, I managed to raise all twelve drums alongside in a fairly short time. I secured the hose to the lifeline again, and picked up the new line I had brought down with me. Once more I worked my way around the wreck, using deck fittings and stanchions and the tangled rigging as best I could to secure the drums in place as they were. The tow would be a short one, but I knew it would be a mistake to underestimate the forces put on a rig of that sort by the sea.

I left the hose trailing bubbles into the water and kicked back to Rosa Janine. When I climbed aboard to switch tanks Cristina and I had to shout over the noise of the compressor.

"How is it?" she asked.

"Fine. Everything's going well." She helped me drop the tank from my back. "I'll take the towline back with me now, and then we'll see if we can float this thing."

She nodded and smiled.

I pointed at the other boat in the distance. "Any movement over there?"

"Nothing. I've been looking at them with the binoculars, but I haven't seen anything."

"Okay. Maybe the fishing's not too bad over there."

I checked to make sure the towline was secured to the small bitts just forward of the transom. Then I passed the other end of the line out through the small towing fairlead and back onboard over the top of the bulwark. I handed it to Cristina.

"This should pay out smoothly when I take it over to the reef."

She nodded again and smiled through the din of the compressor.

We hoisted the second tank onto my back, and I fell back into the water. I was happy I wasn't going to have to do too many more dives. I was nearing exhaustion, but I wanted to beat the weather and get the thing done that afternoon.

When I swam around to the stern, Cristina handed the end of the towline down to me. I tied it to my belt like the tether, using a piece of small line. Then I kicked back to the wreck, marked on the surface by the welter of bubbles breaking from the hose below.

Just past the bubbles I dove with the line until I was a few feet above the wreck. There I detached it from my belt and swam up to the bow with it. Fighting the waving seaweed on the reef, I managed to run the line, which was the heaviest I was using, in through a fairlead and secure it to the small anchor bitts on the foredeck. When the wreck floated free it would pivot 180 degrees and tow bow first.

Now I was ready for the final push. The rig was in place, and Rosa Janine was set to take up the tow. I was tired, even underwater where I normally felt pretty good, but there were still a few good hours of daylight left and it was time to go. There would be time to rest later. Looking back on it, I think I was working partly on adrenaline by then. I was so excited I wanted to laugh into my regulator.

I kicked back along the port side, checking the rig, and the same up the starboard side. Everything looked secure. The drums swayed a little with their slight buoyancy when I pushed on them, but the lines seemed secure. I was confident the rig was more than strong enough for the short tow to Santa Cruz Cabrália.

A LESSON IN GEOGRAPHY

I returned to the hose, which was still spewing a wild stream of bubbles. I untied it from the lifeline and took it to each drum in turn, adding air to each one. It was important to keep the drums about equal in buoyancy because when it floated I wanted it to rise evenly. I did a circuit of the drums, twice each, and each time I carefully replaced the caps. Then I did a third round. That last time I had to tilt the drums a little by pressing down on the end with the opening in order to fill them with as much air as I could.

But still it didn't float. I tied off the hose again and swam around the wreck. The drums strained toward the surface. I tried to push on the side of the hull but I had no leverage and I couldn't put any force behind my body. Nothing moved, damn it. I should have had two more drums.

There was one more thing I could do short of breaking off the salvage to get more drums. I pulled myself up into the cockpit and peered into the darkened cabin. I hadn't gone in there and I didn't want to. I remembered the large eel I had seen the day I had found the wreck, and I shuddered to imagine what else might have taken up residence in there. But if I could get a substantial amount of air into the boat itself it might do the trick.

I took the bubbling hose in one hand and my knife in the other and I bit hard on my mouthpiece and ventured inside. More light filtered into the boat than I had anticipated, but it was still pretty murky. I felt some turbulence next to me which I knew hadn't come from my motions, and I twisted to see something exit behind me. I wasn't sure what it was, fish or eel or something else. My heart was pounding.

I wanted to trap as much air in the boat as I could. I moved forward from the main cabin past the part of the mast which remained in

258

the boat, and up into the small cabin in the bow. The whole time the hose was sending its bubbles up to the overhead where I knew they were forming pockets of air. I hoped the seams in the cabin and in the deck above hadn't opened too much.

I pushed the hose into whatever orifices I could find to try to trap as much air as possible. Then I moved back to the head and the galley and the main cabin to do the same. And finally, there were bunks and storage bins which extended aft under the sides of the cockpit. I pushed the hose as far back into that area as I could.

The problem with filling the boat with air was that I had to be inside to do it. I wasn't thinking very well from fatigue and impatience. A couple of times I thought I felt the wreck shift a fraction, and I was pleased about that. But I never intended to ride it up.

What happened in the end took me completely by surprise. The stern started to shift, and I realized belatedly that I was supposed to be outside watching, not inside. I left the hose stuck far aft in the cabin, and pulled myself toward the light of the hatchway. A loud scraping noise issued from the hull followed by groans and popping sounds from the bow. I pulled myself up the short ladder and through the hatch, but the wreck had already broken free and was on its way up. The cockpit pressed me from below and I remembered to breathe out as I reached the wheel and grabbed onto it.

We broke the surface in a rush, streaming all over, and bobbed a little, riding very low in the water. I was holding onto the lifeless wheel, and I felt more than a little ridiculous, like Neptune riding his scallop shell chariot to the surface—but with a mask and fins. If my navy friends could have seen me they would have laughed themselves sick.

But I decided I might as well make the most of it. I pulled myself upright in the bathtub formed by the cockpit, awkward in my fins, and looked over to Rosa Janine. Cristina was standing on the deck, and I could see her surprise across the twenty yards or so between us. I waved stupidly and she waved back, suddenly laughing.

It may not have been dignified, but we were underway.

PONTA DA COROA VERMELHA 34

The wreck bobbed next to the reef. I held myself awkwardly upright on the wheel for a few moments to survey it. Water still streamed from the tangle of rigging and seaweed lying across the top, and somehow the daylight made the boat look more damaged than it had seemed on the bottom. Weeds lay flat against the deck and the cabin paintwork, and clusters of barnacles stood out like acne on a pale cheek.

But the drums were floating well alongside the gunwales, although mostly under water. I wanted to get the tow away from the reef and the small breaking waves there, so I dropped myself over the side and kicked strongly back to Rosa Janine.

Cristina was laughing as she reached down to me. I climbed out of the water, dropped my tank and vest and gave her a very wet hug. We were both laughing. But there would be time for celebration later. I kissed her and ran over to the wheel. As soon as the engine started, I ran back to the towline and secured it on a cleat where it passed through the bulwark. I didn't want the full length to pay out yet.

Then I throttled forward slowly, bringing the shortened towline taut and swinging the wreck's bow around toward us. Cristina shut down the air compressor and began to pull the hose in from the water.

I was happy the deafening noise from the small engine was gone at last. When we were over the anchor I pulled the throttle back to neutral and swung up onto the foredeck to retrieve the anchor and line. In my enthusiasm it seemed much lighter than it had before. In a few minutes it was stowed in its bracket and I was back behind the wheel.

The sun was edging lower in the west when I moved Rosa Janine ahead again to pay out the rest of the towline. The escarpment looked black with the light behind it, and the rays danced off the water and into my eyes. But it still felt warm on my skin, and I decided there was about an hour and a half left in the day.

That wouldn't be enough to reach the river at Santa Cruz Cabrália, but having gone there once before I thought I could negotiate the channel by the lights of the town. I scanned the sky to the southeast and decided we couldn't wait for dawn. The cloud cover was thickening, and reached overhead on to the north. The blue sky had turned grey, and the sun was warm only because it was reaching us from beneath the high overcast.

I had noticed, too, when I hauled in the anchor that Rosa Janine's bow was pitching more than it had before. A steady breeze had followed below the long fingers of cloud, and ruffled the surface of the sea. So the weather was catching up with us at last. But I looked over at the sun again and decided we would beat it.

When the towline had paid out to its full length we set a course to the east. On that heading Rosa Janine took the swells under her starboard bow. Cristina and I stood side by side with our feet braced against the roll of the deck. We looked ahead through the windshield toward the darkening horizon, and the breeze whipped through the open half and swirled around us and carried on over the side.

I turned to check the tow. The towline was too lightweight to have much of a catenary, but it disappeared into the water nonetheless. With the sun lighting it from behind, the wreck looked like a heap of junk moving slowly behind us. Or it could have been some huge water mammal swimming with its nose just above the surface, hair pushed into disarray by the waves. The drums were barely visible in the water alongside it.

It looked to me that it was doing well back there, so I throttled forward a little and the engine vibrations picked up under our feet. But the most we could do, at least on that course, was three or four knots. I hoped we could pick up some speed when we swung around the reef to a northerly course, but even at a faster rate we would make the mouth of the river in four or five hours. The bow sliced into a wave and scattered spray across the windshield in front of us. More than a few drops passed through the open space and wet my face and chest.

In order to give us plenty of leeway off the reef I had planned to continue to the east for about a half hour before making the turn. But I cut it short by bringing us up a few degrees every five minutes or so to get the swells around abeam where we could ride them more smoothly. In about twenty minutes we were heading northeast, and I throttled forward another knot or two. Now we were rolling more, rather than pitching. That made it a little harder to stand up but reduced the strain on the tow.

After a few minutes on that heading I realized that Cristina and I hadn't spoken since we had gotten the tow underway. The tension had been high in both of us and there had been a lot to do in a short period of time.

"How are you doing?" I spoke over the engine noise and the increasing sounds of the sea and the breeze. I saw that she had put her shorts and shirt back on over her tanga. The breeze suddenly seemed a little colder, and I reached for my clothes.

She had the binoculars to her eyes and was looking behind us. I thought she was watching the wreck. So when she lowered them and I saw the concern in her face, I immediately looked back to see what was wrong. But the tow still looked secure to me.

"That boat's coming this way," she said.

I looked past the tow off into the distance, a little to the left of the sun. It was less than an hour above the horizon now, and I had to squint against the glare and the reflections from the water. But there it was. The big white boat was headed generally in our direction, and the bow wave and the spray it was sending up showed that it was making speed.

"Well, it's time to knock off fishing for the day anyway. I expect they're continuing on up toward Salvador. At that speed they'll be past us in about fifteen minutes." But I was nervous about it too, and I kept my eye on it. I felt like I had the morning after the Candomblé, trying to soothe Janine but feeling a knot of unease inside me.

The other boat followed pretty much in our wake. I made two more course changes in the next ten minutes, which brought us fully up to a northerly heading. I knew the reef ran parallel to our course about a mile and a half toward shore, but I couldn't see it at that range. The swells were now coming in under our starboard quarter and Rosa Janine was pitching again. But we were moving with a following sea now, and the ride was smoother than it had been when we were taking it on the bow.

The moment of truth came when the white boat reached the point of my last course change. If they were continuing on to Salvador they wouldn't make that turn. The way the coast stretched up to the northeast, the only possible destination on our course was Santa Cruz Cabrália. And there was no reason a boat like that would go there. My heart was pounding as I watched them behind us.

When it reached that point it shortened through the turn until its bow pointed directly at us. I suddenly thought of Morgan. It seemed like weeks since I had thought about him. *Shit*! I was a damned fool, and I had been careless. I wanted to tear my hair, but I had to think. And I didn't have much time. By then they were only about five hundred yards astern of us.

I spun the wheel to port, and Rosa Janine's bow came around immediately. I wanted to know for certain if they were after us, whoever they were. They altered course to port as well. So it was definite. They wanted us. Or rather, they wanted our tow.

I shivered a little when I thought about that. I had no way of knowing who else might know about the boat, but if it was Morgan I already knew what he was willing to do to anyone who got in his way. I had no reason to expect easy treatment from him now.

And this time I had Cristina with me. I was almost mad with fear and frustration. I had to find a way to protect her from Morgan. But I didn't even have a gun onboard.

"Cristina! Get my diving knife over there!" I pointed to the deck where I had dropped it when I had unstrapped it from my leg after my last dive. She moved stiffly over to pick it up. Her face looked stony. Then I had a thought.

"And in the cabin; get the signal kit, the red box, quick!" A swell rolled us and she staggered a little on her way back to me. I took the knife, and I saw that her eyes were filled with tears. I tried to grasp her hand, but she ducked into the cabin.

I swung the bow around to the north again, just to gain a few minutes and to keep them guessing. While we were in the turn, I took the knife out of the scabbard and stuck it in the wood next to the wheel where I thought I could reach it if I needed to.

Cristina reached up out of the cabin with the red signal box. Her face was wet with tears, and she looked frightened to death. I thought I knew exactly how she felt.

"Thanks. Now I want you to stay there in the cabin." I didn't want to alarm her any more than she already was, but I was trying to think of anything I could to keep her out of this. But she had already ducked out of sight.

The other boat was by then about a hundred yards off our port quarter and coming up fast. A thick bow wave curled whitely away from the stem and fell back along the side of the hull. I tried to look through the broad windshield, but it was still too far away to see who was onboard.

I crouched down, one hand still on the wheel, and opened the signal box on the deck. Clumsily, I loaded a flare cartridge into the Very pistol. Then I stuck two or three cartridges in the pockets of my shorts and kicked the box aside. It was the closest thing we had to a firearm, and I intended to use it if I had to. I slid the fat little pistol into the waistband of my shorts at the small of my back.

They had slowed considerably, almost even with us now, and were angling in toward us. About fifty yards of rolling water separated the two boats. I could see two people up behind the wheel, but I still couldn't see their features. It looked like one of them had a rifle. I gripped the spokes of the wheel as hard as I could to help me concentrate.

I waited for what seemed like a very long time. When they were about ten yards away, still angling in, I cupped a hand to the side of my mouth and shouted over to them as loudly as I could, "Stand off, idiot! Can't you see I'm towing?"

Morgan walked out of the wheelhouse into view, cradling a rifle in one arm. My gut churned. He was smiling, still trying to look relaxed, but I could see the tension in him and I realized that he didn't know for certain whether I was armed.

"Why don't you just heave to," he shouted across the swells and the engine noise, "and we'll complete this transfer in an orderly fashion."

The sound of his voice broke the shock of seeing him again, and the fear and frustration and anger overflowed within me. I spun Rosa Janine's wheel to port and throttled ahead as much as I dared with the tow. We picked up a little speed with the towline slack in the turn, and I caught whoever was running the other boat by surprise.

But Morgan was paying attention. As soon as our bow started to come around toward them he raised his rifle and fired. The left half of Rosa Janine's windshield shattered and showered me in broken glass. He worked the bolt and I saw the spent cartridge spin up into the air. He aimed and fired again, and one of the roof supports splintered.

We slammed into their starboard side amidships with a glancing blow of our bow. Rosa Janine was about as sturdy as they come, and even though we hadn't come around directly into them, her thick stem smashed into the other boat with a crash, and a large crack appeared in the white fiberglass.

Morgan jumped back out of sight just before we collided. As soon as we hit, I spun the wheel back to starboard and they veered off to port. The distance between us widened rapidly.

We both steadied again on a northerly course, but with about a hundred yards between us. I could see the mark we had made in the otherwise clean white hull, and I hoped they were taking on water. As I watched, Morgan came back out and knelt down at the rail. He was aiming at me.

I crouched again, but while the air compressor gave me a little shelter there really was no place to hide. A moment later I heard a bullet hit the side of the hull like a wet rag on a wooden floor. Then I heard the sharp report from the rifle. Then again. Then a round smashed into the woodwork next to the wheel.

We were still taking the swells from astern, the towline straining and slacking regularly as they passed under us. I looked back at the tow. There was no way I could get back to release it under Morgan's sights. But I knew it was our best chance.

I reached up and pulled the throttle back to idle. The engine noise and vibrations diminished immediately. Another bullet slapped into the hull and the sound of the shot came much louder to my ears. I shifted my crouch to ease the ache in my knees. The broken glass on the deck felt lumpy through the soles of my boat shoes.

The other boat had turned toward us and was heading in fast. They would be on top of us long before I could release the tow. I stayed where I was, crouched behind the wheel, shielded a little by the compressor.

When they were about twenty yards away they swung back to parallel us and backed down sharply. Their stern wave lifted them as their headway disappeared. I could see Morgan still in position behind the bulwark, the dark shape of his rifle still pointing in our direction. I moved a little more behind the compressor.

"That was very stupid, Morrison." He shouted across the water. "The choice is yours. Either you give up now, or I stand off and turn you into matchsticks. I've plenty of ammunition, and either way is fine with me."

"Okay, you can have the wreck, Morgan." I gripped the steel tubing of the compressor frame as I shouted back at him. "Just move off a ways and I'll cast off the tow. You can come in and pick it up after we've gone."

"Not a chance, Morrison. I like the way you've got it rigged now. So stand up with your hands in view and I'll come aboard. Then you and your friend can transfer to this boat and be on your way."

I hesitated. Morgan wasn't going to let us go. I knew that in my bones, and I felt a weight in my chest like lead. I could argue with him, but that would only postpone the inevitable confrontation. And it would put him on his guard. I felt resolve gathering inside me like a sudden hunger. It was now or never.

"What's it going to be, Morrison?" I heard the impatience in his voice across the breeze.

"All right, come aboard." The muscles in my legs hurt as I pushed myself upright off the compressor. The swells were moving us a little out of line with the tow, which sat low in the water astern of us. Rosa Janine's engine idled smoothly and the broken glass crunched under my feet as I shifted my stance on the moving deck. My hands hung at my sides and the breeze ruffled my hair and passed on through the broken windshield. I watched Morgan's boat maneuvering closer. And I waited.

No one else had appeared on the other boat. I decided there was only Morgan and whoever was running it. Morgan and I watched each other grimly as the distance between us narrowed.

The other boat was much larger and had about three feet more freeboard than Rosa Janine. Its captain maneuvered skillfully until they were nearly alongside. Morgan swung up onto the railing, holding his rifle in one hand, ready to jump down onto our deck. At that moment someone else walked out into the open, a short man with a dark complexion. But I couldn't see a gun in his hands, and it didn't matter now anyway. Events started moving by their own accord.

Morgan jumped for our deck. As soon as he moved I reached behind me and pulled out the Very pistol. He hit the deck and braced himself and I fired. But we rode up on a swell at that moment and my shot was about six inches wide. I watched it in slow motion, incandescent and hissing a blinding red. It passed next to Morgan, hit the side of the other boat and ricocheted off into the water where it disappeared in a loud sucking noise.

Even before it hit the water I gave up hope of reloading in time. So I threw the pistol at him as hard as I could and started to move around the compressor toward him. In panic and desperation my vision was narrowing, just as it had at the Candomblé, and the sound of the engines and the breeze seemed to grow into a rushing in my ears. All I could see was Morgan in front of me, staring with wide eyes and swinging his rifle upward with both hands now.

I stepped around the compressor and tensed myself for a final charge. A cry of rage built in my throat. But before it broke free, an explosion of pain and blinding white light blossomed from behind my right ear. A moment later, when my sight cleared, it was to see the wooden deck spin up from my feet and smash itself against my forehead.

THE SOUTH ATLANTIC   35

I was sick. My face was pressed against a coil of damp manila line. Before I opened my eyes I smelled vomit and I knew it was mine. My head exploded in pain each time my heart beat. I didn't open my eyes. I wanted to sleep. I didn't care. I wanted to escape the pain, and I didn't want to think.

But the motion of the boat and the pain wouldn't let me sleep. I wondered vaguely which of the two had awakened me. I moved my arms and legs, and I rubbed my face across the slick cordage. My hands moved over other coils and I guessed I was in Rosa Janine's cabin. The boat rolled violently and I retched and opened my eyes.

Soft light entered the cabin from somewhere behind me, the open hatchway. But even in its dimness my eyes ached as if in a glare. The boat rolled again, and the various coils and other things in the cabin shifted in a loud creaking chorus. I lay still for a while, trying to gather my strength and my wits.

Over the creaking around me I heard the wind. It was now the unmistakable sound of wind, no longer a breeze. And in its roar it carried the sound of the sea with it. All around me now I heard the symphony of noises, wind and water and boat, which means heavy weather at sea.

And then, too, I heard their voices. They were up on deck talking, raising their voices against the weather. I listened, but I couldn't hear their words. But I knew they weren't arguing. I could tell from the tone. And I remembered what I desperately wanted to forget. I retched again, and tasted the acid bile in my mouth.

With that blow Cristina had driven a dagger into my soul. I felt an unbearable emptiness and pain which had nothing to do with sea-sickness or a blow to the head. Now I knew that I had been a fool in a way I had never suspected. And the knowledge overwhelmed me.

I had thought it was amazing good fortune that I had met Cristina so soon after my arrival in Brazil; that she had been so approachable, so beautiful, and so loving. A sense of loss settled over me, but I told myself I couldn't lose what I never had. I pressed my face into the coil of manila and closed my eyes tightly.

It was so obvious now. Morgan was smarter than I was. It was as simple as that. It had been so easy to set me up. He had spotted me when I arrived in Salvador, if not before, and had handed me Cristina on a silver platter. And Cristina had kept him informed all along.

The worst of it was I had fallen in love with her. I had been truly in love for the first time in my life. That joy now seemed a bitter joke, and rage and hatred rose inside me like the bile, and tasted as bad. Now tears came, but they were tears of anger more than of sadness. I clenched my teeth and pressed my face into the coil of rope.

I decided the anger was a good thing. It would make me act. But I hadn't had time to decide what I was going to do when I heard a step at the hatchway. I rolled over and squinted toward the light. It was Cristina. She came down and sat next to me, wearing a look of great concern. Her voice, when she spoke, was lowered in a conspiratorial way, just loud enough to carry above the chaos of noise in the tiny cabin.

"Argus, darling, are you okay?" She reached for my hand. I thought that was taking melodrama too far.

"Go away." My words sounded thick to me and the pain in my head made me blink and made it difficult to focus on her face. "You've done enough. Go away. I don't want to look at you."

She looked stricken. "Argus, you must believe me. If I hadn't hit you Thomas would have killed you."

"Thomas! You know him pretty well then, do you?"

She hesitated a moment, biting her lip and gripping my hand. "Yes, I know him, but it's not what you think, Argus. I used to work for him, but no longer. You must believe me. I love ..."

"Used to! And when did you stop working for him?" My words were thick with sarcasm. "It must have been in the last five minutes. Go away. I'm already ill enough."

"Argus! Don't talk this way. I love you. I love you." Her eyes filled with tears. "You can't know how awful this has been for me. I knew this moment would come, but I hoped it would be later, when we were away from here safely." She glanced back through the hatchway. "It's true I was working for him when I met you. But not later, no; not after I told you I loved you. Not after that. I wouldn't after that."

She hesitated a moment, and I regarded her coldly. She saw my look and continued more rapidly, but still in a hushed tone. "Thomas asked me to help him, and in the beginning I did. I met you as he wanted. And for a while I told him what you were doing; but not later. By the time we went to Cachoeira I hadn't spoken with him for days. I would have told you everything, but I was afraid I'd lose you. And I thought we could do it without him finding us. You see, I never told him where you had found the wreck."

"You never knew until after Cachoeira." I shifted my position away from her.

"That's true, but I knew it wasn't far from Porto Seguro. But Thomas didn't know that, and I hoped he wouldn't find us. I didn't want to tell you until we were away from all this because I knew I would lose you if I did."

"So how did Morgan find us?"

"I don't know. He must have followed us down from Salvador. I tried to be careful. I didn't think he was following me, but I must have been wrong. I'm so sorry." She bit her lip again, and tears rolled down her cheeks. "But I'll prove it to you. He doesn't trust me now, but I've made some excuses and he's not certain what to think. Together we can get out of this. Our chance will come and we'll be able to over-power him."

A thought occurred to me. "Why didn't he just dump me over-board after you knocked me out?"

"He didn't want to do that in front of the other men. He was paying them a lot, but not enough to be witness to a murder. And after they left I wouldn't let him."

A small dim light went on in the darkness of my mind. "You mean the other boat isn't around now?"

"No, they went back to wherever they came from. They left not long after I, um, I hit you."

"That was last night?"

She nodded.

"Where are we now?"

"Heading up north somewhere. I'm not sure exactly where. We can't see land now."

"What time is it?"

"About seven o'clock."

I started to think perhaps she was telling me the truth. I wanted to believe that, and I clung fiercely to the thought. I couldn't believe that Morgan would have hesitated to drop me over the side as soon as the other boat was out of sight. It had to be her influence which had kept me alive through the night. I looked into her eyes and felt some of the warmth return to my blood. She saw the change and reached out to touch my face.

"Oh, my darling, what have I done to you? You look awful."

"I feel awful." I do love you, I thought. But I didn't say it.

"We can get out of this, together."

"There's no one else on board?"

"Only the three of us."

"He's still armed, of course?"

"Yes, but he has a pistol now. He left the rifle on the other boat."

"So how do we go about getting it away from him?"

She glanced back at the hatchway again. "I'm not sure. But he wants you to come up on deck as soon as you can to help him with the tow. He's worried about it. We'll get our chance sooner or later. While he's busy watching you, I'll take his gun."

"He wants my help?" I felt a knot of suspicion growing inside me.

"Yes, the sea is getting rougher, and he's worried about the tow."

So he had some use for me after all. "All right, let's go."

Cristina sensed the coldness back in my voice and she stiffened. But she didn't say anything. She turned and stepped over some things, bent over under the low overhead and bracing herself against the heavy rolls. She leaned out the hatchway and said something to Morgan, who must have been at the wheel. I heard his voice, raised over the wind in brief reply. Cristina climbed out onto the open deck.

By the time I had collected myself and moved the two or three steps aft to the hatchway, Cristina had taken Morgan's place at the wheel. I held myself upright at the opening, clutching at the coamings. My head still crashed with every beat of my pulse, and I felt dizzy. I thought I was going to be sick again. Morgan was standing out on deck, on the port side of the engine hatch. He was watching me.

"Well, the dead do rise, then, don't they?" he said. He was holding a revolver pointed at me. I thought his joke was in poor taste. The emotion I remember feeling was annoyance more than anything else.

I took a deep breath against the nausea which swept over me, and pulled myself up the two steps through the hatch and out onto the wet deck. It was a different world I entered than the one I had left the evening before. The blue was gone, along with the soft warmth of the setting sun. The sky above was heavily overcast, obscuring the horizons, and the sea was a roiling mass around us, cresting in white. The wind whipped the spume in streaks across the broken surface.

I looked around us, but there was no sign of land. A heavy squall line dropped a curtain of rain about a mile off to starboard. It was the only feature in a featureless landscape.

A swell came up on us as I stepped out onto deck, lifting us by the stern and tossing the spray from its crest up against Rosa Janine's transom. The wind took it across the deck with enough force to sting when it hit me in the face. But it was cool and it felt good. I moved to the side of the boat and steadied myself against the heaving deck by taking hold of the roof stanchion behind Cristina. Everything dripped and I was soaked by the time I turned to face Morgan.

"I don't know whether you are the bravest man I've ever met, or simply the stupidest," he said. He was looking at me like he would have looked at an unusual animal in a zoo.

"Let's just say the jury is still out on that." I said it without humor. I had decided to take things as they came. I didn't think anything would surprise me again.

Only then I thought to look back at the tow. It was all but invisible, riding very low in the water, almost submerged and washed by the swells. The tow line strained straight into the water from Rosa Janine, and her engine labored and raced as the seas passed under us.

"Looks like you've got a problem with your tow," I said. I wanted to sound unconcerned, but it was difficult, having to raise my voice above the wind.

"That's a perceptive observation." The dryness in his voice contrasted with the spray which leapt up from another swell and slapped into his back. He shifted his stance. "In fact, if you help me secure the wreck alongside, I would think it only fair to share some of its contents with you, in spite of all the trouble you've caused me."

I wanted to ask him if he intended to do that before or after dumping me overboard, but I decided to play things out a little more. "And just exactly what are the contents?"

He looked at me blankly for a moment. "Didn't Haverton tell you?"

"Not exactly."

"You mean you did all this without knowing what you were after?"

"I guess I figured I didn't have anything better to do."

The look on his face told me he thought I was crazy. "Well, there's no harm in telling you now. *Bobotie*'s ballast is gold; forty-five hundred pounds of gold. That's about sixteen million dollars."

I was a little disappointed. The figures seemed crude, and the mystery which had shrouded the wrecked boat seemed to strip away and disappear in the streaming wind. But I knew for sure then that Morgan would never let me go. Otherwise he wouldn't have been honest with me. I looked over at Cristina. She had turned from the wheel and was eyeing Morgan strangely. Looking back on it I think she had just come to the same conclusion, but I didn't see it at the time. I gripped the stanchion and felt the water run down my body and all I saw in her look was betrayal. I decided it was time to play out whatever was going to come.

"Why don't you secure the tow yourself?"

Morgan stared at me without expression.

"Oh, yes," I continued, "I remember now. If you were a master seaman you wouldn't have hired old Haverton to do your sailing for you, would you? After all, he proved to be somewhat less than reliable."

Morgan shifted his stance again as another swell passed under us, and I savored the sting of the spray on my face. He still held the revolver on me.

"Okay, I have a great idea. You give me that gun and I'll help you with the tow. Otherwise, you're right, you're going to lose it. That rig was marginal even for a short coastal tow in good weather. I'm surprised it's still afloat. And at this rate you're going nowhere. You've got a very large sea anchor back there and you're just using up fuel trying to tow it. So how about it?"

"That's more than I'm willing to pay, old fellow. After all, you have tried to kill me before."

That surprised me. "If I had wanted to kill you I would have done it in Nairobi." I waited a moment and he watched me silently. "All right, then, you don't have to give me the gun. Just toss it over the side and we can get to work."

"I keep the gun, full stop."

I wasn't feeling well enough to have much patience. "Fine. Then you can do it yourself. If you think I'm going to do more of your work for you just to get a bullet in the back of the head, you're nuts." In any case I had already written off the tow. I don't think we could have secured it alongside in that weather, and it was going down. Already it was even less visible than it had been when I had come up on deck. I enjoyed the thought that Morgan was going to lose the gold, and I understood then what small pleasures mean to a dying man.

As far as I was concerned the gold meant nothing. I realized that it had always been something abstract to me. I had found something much more valuable on the beaches of Salvador and in the churches of Cachoeira and in the dark currents of All Saint's Bay. But I had lost my love for Cristina now and the other seemed unimportant to me.

Morgan was visibly angry now. I saw that the plot had about played itself out, and my instincts belatedly turned to survival. My wits really had been dulled by pain and nausea. I realized too late that I had missed a chance by turning down Morgan's offer. Perhaps I could have taken him off guard while we were working to secure the tow. But there was no point in thinking about it now. I had said too much to go back.

Gradually I became aware that Morgan and Cristina had been speaking. But their words to one another seemed irrelevant to me. I took the opportunity to look around me for some kind of weapon. My knife was gone from the woodwork next to the wheel. I tried to think. I knew Anísio kept some old tools in an open section of the bulwark. I could just see them there, rusty and wet only a short step from where I was standing.

Then there was something in the tone of Cristina's words which pulled my attention back to her. She was speaking with a force and intensity which I had never heard in her voice before. She had turned entirely from the wheel and was facing Morgan, one hand on a spoke and the other on the stanchion, barely touching mine. Another sheet of spray flew across us.

"I won't hear of it Thomas. We agreed."

"Yes, we agreed, but he's worse than useless now. He's dangerous. Aren't you, Morrison? I hate to tell you this, but your time has come. The jury is in, and the vote is for stupidity."

Morgan's arm tensed as he raised the revolver a little. I dove for the tools next to the wheel and at the same instant Cristina stepped forward. My knife was suddenly in her hand. I don't know where it came from. She raised her arm to throw and Morgan fired.

Her arm came down and released the knife as the revolver in Morgan's hand exploded. I watched her in a grotesque dance. Her head snapped back and she staggered backward a step. The spray which spattered across my shirt was bright red. Rosa Janine rose on another swell and without losing momentum Cristina plunged over the side into the opaque churning water.

I heard a wild animal cry and I looked at Morgan. He was staring with wide, shocked eyes at the spot in the water where Cristina had disappeared. But his mouth was closed in a tight line, and I knew the scream was coming from me.

He tore his eyes away from the water and started to bring his aim around toward me. My hand had closed on a wrench. I brought it up and threw with the strength and accuracy of a madman in a dream.

It hit him full force in the chest and at that moment I heard another pistol shot. But Morgan hadn't fired. It was the towline. It had parted under the strain a few feet astern of us, and Rosa Janine lurched violently.

I can still see his face clearly as he went over the side. He never opened his mouth. He staggered backward under the blow from the wrench and from the sudden movement of the deck. The top of the bulwark caught him behind the knees and he pitched over the side and disappeared under the waves like a sack of shot. He never came up.

I staggered to the wheel and spun it to starboard, looking for any sign of Cristina in that direction. Free of the tow, Rosa Janine came around rapidly. I tried to focus on the point in the cresting waves where I thought she had gone overboard.

What was it? I tried to concentrate on the words. I tried to picture the slowly-working lips of the sleeping man who had spoken so clearly to me so long ago. But he slept soundly now, and mutely, and I couldn't hear anything over the screaming of the wind in my ears.

What was it? What was the thing I had forgotten without knowing it? I stood there, my stance wide against the heave of the boat, as everything swirled around me.

What was it? I was totally alone, more profoundly than I had ever been in my life before. A numbness began deep inside me and spread outward until I was a burned out husk. I felt the press of the wind on me and the cold sting of the spray. But inside I felt nothing. And the words wouldn't come. The shades of grey around me seemed to grow closer to one another until the whole world became a dark and colorless place.

I circled aimlessly for a long time—it must have been hours— scanning the endless breaking seas and the dark impenetrable troughs for any sign of Cristina. Eventually, feeling a cold numbness in the core of my being, I set a course to the southwest.

TERRA INCOGNITA   36

I am walking on a city street in the late autumn. It is evening in the Chelsea neighborhood of Manhattan. Unlike my imaginary visits to Jamba, this is real, with passersby making their way to meet friends for drinks or dinner, and busy street traffic. But as is so often the case, my thoughts drift back to the hours after that terrible day thirty-five hundred miles to the south.

The worst of the storm had passed when I reached Porto Seguro. I remember clearly every feature of its estuary and of the small houses lining the broad sandy beach and the bank of the river. It had stopped raining. The overcast was still heavy, black clouds scudding fast overhead, and the painted colors of the houses which seemed so bright in the sunlight were subdued. The wetness of the storm lay over everything.

I turned past the channel buoy and motored slowly upriver, and I was thankful for the shelter of the channel bar after the long hours of heavy weather. The tide was ebbing, and the boats at their moorings trailed toward me as I moved slowly into the estuary. After completing the turn at the foot of the village I could see the quaywall extending ahead on my right. I brought Rosa Janine gently up against it.

As I tied up and shut down the engine I realized dumbly that I hadn't the faintest idea what I was going to do. I climbed up onto the quay and turned to look down at Rosa Janine. The marks of violence on her seemed to have been softened a little by the storm. Half the windshield was missing, and I could see a few glass fragments which hadn't been washed overboard, glinting dully in the grey light. And the roof support was splintered where Morgan's rifle shot had caught it. But I couldn't see the bullet holes in the port side of the hull, and altogether the damage wasn't very obvious. What was left of the tow-line still trailed slackly into the water astern.

I turned and started walking without thinking of a destination. The truck was nearby, but I wouldn't have known where to drive. I walked on, and in several minutes I found myself standing in front of Anísio's door. I reached out and pulled the bell rope.

But now I am standing in front of the door to a brightly lit Chelsea art gallery. The large poster in the window announces the latest New York show of the well-known Brazilian artist Anísio Dantas. I pull the door open and step into the minimalist space, past a waiter holding a tray full of glasses of Prosecco. Anísio's immediately recognizable work is everywhere on the white walls.

I scan the room, taking in the well-dressed couples sipping their wine and conversing in quiet voices. Toward the rear of the gallery, I spot Anísio and move in his direction. He looks much the same as the last time I saw him, except he is dressed for cold weather in a city. This is the first time I have seen him wearing dress shoes.

As I approach him, his face brightens and he turns toward me.

"Argus! Thank you for coming to my opening!"

"I wouldn't miss it for the world. It's been far too long, my friend. And besides, after five years it's well past time we saw each other again in the flesh. I'm happy you allowed your agent to talk you into another show in New York."

"It was inevitable. How are you doing these days?"

"Getting along, thanks. I'll tell you more over dinner if you have a free evening while you're up here."

"Of course. I promised Janine that I would let her know how you are doing."

"Is she enjoying her time at the university? I think you wrote that she had entered UFBA?"

"Ah, she has graduated now. She received her law degree with honors. In fact, she finished it in four years, one year less than is normal. But then I always knew she is much more intelligent than her father."

"Wow. Please give her my congratulations. I'm happy to hear things are going well for her."

"Well, her degree is the least of it. She has accepted an offer of a position at a law firm, and—most importantly—next month she will marry one of her fellow lawyers. My only complaint is that she will be living in São Paulo. Rio would be better, but all the money is in São Paulo these days, so it is natural that all the lawyers will be there."

"She must be very happy. That's great."

"Yes, her fiancé is a very nice young man, and she seems to enjoy her work. Personally, of course, I couldn't stand being a lawyer. But it suits her."

Several others have gathered to speak with Anísio, so I decide it is time to sample the Prosecco and move around the gallery.

"I'll come back before leaving and we can decide when we can have dinner later this week." He acknowledges with his eyebrows as he shakes hands with his next admirer.

I move to the nearest waiter and lift a glass from his tray. As I take a first sip and look around to decide how to navigate the gallery, my eyes meet those of someone I dully recognize as Rebecca. At first I am certain that I am hallucinating, but after two heartbeats it is clear that I am not.

"Argus! My God, you are alive!"

"Yes," I reply stupidly, not having any idea of what else to say.

After an awkward pause, Rebecca gestures to her companion.

"You remember my husband, Geoff? He was at the UK High Commission in Nairobi when you were there."

"Of course. Hello, Geoff, how's your tennis?" We shake hands.

"I don't get much time for tennis these days. I've been with our UN mission for a couple of years now. That keeps me busier than I was in Nairobi.

"But more importantly, how are you? Your sudden disappearance certainly created a major kerfuffle in the dip corps in Nairobi. You are probably still a major topic of cocktail party conversation there."

"I always try to be entertaining," I reply with a thin smile. Rebecca is looking at me with a strange expression as Geoff continues.

"But our news is more on Rebecca's side. She is opening in a play on Broadway next month."

"It's not the lead," Rebecca interjects. "But it *is* a pretty good supporting role. I was lucky to land it."

"I doubt luck had anything to do with it." I have recovered some of my balance.

Another awkward pause. None of the three of us seems able to come up with anything appropriate to say. Finally, Geoff breaks the silence.

"Well, it was good to see you, Argus. What a surprise, after all this time. But I'm afraid we have to get to our dinner."

We shake hands, and he turns to go, expecting Rebecca to follow suit. But she is still looking at me.

"Did you find what you were looking for, Argus?"

I look back at her, at Geoff, and then back at Rebecca. After several moments I respond.

"Yes. I did. Yes."

Charles Jamison has been a naval officer and a diplomat, and has lived in Kenya and Brazil, among other countries.